HER AUSSIE PROTECTOR
Rosie Miles

Cover Art Design by: Kelly Moran/Rowan Prose Publishing
Photo Credit: Adobe Images/Deposit Photos
First Edition
ISBN: 9781961967519
Rowan Prose Publishing, LLC: Peridot Imprint
www.RowanProsePublishing.com
Published in the United States of America

PRAISE FOR ROSIE MILES:

"Palpable chemistry between characters."
-Little Miss Bookmark

"A highly entertaining read."
-Bookaholics Not So Anonymous

"An enjoyable story."
-The Sassy Bookstr

"Suspense, romance, and all round action."
-Author Eleni Konstantine

CHAPTER 1

R *idgeleigh. Suburbia. Southeast Queensland. Australia.*

Some parents should be shot.

Mitchell Buchanan strode to the van, his footsteps striking hard against the concrete. He grabbed blankets before heading back to the three boys who'd just shuffled into Mates and Eats, an open-air drop-in center, at eight-thirty at night, in the middle of winter, wearing tank tops, shorts, and filthy, worn sneakers. "Here." He tossed a blanket to the oldest of the group, who looked about fourteen. His eyes said fifty.

Mitch settled the boys into seats and draped the two younger ones in blankets, hoping it would stop the wind cutting into them. "Wait here." Hurrying to the food truck, past a group of youths leaning against each other to block out the wind, he grabbed a tray and filled paper cups with hot chocolate. He sniffed the sweet aroma of warm donuts and snatched a few of them too. Not the best food for kids, but it would fill their bellies. With the tray piled high, he headed back across the quadrangle.

He towered over the kids as he doled out their dinner but was careful not to question them as though they were in trouble. Once a cop...

The boys scarfed down the donuts, curled their fingers around the cups, and blew on the hot drink.

"So, guys." Mitch rested his butt on the back of a chair and relaxed his frown. "Where's home?"

The two younger ones zeroed their gaze on the big brother who, by the terrified look in his eyes, didn't have a believable lie to share.

Mitch strummed his fingers against his knee. *Go easy.* "Are you safe? Is there someone at home?" He kept his voice low, gentle.

After a moment, the oldest kid raised his eyes to meet Mitch's and whispered. "Yeah. They've been drinking."

"Okay. Remember, if you need something to eat or someone to talk to, the van's here most nights."

A quick nod.

Why couldn't you just ask them who's their favorite soccer team? They don't come here to be interrogated like they are criminals.

His gut churned, and he longed to punch something to ease the uselessness roiling deep inside him.

Mitch stood and stalked toward Hamish, the volunteer co-ordinator for this hub, which welcomed anyone needing food, drink, and someone to talk to. No judgment attached.

Hamish slapped Mitch on the back. "Hey, man, why the frown? You're doing fine."

"Not from where I'm standing."

"I've been observing. You spend time with the kids, they need that. We'll work on your communication skills as you go." Hamish gifted him with the toothy grin that made the young, dreaded guy a favorite with the kids.

"Thanks." He turned away and stared at the old, revamped ambulance across the parking lot. He'd been here almost a week, and there hadn't been a sighting. He knew his bloody plan would work. He sighed. He just needed to give it time. Jones would turn up to see his only living relative, his sister, the doctor. Sooner or later. Hopefully sooner.

Mitch rubbed his thigh. The cold ate its way through his jeans and into his skin. The wound had healed, but it still throbbed to the marrow. They'd assured him he'd have a one hundred percent recovery. Eventually.

Mitch checked out the doctor as she squatted next to a toddler and mussed her hair. The dossier photos didn't do justice to the flesh-and-blood, long-legged woman. The black-and-white didn't show the flush on her cheeks or the sparkle in her eyes. Mitch figured he'd continue to tail her, and when her brother rocked up, he'd grab him.

He scrutinized the area and slanted another look at the lush doctor and speculated on her involvement. How did she subsidize the mobile clinic? By being a part of, and accepting funds from, her brother's deadly smuggling racket? The organization she headed would be expensive to maintain.

The hub emptied, one homeless person at a time. At ten o'clock, he stepped out of the shelter of the food truck, zipped his leather jacket, pulled his beanie down over his ears, and leaned into the icy wind howling down the street. As he collapsed chairs and loaded them into the trailer, he watched Doctor Jardine, and her nurse shut up shop.

She stripped off her high-vis jacket with *doctor* emblazoned across the back, revealing a black jumper that clung to her breasts. His sigh whistled out between his teeth. Statuesque described her to a tee. His gaze trailed down the length of her jeans-clad legs, stopping at the lace-up commando boots. She climbed into the van.

He began a last perimeter check for the night. Edging through a narrow space between the manicured shrubs, he slid down a grassy slope toward the car park. He gave the vehicles a cursory glance noticing nothing out of place. He continued past the cars and onto the bitumen road that led back up the hill to one of the hub's two entrances, both of which were cordoned off by traffic cones. The only vehicles inside the hub were the ambulance and the food truck. According to Hamish, they were considering working with a charity that provided clothes washing and drying service – via another van. But it wasn't a done deal. He finished the perimeter check and was heading back to the food van when a rustling in the bushes bordering the side entry into the hub triggered his senses that had been on high alert for too many years for him to ignore the sound.

Someone crept along the hedge.

Jones? Too small. Mitch narrowed his eyes as the skinniest, most pregnant teen he'd ever seen emerged from the shadows and stumbled into the parking lot, bent almost double and dragging her feet.

The ambulance roared to life and started reversing. "Shit," Mitch muttered. He couldn't let the doctor leave when someone really needed her. He bolted across the allotment, thumped hard on the side of the vehicle, raced back, and dropped to his knees beside the girl.

The van jerked to a halt. A door slammed, then Doctor Jardine was beside him on the ground.

"Charli. Love. C'mon, talk to me." Doctor Jardine pushed the young girl's hair out of her eyes.

Her deep, throaty voice, almost a purr, upped her statuesque status to siren.

He shook his head and buried his inappropriate notions. "Can I help?"

Doctor Jardine's navy-blue gaze focused on him for a second before dropping to his volunteer lanyard, then she refocused her attention on the child doubled up and crying.

"Let me check her." Doctor Jardine kicked into gear. The nurse arrived and shoved him out of the way to move beside the doctor. A quiet urgency thrummed between them.

Doctor Jardine dug around in her pocket and handed the keys to the nurse. "Open up, Bridge."

Mitch stepped up, offering himself without words.

She said, "Get her inside."

Bending, he scooped up the pregnant teen as though she were a feather and stepped up into the ambulance, Jardine on his heels. Bridget pulled a sheet from under the bed and covered the patient when Mitch laid her down.

As another wave of pain washed over the girl, his hand must have been the closest object, so she grabbed it and hung on with her nails digging into his palm. He squeezed back because he couldn't think of anything more useful to do.

"Thank you." Doctor Jardine eased past him and touched the young girl's arm. "Charli, I'll check and see how you're doing, okay?"

The girl nodded.

"Take a big breath, and we'll get started." She moved to the bottom of the bed and began her examination.

Mitch sniffed, and the coppery stench of blood filled his senses. He rubbed at the healing wound on his leg as the recollection of that night snuck into his mind like a thief. *I hate that smell.* He shut it down.

"You're in labor." The doctor looked at Charli and smiled. "We can't have this baby tonight, love. It's way too early."

Doctor Jardine looked up at him. "What's your name?"

"Mitch." He held her gaze.

"Hi, Mitch. I appreciate your help. But we've got it covered. You can go."

"No." Charli hung onto Mitch's hand for grim death as another contraction hit and didn't let go. "Please don't leave. Travis might come. He won't hurt me if you're here."

Doctor Jardine shrugged, then squared her shoulders. "Okay, Charli." She turned to her nurse. "Bridge, will you drive?"

"Asher, you know we're not supposed to transport." Bridget passed the doctor a blanket to wrap around their patient.

"I know."

The unspoken communication between them said the young girl's condition wasn't good.

Bridget nodded, leapt to the ground, and slammed the door closed behind her. The engine rumbled as it fired up, and Charli crushed his hand tighter.

Mitch crouched by the top end of the gurney and focused his attention on the terrified young woman. "You'll be okay." He squeezed her fingers. As the kid groaned deep in her throat, he clenched his jaw. *I hate feeling so useless.*

"He wouldn't let me come." Charli's voice quivered.

"Who?" he asked.

"Travis..."

"Her boyfriend," Doctor Jardine muttered in his direction as she arranged the strap around the girl to keep her safe during transport. "Don't you worry about him. You're here, and we'll look after you. Okay?" She patted Charli's arm.

"But ... he said ... the baby ..." Her words deteriorated into a jumbled mess.

Mitch held her hand as her body bowed.

"Don't let him..." Another harsh groan. "My baby. My baby."

Mitch shook his head and said a silent prayer for the kid and her child.

CHAPTER 2

Doctor Asher Jardine slipped into the hospital room and read her patient's chart. Charli's vitals were strong. The resident had signed off on the medication chart. Mom and her baby would be okay. It had taken hours, but the emergency team had stopped the hemorrhaging and the labor that was ripping Charli to bits. Asher thanked the nurses at the desk as she grabbed her bag and slipped it over her shoulder.

Bridge had gone home with Ethan, her brand-new husband, whereas Asher only had Peaches, her ginger tom, waiting for her. They had a cruisy relationship. She did his bidding, and he allowed her to scratch his ears. It worked well. She headed toward the exit.

A man in a leather jacket sat stuffed into a plastic waiting room chair. *Uh oh. Forgot about him.*

He untangled himself and rose to meet her. "How's the kid?"

She'd managed to ignore his deep, mellow voice while she'd triaged Charli. Now, with the crisis over, it sent shivers along her nerve endings. She'd turn on the radio to listen to that voice.

"They're fine, thanks. They stopped the labor. Baby can cook a few more weeks." She gave him a bright professional smile that belied the seriousness of Charli's condition. "You helped save two lives tonight."

"No problem." His gaze never left her face.

She gave him another smile and turned away.

"You'll need these."

That voice stopped her.

She turned at the distinct jangle of keys and raised her brow. "I have my set. Why do you have those? And why are you still here? Bridge said she'd give you a lift to wherever you had to go." She plucked the keys dangling from his fingers and clasped them in her palm, feeling his warmth from the metal seep into her skin.

"I didn't see her. Mind you, I went looking for coffee."

Ask if he needs a lift. She tried to ignore that voice, but her ingrained manners insisted. Besides, she could use the time to pry some information from him. He'd been around the hub this past week, and she'd like to know why. His sheer size made him hard to miss. "Can I give you a lift?"

"I'd appreciate it." He smiled.

She didn't respond to the invitation in his smile. "Where to?"

"I'm parked at the hub."

"Okay." She took a couple of steps, then turned back to face him. "Formal introduction time, I'm Asher Jardine." She held out her hand.

He clasped it in his. "Mitch Buchanan."

Her hand looked tiny wrapped in his firm grip. She withdrew it and turned away. "Are we still parked in the ambulance bay?"

He shook his head. "Your nurse gave me the keys when you took the kid to emergency and asked me to move it. We're in the main parking lot."

"Okay. Let's go." When he fell into step beside her, his size swamped her. She straightened her spine and squared her shoulders and still only just reached his chin. And it didn't bother her. *Most unusual.* She pulled in a breath, and his clean scent wiped out the antiseptic hospital smell as they travelled the long corridor. Fixing a smile to her lips, she asked, "What sort of work do you do?"

"Defense Force."

"On leave?"

"No." Tension edged his answer. "I'm in rehab."

Sensing she shouldn't prod, Asher asked regardless, "Regular army?"

"ADFI."

She glanced at him, taking in his military bearing and tight physique. "Australian Defense Force Investigator. Cool."

"I'm impressed. Most people ask what it is."

She shrugged. "Some of our young volunteers last year were thinking about joining. I read the careers list.

His lips curved, drawing her attention to the cushioned fullness of his bottom lip.

"Why are you volunteering at Mates and Eats?" Asher pushed the button for the glass exit doors to open.

Mitch stepped back, gesturing for Asher to step through first. "I'm convalescing. I was going nuts doing nothing but rehab sessions, so I thought I'd have a go at doing some volunteer work."

As she stepped out into the night, the wind sliced through her thin medical jacket, and she shivered.

"Here." He unzipped his leather jacket and slipped it off, holding it out to her. "Put this on. *Was this guy for real?* "That's unnecessary." She shook her head. "Thank you, but no. I'm fine."

He shrugged those big shoulders, the black T-shirt pulled taut across the width of his chest.

Asher cleared her throat. "So, you have an injury to your leg?"

"Why would you think that?" He slid his arms into the jacket and pulled the zipper back up.

She looked straight at him, then dropped her gaze to his legs. "You're limping."

Mitch narrowed his eyes and gestured into the dark. "The ambulance is this way." He turned and moved in the direction he'd pointed.

Left with no choice but to follow, Asher quick-stepped to catch up. "And Hamish knows why you're volunteering?"

A brief nod. "He said it makes sense to help while I'm here."

"He's not worried that you look like a cop?"

He turned toward her. "What?"

She paused and lifted her chin. "Our area, well, it's a sanctuary for those who believe that 'the authorities' are out to get them. Unless they're requested, the cops don't come near us." She held his stare. "I don't want our people, especially the kids, scared off because there's a cop hanging around."

He drew back. "If anyone asks, I tell them I'm a soldier." His brown eyes bored into hers and his tone dropped low. "And I don't scare them."

She raised her palms. "No offense. Sometimes my mouth has a habit of running free." *Why are you explaining yourself? He helped, that's it, you don't owe him anything.* She strode toward the ambulance.

As he matched his step to hers, a shiver of awareness nudged her. She slanted a glance toward him. *Holly Molly, he's huge.* She managed a breath past the lump lodged in her throat. Thankfully, he didn't notice her discomfort. Just as well she didn't fancy big guys, or she could find him very interesting. *Shut up, Asher.*

Shoving the crazy thoughts aside, her lips curved with pride as she approached her mobile clinic. "Health for the Homeless" had gone from a dream to a reality, an up and running entity. She'd worked her butt off to make her dream come true. She pushed the button on the keypad, unlocked the ambulance, and sprung up into the cabin as soon as she heard the beep. Mitch hauled himself into the passenger seat. She turned to speak to him. He was staring out the window, scrutinizing the parking lot.

"Are you looking for someone? Something?"

He faced her. "No." Then gave his attention back outside.

She switched on the ignition and, when the beast rumbled to life, twisted some knobs to turn up the heat. "Tell me about your time in the army."

He turned toward her. "Not much to tell."

Great communicator. She pushed again. "Were you a cop before you enlisted?"

His almost black eyes held her gaze with such intensity, Asher swore he was in her head. She pressed her lips together.

"Yes."

The ambulance idled as she stared at him. He didn't drop his gaze, showing no sign of discomfort from her questions.

"Okay then." Accepting he would share nothing other than basic information, she reversed the ambulance onto the road. She slanted a look at him as she drove. He might tell the truth about himself, but her inner sense of something wasn't quite right screamed for attention. Asher believed he was telling the truth, but not the full story.

His deep voice broke the silence. "Tell me about this organization you're involved in."

"What do you want to know?"

"Are you funded?"

"There are some backers. Hamish and the crew pick up the food donations from various companies within the area. The volunteers meet with Hamish at the local school hall and prepare all the donations, fill the urns with boiling water, and bag up the sliced bread. Then they load up the van and drive down together. At the end of the shift, they all go back and clean up. It's a terrific service, and the community is so grateful."

"What about the ambulance?"

Asher patted the steering wheel with pride. "Some GP surgeries donate supplies like antibiotics and dressings. We also have a major fundraising venture which brings in much-needed cash."

She steered the ambulance into the Ridgeleigh parking lot. "Which car's yours?"

He pointed to a big older Ford truck.

It suited him, looking tough and powerful.

Asher parked beside the truck, which was in damn good condition. but didn't turn off the ignition. "Thanks for tonight."

"No worries." He drew a beanie from his pocket, pulled it on, and pushed the door open. Icy wind swirled into the cabin as he stepped out.

"So, Mitch, why don't you travel down to the hub with the other volunteers?" Asher tapped her fingers against the steering wheel.

"I prefer not to." He pulled the jacket collar up as high as it would go.

"Okay. So how long are you going to be around?"

His eyes captured hers and her stomach knotted.

"As long as it takes." His big hand grabbed the door.

"Well, I hope your recovery is quick." Asher gave him a bright smile.

His smile didn't reach his eyes. "Me too."

Asher sat in the idling ambulance till Mitch drove out of the parking lot before heading for home. Ten minutes later, she pulled the ambulance into her driveway and turned it off.

She grabbed her gear, climbed out, and pressed the button to lock her pride and joy. Trudging up the few steps to her front door, she unlocked it, stepped inside, then kicked it shut behind her. Her boots tapped against the polished timber floorboards as she headed into the lounge room, where she dumped her bag onto the big leather couch.

Peaches, her ginger tom, pounced into her arms and she hugged him close. "Hello, your magnificent creature," she whispered to him as he purred long and hard. She placed him on the couch.

Strolling into the kitchen she popped the kettle on. Her thoughts raced in a million directions as she found her favorite mug and an herbal tea bag. As she poured the boiling water, she sniffed the aroma of ginger.

Back in the lounge room, she settled onto the leather couch and sipped the hot medicinal brew. Peaches sprung into her lap and purred. She trailed her fingers through his fur with one hand and held the mug in the other.

Mitch Buchanan's strong features filled her mind. There was way more to him than he was letting on. What wasn't he telling her? He'd looked her straight in the eye. He was solicitous. But. She shook her head. She really needed to stop overthinking. He may be the real deal. After all, he was patient and attentive to Charli. Still, she'd ask Bridget to get Ethan to check him out. Just to be safe.

Her home phone rang, Asher jumped, disturbing Peaches, who leapt to the floor. She glanced at her watch. Two-thirty a.m. "Please let it be the hospital." She grabbed the phone, and steeling her spine, whispered. "Hello."

Nothing. *Not again*. She bit her lip. "Dr Jardine speaking."

When the breathing on the other end of the line deepened, goosebumps rose on her arms she shivered and replaced the phone onto the cradle. It shrilled immediately. This time, she didn't answer. If the hospital needed her, they had her mobile number. She pulled the connection chord from the wall socket.

She rubbed the goosebumps on her arms and stared at the phone. Three nights in a row. *Why does someone do this? And how in hell did they get my private number?*

Asher dragged herself to her office, fired up her computer, and opened it to the Street Doctor file. She scrolled through until she found Charli and updated her medical information. *What would it take to get this girl home?* Asher believed when she started this organisation, that she would help those who had strayed off their path to get home. That she'd work with like-minded people, with the same passion to help save young children from a life of poverty and despair being homeless created.

A life no one deserved.

Asher stretched her arms high above her head, then dropped them into her lap. "I'm exhausted." With that, she saved her notes and closed the computer. She showered quickly, donned her pj's and crawled into bed. Thumping her pillow into shape, Asher glanced at the clock: three-thirty a.m. "Please let me sleep straight through."

CHAPTER 3

I cy winds howled through the quadrangle housing the hub. Asher tugged her jacket sleeves down and fastened the top button of her vest to ward off the blasting cold. Leaning against the hood of the ambulance, she took in the area. A menagerie of people accessed what was on offer at the food truck. Tonight, there were more younger kids than usual. She sighed. They should be at home with parents who loved them. *Yeah right. In a perfect world.*

Across the expanse of the hub her gaze found Mitch amongst a group of kids. He drew her like a magnet. He raised his fingers to his brow, and Asher returned the salute, allowing herself another few seconds of just looking at him and wondering *what if?*

"Made a new friend, have we?" Bridge stepped up beside her, holding out a cup of steaming coffee.

Asher smiled at her bestie, pulled up the zipper on her parka, then took the disposable cup from her hand. "He helped us out last night, so I gave him a lift back here. We had a conversation of sorts." Asher looked around the waiting area. "I'll fill you in later. We have our first patient."

Stepping to the side of the ambulance. She gave a bright smile to a tattered man who had approached her waiting area.

Although the annex was pulled to ward off the wind, it was still cold. "Come on in." She gestured at the van, leading the way into its warm interior.

He stepped up into the ambulance. Thirties maybe, a matted beard, and wearing a threadbare sweatshirt that wouldn't protect him from the cold. His deep blue eyes still contained a spark of life.

"I'm Doctor Jardine. Please, sit." Asher smiled and patted the gurney. "How can I help?"

"I haven't filled out your form." He handed her the clipboard that Bridget usually helped patients with.

"I can create a file for you, if that's ok?"

"Sure. My name's Rick. Feels like I'm swallowing razor blades. Can't shake the cough."

She smiled and pointed a thermometer at his forehead. "Temp's up. I just need to check your throat. Open wide." Asher depressed his tongue with a candy lollypop, cola flavored this time and shone the torch down his throat. "No wonder you're having trouble swallowing, there's pus on your tonsils."

When he rose to leave, Asher put her hand on his arm to stop him. "If you're coughing, I'll check your chest, just to make sure there's no sign of anything sinister." She finished the examination and smiled. "You have tonsillitis, but your chest is clear. You'll need antibiotics." She unlocked and opened a drawer. "Any allergies?"

"No."

"Good." Asher grabbed out a box of penicillin, a blister pack of pain pills, and a small bottle of cough medicine and handed the man the medications. "There's a full course there. Follow the instructions on the package. They should kick in within twenty-four hours. If you're not feeling better in a few days, come back. Okay?"

He nodded.

"Do you have somewhere to stay?"

He held her gaze then shook his head.

Asher didn't push it. She respected her patient's privacy. "See the people at the van across the way. They'll give you a blanket and some warm clothes."

"I don't need them." He straightened his tattered sweatshirt and squared his shoulders.

Asher looked at him and her lips curved. "They have soup and rolls tonight and donuts for dessert." She met his shadowed eyes and pushed on. "We're here most nights. Come see us if you need anything. Okay?"

He nodded, stood, and stepped from the van.

"Another coffee?" Bridge asked from the door.

Asher nodded. "And a gooey donut?"

Bridget smiled. "I'll be back in a tic."

Asher recognized her next patient. "You're up, Serina."

"I'm late."

"How late?"

Serina chewed her lip. "A week."

Asher met the graceful young girl's worried eyes, then moved back to her desk and withdrew a specimen jar. Handing it to her patient, Asher said, "Speak to Hamish, he'll escort you to the bathroom."

Serina bit her lip. "Okay."

"Come straight back." Asher smiled at her patient. "Go."

Serina returned a few minutes later and handed the urine filled jar to Asher.

Asher dipped the testing strip into the sample. "Negative."

They both sighed in relief. "I gave you some birth control pills last time you were in. Did you have a problem with them?"

Serina nibbled her lip, then spoke. "I keep forgetting to take them."

"Oh dear. At your last consult, I mentioned there are heaps of options for birth control available. We can go over them again now if you like?"

"Sure."

At the end of the discussion, Asher handed the pamphlet to Serina. "When you decide what you want to do, come see me. Serina?"

The young girl met Asher's eyes.

"Remember, take those birth control pills till you come back. Ok?"

"I will." Serina turned away and jumped to the ground.

Asher grabbed the antiseptic wipes and started cleaning the treatment area. When the step into the van squeaked, she fixed a smile on her lips and turned. Her stomach lurched when she recognized Charli's boyfriend. Squaring her shoulders she fixed her professional smile into place. She could understand what Charli saw in him. His good looks and muscular build could turn a young girl's head. But something in his pale blue eyes made Asher wary. She didn't trust him, not one bit.

He stepped into Asher's personal space, menace radiating from his brawny frame.

She refused to step away. No way would she allow the creep to intimidate her. She lifted the clipboard. "Fill out a form and I'll be with you in a minute."

"You think you're so damn smart."

Gloves off. "Look, Travis." She crossed her arms. "If you're not here for treatment, piss off. I have things to do." She stepped further away.

His hand shot out, gripping her arm hard. She winced in pain but refused to cry out.

Her legs trembled as her blood boiled. She pulled herself straight and clenched her fists. "Take your hands off me."

"Make me."

Her lips curved. "I don't have to. My nurse will be back in a minute, and you'll disappear, that's how bullies work. They only intimidate those smaller, weaker than themselves. I'm neither. So, get your damn hands off me."

He smirked at her and repeated in an ugly tone. "Make me."

Anger, like dark poison, surged through her. *Stay calm.* She pulled in a deep, cleansing breath. "Take your hands off me. Don't make me say it again." And tried tugging her arm from his grip.

"Everything okay, Doc?" Mitch's voice filled the van and eased her anxiety.

She dragged her gaze from Travis to Mitch, who stood at the back door of the ambulance. "Fine. Nothing I can't handle." She gave her attention back to Travis. "If you have a medical condition, I can help you with, fill out the form and take a seat, otherwise please leave now."

"Where's Charli?" Travis demanded.

"I don't know."

"Lying bitch. You took her away last night. She didn't come home. Where is she?" Travis squeezed her arm harder.

"Let go of my bloody arm." Asher bit back her groan of pain.

Mitch strode toward them. Travis, still clutching Asher's arm, turned to face Mitch. "Piss off. Mind your business."

Mitch took another step. "Let her go."

Travis released his grip on Asher, turned, and swung a fist at Mitch.

"Bad choice." Mitch grabbed the thug's fist, twisted him in his arms and employed a choke hold.

Travis went limp in seconds.

"Where do you want me to dump him?"

"What in hell have you done? You can't come in here and manhandle a patient because he's being an ass." She shoved her fingers through her hair and tightened her ponytail. "I've worked hard for twelve months to gain their trust." Clenching her fists at her sides and struggling to reign in her temper, glaring at the man-mountain before her.

"But it's okay for disgruntled boyfriends of young pregnant girls to come in here and not only threaten, but assault you?" Mitch lowered Travis to the floor, crossed his arms over his chest, and rocked back on his heels.

"He's just pissed off."

"Doesn't give him the right to lay hands on you."

She held his gaze. "I know that. But that doesn't make it right for you to lay hands on him." Hearing her sarcastic bitch voice pulled her up. She took a deep breath. "So, what do you suggest I do?" She tapped her fingers against the bench.

"Get a bodyguard."

"You have got to be kidding."

"No, I'm serious. As strong and independent as you are, you are still female, and in some people's eyes, that makes you a target." He dropped his arms to his sides.

"Mitch, I understand your point of view. I've heard that argument since the day I started offering this service. In all honesty, I've never had the need for a bodyguard. Until the past few weeks." She clamped her mouth shut.

Mitch shook his head. "Look, Doc. You do a fine job. If you want to continue, find yourself a bodyguard, or if that's too intimidating a word for you, call him a driver." Mitch stared at her. "I thought you had a driver. What happened to him?"

"How do you know that?"

No answer.

"I asked you a question." When he didn't respond she slammed her hand against his chest, then snatched it back when his heartbeat thumped against her fingers. Then in a sharp tone, demanded. "I asked you a question."

"Hamish filled me in when I started here. So, what happened?"

Asher glared at him. "That's none of your damn business."

Travis groaned.

"We've finished this conversation." Asher told him and edged toward Travis.

The minute Travis opened his eyes, he rose.

Asher stared at him. "I don't know where Charli is." She wasn't lying. She didn't know if they had transferred her to Lily's yet. "But I couldn't tell you if I did. Doctor patient confidentiality."

Travis shoved past her.

Mitch had moved to the back of the ambulance. When Travis tried elbowing his way past, Mitch grabbed him. "Don't come back. You don't get to hurt her again. Understand?" Mitch stepped aside and allowed Travis to slink away into the night. He followed him outside, shook his head and stalked back across to the opposite end of the quadrangle.

Bridge arrived with the coffees and stared at Asher. "What happened? You're chalk white."

Asher shrugged. "Honestly, Bridge, it's not worth talking about."

Mitch hunched further into his jacket, turned, and headed over to the food truck. He grabbed a coffee, then settled against the hood. Wrapping his hands around the cup, he inhaled the aroma of the strong brew, blew into the hot drink, and sipped its dark deliciousness.

His search for Corporal Jones had stalled. He'd followed every lead, searched every bar and brothel. Jones seemed to have turned to ether. So, he would continue to play his hunch that Jones would rock up here to see his sister. Couldn't happen soon enough. That woman did his head in.

When that creep, Travis, grabbed her earlier, Mitch had seen red. But she'd handled it like a pro and hadn't appreciated him stepping up. In his world, men didn't intimidate or lay hands-on women. *It's nothing to do with you, Buchanan.*

From the conversation he'd overheard, the young girl from last night had the misfortune of being Travis's girlfriend. He hoped the guy would be smart enough to stay away.

Two more streetlights had blown in the cul-de-sac since last night, and the icy wind blasted its breath over everything and everyone, making this precinct an even more miserable, depressing place. And the kids out tonight looked younger and hungrier than the ones last night. He scrutinized Asher and Bridge pack up the van, getting ready to travel, and set up in an even rougher part of the city.

As he sipped his coffee, six teenage boys sauntered into the area, shoving each other, and cursing at the top of their voices. Sensing trouble, Mitch dumped his cup into the trash and moved to intervene. "Have you lot eaten?"

Nods and grunts were the response. He pointed toward the food truck when he noticed one lad hunched over. "You okay, buddy?"

The kid stepped away and didn't make eye contact.

Another boy, an older teenager, all swagger and attitude, stepped into Mitch's space. "Why's that your business, army jerk?" He laughed and nudged one of his mates for backup.

Mitch looked around. Most volunteers hovered close to the food truck. The few kids sitting at tables stopped talking, their gazes dropping to their toes. Swallowing the urge to forcibly remove the little pricks from the area, he motioned toward the ambulance. "There's a doctor over there. She can make sure your friend's doing okay. He looks like crap."

Big Mouth strutted back. "Bitch banned us...told me she didn't treat crack heads. Bitch thinks she's above everybody."

"Your mate needs help."

"Fuck off." Big Mouth turned and headed toward the food area. His mates fell into line behind him.

Half an hour later, Mitch and the rest of the volunteers were eating before they closed when he heard a commotion. Mitch looked toward the ambulance and recognized the group of boys from earlier. They were louder and their language even more foul as they strutted toward the ambulance. Mitch kept his eyes on them, hoping they were just passing through.

When Big Mouth bashed on the side of the ambulance and his profanities escalated, Mitch rushed toward them.

Asher jumped from the van to stand in front of Big Mouth and spoke in a rational voice. "I've told you before, if you need my help to get your life back on track, you're welcome. If not, stay away."

He lunged toward her, but she side-stepped him, turned, and reached into the van. Bringing out a battered baseball bat, she smashed it hard against the trash can. The sound reverberated through the area and had the required effect. He stopped dead in his tracks. A flush brightened Asher's cheeks.

"Get out. If I see you back here, I'm calling the cops." She shouldered the bat.

Mitch stood close enough to intervene. Unwilling to undermine Asher's ability to control the situation, he remained in the shadows, ready to pounce. The group of boys scuttled into the night at her threat, and she hauled herself into the driver's seat.

He shook his head. He couldn't allow this woman to do her job unprotected. It went against everything ingrained in him.

The Sentinel Bureau had assigned Mitch to Health for the Homeless, undercover, and under orders, his mission was to find and apprehend Corporal Greg Jones. Believing in his gut that Jones would contact his sister made Asher Mitch's one remaining lead. Without her as bait, Jones might remain invisible. Asher's safety became a priority.

Mitch strode to the ambulance, thumped on the door, and opened it. "Meet your new driver. Shove over."

CHAPTER 4

Asher shuffled across the bench seat–not that she had much choice. Those blue jeans encased hips weren't taking no for an answer. If she didn't move, he'd end up on her lap. As tempting as that might be in different circumstances, she wouldn't allow him to meddle with her ambulance. Her life. She stared at him. "Are you serious? We don't—"

Bridge, sitting next to her, jammed her elbow into Asher's ribs. "Thanks. We appreciate your offer."

Heat seeped from his denim, through her denim, and into her skin, and she shuffled over more. *I should have found the money for an ambulance with separate seats.* Everything about him screamed danger and to get him out of the life she'd planned for so long. A life she'd created. To suit her. Her plan. Her beliefs. Free from being dominated by men who believed they knew what was best for her.

But as much as she hated to admit it, tonight's altercations with Travis and the crack gang had rattled her.

Mitch had his hand on the ignition, waiting for her answer. Waiting for permission. Dammit, why did he have to be so nice about it? Why couldn't he just continue being one of those "take over jerks" so she could push him out the door and tell him to get lost?

She sighed. "Yeah, ok, thanks." Asher crossed her arms. "I accept your offer. For tonight. But that's it."

He shrugged and kept his gaze on her. "You're welcome." His lips compressed into a straight, stern line. "Where to?"

Bridge gave directions as he drove. Now squished in the middle of Bridge and Mitch, she sat as still as possible to make sure she couldn't touch him. It wasn't enough. His body heat still radiated toward her, and she couldn't get any further away from him. Citrus tinged her next in breath. *It will be a long night.* She reached over and grabbed some paperwork from the glove box, hoping it would take her focus from the man a heartbeat away from her.

At St Paddy's, Mitch switched off the ignition, slipped the keys into his pocket, pushed open the door and climbed out. Asher climbed out too, ignoring the warmth in the vinyl where he'd been sitting. She followed him until Bridget grabbed her arm.

"What?" Asher turned.

Bridget stood with her fists resting on her generous hips, her eyes spitting, and her lips pursed.

"Okay. Spill it." Asher crossed her arms over her chest. She'd seen that look before.

"I will, but you have to listen."

Asher gaped. "I always listen."

"No, you don't, and you still aren't." Bridget's gaze froze Asher to the spot.

"But—"

Bridget raised her palm. "You are under attack, my friend, and we will let nobody hurt you."

"We?"

Again, the hand. Asher rolled her eyes.

"Mitch has offered to drive."

"Yeah, for tonight. That's it."

"We need a driver, Asher. You should be damn grateful Mitch showed up earlier. Charli's boyfriend could've hurt you. And those thugs…"

Asher jammed her hands into the jeans pockets and paced back and forth to let off some steam. "I handled it."

"You shouldn't have to." Bridget's voice wavered.

Asher spun round. "I've built up rapport with these people, they come to me because they feel safe."

"They're not the ones threatening you." Bridget grabbed Asher's shirt and pulled her close. Glaring up at her she growled. "Wise up, Asher. You don't have to do everything alone."

"But—"

"Bottom line, you either ask Mitch to drive for us permanently, or I'm off the roster." She pushed away. "I don't want your selfish 'I can do it myself' attitude to get in the way of what we've built. Or endanger our lives." Bridget turned and stalked toward the hall.

"Is that how you see me?" She folded her arms across her chest. The quiver in her own voice threw Asher. She wasn't a quivery female. She was hard, fast, and decisive. Always had been. So why go to bits now because Bridge pointed it out to her?

Bridget paused mid stride, turned, and strode back to Asher. "You have trouble listening to what you don't want to hear. But I'm telling you. You need a driver. Not just tonight. Every shift."

"Bridget." Asher held Bridge's gaze, acknowledged the pain and love in her eyes. She bit her lip and swallowed the lump lodged in her throat. "Why Mitch?"

Bridget counted off on her fingers. "One, he offered. Two, he met my old man last night at the hospital and they hit it off."

They would. Macho males.

"Three, he's military. He knows how to recognize trouble and how to handle himself."

"He's only hanging around until he's fit." Asher dropped her gaze and focused on the scuff marks on her boots. *Damn, I hate feeling weak.*

"Good, then he'll work for free. More funds for the van."

"That's a positive," Asher admitted.

Bridget laid her hand on Asher's shoulder. "Why are you so against him?"

Asher squeezed her eyes shut as his tall, muscular frame filled her head. *He makes me want to play.* Play the type of games where bare skin and wet kisses took over her sensible, professional self.

"Get to know the man," said Bridge. "He may surprise you."

Asher blew out a breath. "I hate surprises."

"Asher. Please, ask him."

"Fine." A sigh fell from her lips. "I'll talk to him."

"Before next shift?"

Asher smothered a groan. "Yes, Bridge, I'll do anything rather than lose you."

She pulled Asher in for a hug. "Good. Let's get set up. We have patients to see."

Asher smiled at the mother and her baby before giving her attention to reading the blood results. She drew a breath a calming breath, then spoke to the young mother. "Damari, Angie needs further tests. Here." Asher scrawled out a referral, then stood and stepped toward the nervous woman. She placed the referral into Damari's backpack. "Take her to see Doctor Helene. The address is in the referral. She's my friend, and she'll look after you both."

"But—"

"Please." Asher met the young mother's troubled gaze. "They won't take her away from you. You're a wonderful mum. Okay?"

Damari chewed her lip, nodded, tucked her precious baby against her chest, and left the consultation. From the door, Asher noticed the young mother hug her baby tighter against her body to shield her against the fierce wind and push toward the revamped church hall that was their home. As Damari drew closer to the entrance, Mitch peeled himself off the wall he looked to be supporting with his huge shoulder and approached mum and baby. He took off his big leather jacket and draped it over the woman's bony shoulders, escorting her inside.

He's such a conundrum. Not that she cared. He meant nothing to her. So why couldn't she drag her attention away from his sheer physicality? She blew out a breath and stared at its dance in the icy air. *Let it go, Asher.*

She stepped out of the ambulance and wrapped her arms around herself for warmth. So far, this winter was the coldest on record for Queensland. Normally the winters in the sub-tropical paradise were very mild. Asher dashed across the car park and ran up the few wooden steps, pushing open the door of the church hall. Her gaze fell onto the children on makeshift beds, their exhausted mothers sitting beside them, patting them to sleep. Their misery of being homeless tore at Asher and resurrected memories of her time on the street. She wrapped her arms around her middle, and drew in one deep breath, then another. She blinked, furiously determined to stop the tears burning her eyes from falling. *So many kids. How can I help them all?* She scrunched her eyes, refusing to allow pity to direct her. She'd figure it out.

Somehow.

Because that's what she did.

Always had.

Back inside her ambulance, Asher shut all but one back door to stop the bitter wind seeping into every orifice. She rubbed her arms, trying to generate some heat. It didn't work, so she grabbed her spare hoodie from under the stretcher and pulled it on. She did a quick stock take on the antibiotics. Damn it, not enough to see her through a couple more shifts. Time to approach and plead with pharmaceutical companies for more samples. Not the best part of running this service, but she wasn't proud. She'd do whatever it took to keep her patients healthy.

She'd packed up the ambulance and they were ready to go. In the night's silence, her promise to Bridge that she'd speak with Mitch played in her mind. How would she ask, and what would be his response? And why did she care? No point stressing over it, just do it.

"You ready to go, Doc?"

She clutched her chest and stepped back at the sound of Mitch's voice. She whirled toward him. "Don't sneak up on me."

"I didn't mean to scare you." He stood outside the ambulance, in the cold, muscled arms bare. "Tough night?"

She gaped at him. *He must be freezing*. Asher shook her head and blinked back tears. "It's been a miserable night."

"Did you grab a coffee?" His somber gaze held hers.

"No. Way too busy. Aren't you cold?" *Shut up, Asher*.

A shrug. "I've been colder."

She blew into her hands. "Where?" *Don't ask personal questions.*

"Afghanistan."

So, they deployed him. "In winter? I guess that explains it."

He narrowed his eyes, pulled the keys from his pocket. "You ready to leave?"

Sweet Mary. His velvet voice warmed her from the inside out. "Yeah." Asher stepped around him, making sure not to touch one inch of his welcoming frame. "I'll go round up Bridge. Back in a tic."

Bridget stood just inside the hall chatting with a few of the mothers, sipping a drink.

"Time for us to go."

"Sure." Bridget turned back to the group. "Remember, we'll be back on Friday. If you need anything, ask. Someone will help." She placed her cup on top of the cupboard.

Asher and Bridge said goodbye to the staff and, linking arms, rushed back to the ambulance. Mitch had the motor running, and when Asher opened the door, heat welcomed her.

Ash stepped back and looked at Bridget standing beside her. "After you."

Bridget gave Asher a shove into the ambulance. "No, after you."

Again, Asher found herself seated between Mitch and Bridge. Obviously, Bridget's way of getting her to talk to him.

"Where to?" Mitch asked, putting the ambulance in reverse.

"Home base." Asher stated, reaching for paperwork.

He nodded.

Asher gave him the address to the semi-industrial estate and settled back into the seat. The heat from the vents blowing against her face enticed her to close her eyes for a minute. She wanted to. But the thought of maybe nodding off and waking up on Mitch's chest kept her awake. And had her wishing again, she'd found the money to purchase a newer van. One that didn't have a bench seat.

She still had heaps to do before heading home. Which included broaching the subject of Mitch driving for them. Bridge had reminded her five thousand times since Asher said she'd ask.

Just ask him.

"So, Asher," Bridge said. "You decided what you're wearing to the fundraiser?"

Asher rolled her eyes. "Not tonight, Bridget."

"Yes. Tonight. And again tomorrow, until you give me an answer that doesn't involve black T-shirt, black jeans, and Doc Martens."

"You crack me up." Asher received an elbow in the side for her effort.

"Okay, have you written a speech?"

Asher couldn't hold in a groan. "I hate this."

"What?" Mitch asked.

"Trying to be something I'm not."

"You've lost me."

"Me too," said Bridge.

She gave a big shrug. "All I want is to help people. Why do I have to be the spokesperson responsible for raising money?"

"Because this baby is your venture. You started it because you want to"—Bridge raised her fingers in air quotes— help people. And sometimes that means doing something that makes us uncomfortable, so we *can* help. This event will raise heaps, Asher."

"I know." A tremendous sigh escaped from her. "I'm just not comfortable..."

"Taking off the black jeans and Doc Martens?" Mitch asked.

Asher gaped and glanced sideways at Mitch. *Was that an innuendo?*

"Showing your glamorous side?" Bridget threw in.

She shook her head. "Look, I hate talking in front of large groups of people. It makes me feel"—she shuddered— "insecure."

"Why?" Mitch shot her a quick glance.

"Being under the spotlight. The focus of all those people, nowhere to hide. What if I say something wrong? What if I can't get people to understand how important this endeavor is? What if they don't donate and I have to shut this service down? I'll blame myself." She bowed her head. "I hate that pressure."

"Asher. You did it last year, and you were brilliant." Bridge patted her knee. "You will be again."

"Last year, there were a few dozen people sitting around a table in a pub, having lunch. Hell of a difference between that and the three hundred odd people they have planned for this year."

Mitch pulled the van into the estate and followed Asher's direction to the building. He stopped at the enormous roller door, and Bridget climbed out, unlocked the padlock, and heaved on the heavy chain. The door inched open.

"That looks like hard work." Mitch turned and faced Asher. "I'll give her a hand." With that he leaped out of the ambulance and took over.

When the door was fully open, Asher slid across the seat and drove in.

"I'm going," Bridget announced as soon as Asher jumped down from the ambulance. "Ethan will be home, waiting for me."

"Night." Mitch pulled the chain to drop the door back down.

"I'll walk you to your car." Asher linked her arm with Bridget's and left through the side entrance.

"Remember what we talked about." Bridge climbed into her car and put on her seat belt.

"As if I could forget." Asher smiled, then shut the car door. "See you tomorrow."

• • • • • • • • •

Mitch leaned back against the rendered wall and enjoyed the sway of Asher's hips as she hurried towards him.

Her cheeks glowed pink when she entered the building. "Are you in a hurry?" Her voice carried an odd tone as she twisted a ring on her pinky.

If she twisted it harder, it'd saw right through. "No. There's no-one waiting for me."

"Then come back into the office. I'll make a hot drink."

He nodded and followed her. As he trailed behind her, he struggled to keep his eyes off her lush butt. *Focus, Buchanan.*

"This isn't too bad." She held up the instant coffee jar. "How do you like it?"

"As long as it has caffeine. Strong. Black. No sugar."

After a minute, she handed him a mug.

"Thanks."

"Mitch."

"Doc." He mimicked, eying her over the rim of the mug. He could see the question in her eyes. So why didn't she just ask?

She lifted her head, squared her shoulders, and stared right at him. "Will you drive for us?"

Wasn't expecting that. "You were adamant my driving was a one-night thing." He sipped his coffee. "What's changed your mind?"

"Bridge threatened to quit."

"And?"

"And I'm not stupid."

"Never thought you were." He smiled. "Stubborn maybe."

"I'm not stubborn." She thrust out her chin. "I'm determined."

Whatever you believe. Choosing to leave the next move up to her, he took another sip of his disgusting instant coffee and looked around the compact office.

Two computers and a laptop sat alongside a phone-fax machine on a wooden bench that covered the length of one wall. A four-drawer metal filing cabinet stood at the end of the bench.

Two basic office chairs. The only thing out of place was the huge, scarlet couch overloaded with rainbow-colored cushions.

"Do you sleep here?"

"When I'm too tired to drive home. By the time I finish doing paperwork and restocking, I'm shagged." She sucked in a breath. "I meant exhausted."

"I can understand that." He smiled, couldn't help it. "After all the hours you put into your patients and the service you offer the homeless, I'm not surprised you're too," he paused and met her baby blues, "exhausted to travel home some nights."

He took a swallow of the hot drink, "You're right about this. For an instant, it's not gut destroying." To hide the grimace as he finished the drink, he crossed to the opposite side of the room and stopped in front of a white-washed brick wall, holding a huge corkboard covered in pictures.

"What's all this?" He motioned toward a framed photo of Asher and Bridget beside an article from the local paper about the work they did. In another frame hung a blown-up print of the revamped ambulance, with a huge smiley face and a big number one drawn beside it.

"My vision wall."

She crossed the room and stood beside him. Her delicate scent enticed him to move closer. He stepped away.

"You into real estate?"

She snorted. "Hell no."

He motioned toward a picture of a dilapidated apartment block. "What's this?"

"Goal two. I will buy that block of units and turn it into a home for teenage girls down on their luck. It will be a haven where they can find themselves and learn to believe they can achieve their dreams."

Mitch focused on her face as she spoke. Her eyes sparkled, her gestures were wide, and her voice filled with conviction, so different from the persona she presented at work. Seeing her expressive side had him wondering why she kept it hidden.

"I've achieved my first goal; Health for the Homeless is up and running." She turned toward him. "Do you use a vision board?"

"Nope. I don't need reminders of what I want in my life."

"Fair enough." She smiled.

"Have you always used them?" He couldn't contain his curiosity.

She shook her head. "Only since medical school. They keep me focused."

"The decrepit, crumbling apartment block with the unreal price tag is your next goal?"

"It is. All I have to do is find the deposit and I can make the second part of my dream come true." She tipped her head and screwed her eyes shut. "I *will* buy that block of units, and I don't care what I have to do to get the money."

Does that include taking money from illegal dealings your brother's involved in? And justifying it because you help others? "So, Doc, about me driving for you."

The animation drained from her face, and his gut twisted. *Just do your job, Buchanan.* "How long for?"

"I don't know. Until I can arrange for another driver. A couple of weeks, maybe longer. You told me you're"—she made air quotes with her fingers— "sick of rehab, but could you somehow combine driving for us with your rehab sessions? It's only three, sometimes four shifts a week."

"Why me?" He held her gaze.

"As I said earlier, Bridget told me to, and besides, "She twisted her pinky ring. "You know how to render people unconscious." Asher pulled her bottom lip between her teeth. "It's scary out there." She gestured toward the door. "It never used to be, but something's changed. And…"

"And?" He quirked his brow.

Her shoulders slumped. "It makes me want to be more cautious."

And you don't like to admit it. "What's scary out there?"

"I think I'm being watched, not just at work, but at home. What's freaking me out are the hang ups. Three times this week. Every time I answer my home phone." She hugged herself. "It's creeping me out."

She had his full attention now, but he kept his expression neutral. "Have you mentioned it to Bridge's husband? He's a cop, isn't he?"

Mitch studied her. The continuous twisting of that pinky ring, the rapid rise and fall of her chest, and the shadows in her eyes. More than scared. She was terrified. Seeing her at the clinic, he'd never guess it, but she'd shown him a part of herself, a vulnerable part.

"You know what it's like. Until there has been a crime committed, there's nothing to be done. Blah, blah, blah." She flung her arms out in frustration. "Seems like you have to have a dead body, before they can investigate your complaint."

He took some time, as if considering her proposal. Of course, he'd be her driver. What better way to stay close while looking for her brother? "I'll have to check my schedule, but I'll let you know."

The dark shadow lifted from her eyes. "Thanks." She smiled.

As their gazes locked, Mitch glimpsed a flash of vulnerability in the depths of her eyes. "No worries." He expected to feel elated when his strategy of staying close to Asher paid off. Not deceitful. He hated not being able to be completely honest. Especially after all she'd revealed to him during their earlier conversation. But orders are orders. At least now he could keep her safe while waiting for her brother to show up. Jones's unstable mental state made him dangerous. So why did he feel like a prick? *Just do your job, Buchanan.*

CHAPTER 5

Asher parked her beat-up Ford Focus out front of the huge, old Queenslander and waved to Lily, who waited for her by the home's front door, her smile as welcoming as the contents of the cup she held. Asher climbed the dozen steps to the veranda and, after taking the proffered cup, hugged her friend.

"Has Charli arrived?" Asher trailed behind Lily along the hallway that ran down the full length of the house. Their footsteps echoed on the timber floors.

"I've put her in the blue room."

Lily had renovated six rooms of the house into small versions of self-contained units, each with a tiny bathroom, a bed, a comfy chair, and coffee table. Only the main living room, dining room, and kitchen were common areas. Each room now homed a young pregnant girl, and Lily loved being house mum. Lily had renovated under the house for her own living space.

Stepping out onto the huge back deck, Asher took a sip of her coffee, rested her elbows on the timber rail and cupped her drink in both hands. She glanced toward Lily. "Those evergreens you've planted around the fence line are a great privacy screen."

"That's exactly why we chose them." Lily said as she joined Asher at the railing. "But honestly," she pointed to the corner of the yard. "I prefer that beauty."

"I can't say that I blame you. Those red and brown leaves are stunning." Asher said then continued her visual exploration. "The strawberry patch is coming along."

"The girls enjoy tending it." Lily dropped her arm across Asher's shoulder. "And it's good for them being outside in this glorious winter sunshine."

"True. I still can't believe you've done all this in just over eighteen months." Asher motioned toward the house and gardens. "It's spectacular."

"And useful." Lily met Asher's gaze, and her lips quirked up. "I'd been searching for something worthwhile to do since they killed Simon. He'd approve of my commitment to this project."

"I'm sure he would." Asher had only seen Simon once. The night she'd worked to save his life after some crackhead had beaten him senseless. "If I could give him back to you, I would." Asher sunk her teeth into her lip.

Lily pulled Asher in for a hug. "You did everything you could. I saw you fight like a demon even after you were told to call it." The hug turned to patting. "I'll always be grateful to you for trying to save him. That night-haunts me." Lily looked skyward; her voice softened. "Strange how life works out. In losing him, I made the friend of a lifetime." She stared intently into Asher's face "Every shadow needs a light. And you and this place are mine."

"I should be comforting you." She shuddered as she remembered the grief and pain etched into Lily's face the night her husband died.

"You have. You've helped fill my life. I haven't been this happy in forever. Thank you."

Asher blew into her coffee. "How's Charli doing?" She sat on the backsteps.

Lily plopped down beside her. "She slept through the night and when I checked her earlier, she was still out of it. On a positive, there's color in her cheeks."

"I'll go see her."

"And I'll see you when you finish your rounds."

Asher stopped at the storage cupboard and stocked a metal trolley, then headed to Charli's room. After a quick tap, she pushed open the door and stepped inside. "Good morning."

Charli dragged herself up on the bed and rested against the pillows.

"How are you feeling?" Asher held Charli's slender wrist and took her pulse.

"I'm okay."

"Great." Asher grabbed the stethoscope from the trolley and listened to Charli's heartbeat, then her baby's. "Good and strong." She jotted the young girl's vitals onto the chart and sat on the end of the bed. "As I explained last night, we stopped the labor, and I'm very glad, because you're only thirty weeks, and the baby is tiny. Now baby can grow for a few more weeks."

The young girl nodded, and her thick blond hair fell out of its ponytail and veiled her face. "I was so frightened," she whispered.

"Are you up to telling me what happened?"

Charli dipped her head. "He...He's going to sell our baby." Her words were barely audible.

A hot stab of anger burned into Asher's gut. *Breathe, Ash, breathe. Don't scowl. You'll terrify the kid.*

"He said the money we'll get would set us up for life."

Bastard. Asher counted to ten and sucked in her breath.

"I told him no. He got angry and pushed me. I fell over, and he stormed out. I just lay there for a while but when I stood up, a...a sort of cramp ran through me." Her breathing stuttered, and she placed her hands over her belly before she continued, her voice rising. "Then I bled." She finally looked up for a second. "I thought my baby died." Her head dropped back down, and she twisted her fingers together. "Then I remembered it was Wednesday and you'd be at the hub."

"I'm so very glad you came to me, Charli. Your quick thinking saved your baby's life. And yours." Asher pushed Charli's hair back off her face. "Look, you're both safe here. You and your baby's health are what's important now. Don't worry about other stuff or you'll slow down your recovery. You are safe here." She smiled. "If you need anything, let Lily know."

Again, the young woman ducked her head.

"What's wrong?" Asher kept her voice calm and made sure her lips curved up.

Charli shook her head.

"Okay." Asher stood. "I'll see you later." She'd reached the door when Charli's voice stopped her.

"There are more of us."

"More?" She turned and looked at Charli. "More what?"

Charli swung her legs to the floor and tried to stand, but in her weakened state, she faltered. Asher reached her before she fell and settled her back on the bed.

"He told me that there's at least three more."

"More what?" The minute she asked, Asher knew. *Shit. Bastard.*

"Girls like me."

"Where?"

Charli shrugged. "In a house. Like this one, I suppose." She pulled her knees up and rested her chin on them. "The girls, they're going to stay there 'til the babies are born, sign them over, then walk away. Those people in charge of the houses take care of all the expenses. That's what Travis wanted me to do."

"They? Do you know who they are?" Asher settled on the side of the bed and took Charli's hand. "How did your boyfriend organize it?"

Charli shrugged. "They're not all his."

"I never considered that." Asher held the young girl's gaze, "But your defensive tone makes me think you have. Are you sure they're not his?"

Charli's eyes rounded. Then her shoulders sagged. "I don't know. He's just decided I had to give my baby up. He's already taken money for it." She shook her head. "That's all our baby is to him. Money. He keeps saying he loves me, and it'll be better afterward, but he can't really love me if he wants to sell my baby, can he?" Tears trickled down her face. "I thought he loved me."

"He told you all this stuff?"

Charli shook her head. "I heard him on the phone. And I asked him." A sigh fell from her pale, pinched mouth. "How could I have been so stupid?" She dropped back onto the bed and sobbed.

Asher touched Charli's arm. "I'll come see you soon. In the meantime, remember, you're safe here." She slipped from the room. *How the hell am I going to handle this?*

She'd have to call Ethan. Maybe he could unofficially find Charli's boyfriend and question him about selling babies. Then what? Asher shook her head and vowed there was no way in this world that creep would get his hands-on Charli's baby.

Asher went to find Lily. They sat together at the communal kitchen table and discussed Charli's situation.

"Private adoptions? Are they even legit? We need more information." Asher cradled her head in her hands.

"I have a friend in child safety. I'll call her, see if she's heard anything." Lily replied and grabbed a note pad to jot down a reminder.

Asher checked her watch. "I have to go. I've got a meeting with a pharmaceutical rep. And a list of doctors to visit. Call me if your friend knows anything."

"Of course." Lily pushed back her chair and stood.

"Thanks." She rose, hugged Lily goodbye, and headed to her car.

She'd climbed inside and grabbed her phone. No message from Mitch. She hated waiting, but he said he'd let her know before the next shift, which was tomorrow. Fingers crossed.

She drove toward the first doctor's surgery on her list. She hoped more local doctors would get behind her cause and offer some of their antibiotic samples. *Won't know till I ask.*

CHAPTER 6

Early the next morning, after checking her phone for a message from Mitch for the millionth time, she stuffed it and her house key into her running belt and stepped outside. After tying her shoelaces, she pulled her front door closed. A stiff, cold wind lashed her, and she almost changed her mind and went back indoors. But clearing her head was more important than staying warm.

The changing color of the clouds from pewter to gold heralded the sun's imminent arrival. She started her slow, rhythmic run up her driveway and out onto the road.

Birds twittered a chorus of life as she lengthened her stride and glanced around. Usually there were a few other runners about this early. Maybe they were smart enough not to come out in the middle of winter.

Not her. She needed to be outside to unwind. She sucked in another lungful of frigid air.

Running helped clear her head. And there was a lot for her to work out right now. Mitch, for one. She really needed a driver, but if he accepted the driving role, she'd have to figure out how to manage the attraction gnawing at her insides for him. It shouldn't be too hard. She'd frozen off others who'd shown an interest, usually before they'd even acted on that interest.

Yeah, Ash, but he attracts you. Why? She blew out a noisy breath. *Because he's not like the others.*

There was no point thinking about him. She didn't have time for a relationship. *But what about just good old sex?* When that thought thundered into her mind, she stepped off the path and almost lost her balance. *Focus, Asher. Think about something else.* She turned her thoughts away from the man who was in her mind too often and headed toward the park.

How was she going to oversee that gang of crack addicts coming to her service? It's not as if they were there for help, they were just out for trouble. Until a couple of weeks ago, they only caused minor problems. Most addicts dropped by, ate, then left. But there was something menacing about this gang. They'd created aggressive disturbances the last few times they'd dropped in, but the other night, their violent behavior escalated to scary. So, what caused the escalation in violence? Sure, it was a tough area, but lately, the aggression had changed. It seemed more organized if those two concepts could go together. Almost as if it were...orchestrated. A shiver trailed her spine.

And now finding out that there were people out there offering to buy babies from young single girls. It wasn't good. What sort of people bought babies? Desperate childless couples? Pedophiles? Bile rose in her throat. She'd asked Ethan if he could help, but as usual, without evidence, there wasn't much he could do. The joy of being outside fizzled. She sucked in another lungful of frigid air. *Just run, Asher. Just run.*

Thirty minutes later, she slowed to a fast walk. Icy wind whistled along the path and across her bare arms. She rubbed them and picked up her pace. She forged her way up the grassy hill, her muscles protesting as she climbed. She plowed on rather than using the stairs.

At the turnaround point, she stopped for a breather before the return trip. She was stretching when unease prickled her skin. She straightened and looked around. No one. Not even another jogger. She hadn't realized how alone she was. *Time to go.*

She took half a dozen steps when a hand clamped her mouth and an arm around her waist hauled her hard against a solid body.

Asher thrashed but couldn't break free from the vice-like grip trapping her. Her heart hammered. Her breathing fractured as panic ripped at her insides. *Calm down. Breathe. Think. Count.* Nothing helped.

The sickening stench of cheap aftershave curled her stomach. She struggled again, but his sheer strength held her tight.

He spoke against her ear. "You scream, I'll snap your neck."

She believed him and nodded against the pressure over her mouth. His grip loosened enough for her to inhale but only dropped to her neck. She knew anatomy, and from there, he could not only dislocate her jaw with a slight movement but could carry out his threat to break her neck or cut her air supply.

Asher hauled in a breath. *Stay calm.*

"Where's your brother?" The guttural voice dripped with malice.

She shivered. "I don't know." It came out strong. Good, he didn't need to know she was terrified.

"He has something we want."

"I can't help you." She glanced down at the arm across her chest. Ordinary black sleeves, probably a hoodie. No tats. She was hoping for a distinguishing feature.

"Tell your brother." His hot breath fanned her temple, making her want to retch. "If he doesn't give us what we want, you suffer."

"I haven't spoken to my brother in a year. I have nothing to do with Greg."

The arm across her neck pulled, and pain shot through her throat and cut off her breath. "Tell your brother to give back what's mine or you'll lose everything that's yours." His grip eased a fraction.

She coughed as she fought for oxygen. Anger coiled in her gut, unraveled, and seeped through her. Acid words threatened to rip loose. She wanted to break free, to claw at his face. Her body trembled as she visualized him lying on the ground bleeding from deep gouges.

Asher reined it in. This guy wasn't worth dying for. "I don't know where my brother is."

"Well, find him. We'll be watching."

Her phone rang. Thank God. If she could just hit the answer button, someone would hear, someone would help. She wriggled, squirmed, trying to get her hand free.

He must have guessed her intent, and with "stupid bitch," threw her away from him. She stumbled, thrusting her hands out to keep from falling onto the stone path, but gravity won, and she tumbled to the ground only to feel the sting of something stabbing her head. And then nothing.

Mitch strode out of the office and toward the gym. The investigation for Jones continued. Mitch had a couple of new leads to follow and being Asher's driver would certainly help. The last guy Jones had extorted had hung himself. Mitch had to find Jones. He would. How many more were going to die because of this demented prick?

He shook his head. No, keep it professional. Dr. Asher Jardine was no longer a suspect in receiving stolen property, and the Colonel had given the go ahead for Mitch to drive for her. Even if the Colonel had refused the request, it wouldn't have stopped Mitch. He'd have done it unofficially so he could protect her while he looked for her brother.

He paused as he pulled the door open. Why her? There were a hundred-other people at risk in this case. *Why was he so fixated on keeping her safe?*

Before he could plan an answer that made sense, he heard the shouts "Hey, man" and "Mitch, buddy." It felt good to be here. Equipment that helped people with broken bodies heal filled the ultra-modern gym. The smell of strong liniment flicked a memory of a time when his body was being pummeled into recovering.

"Sorry I had to bail last week guys." He grimaced. "And I'm going to have to bail again today. How about a rain check?"

Jace wheeled over, shook his hand. "No worries. The weather's been lousy for gliding, anyway."

"I checked the forecast for the next couple of days. Friday onwards looks good," Pete slapped Mitch on the back.

"Cool." Mitch grabbed his truck keys from his pocket. "I'll meet you on the mountain. I'm looking forward to gliding with you lot. It's been way to long." He looked into his mates' smiling faces. "Have all the equipment ready by lunch."

"Will do."

"Okay. I have to get going." He gave a salute, exited through the side door, and headed along the paved stone pathway toward his truck.

Climbing into the cabin, he plugged his phone into the connector and called Asher to give her his answer and arrange a time for tonight. It rang out. He backed out but stopped at the gates and tried again.

"Hello."

She sounded odd. "Doc? Are you all right?"

Nothing. There was the sound of traffic, muted voices, even birds. His heart thudded harder as adrenalin spiked his system. "Doc? Doc, talk to me."

"Mitch. I... I..." Her voice faded.

"Asher. Where are you?"

"I think I need a doctor."

"Asher, where are you?" He repeated, keeping his voice even. It took a while, but she gave him her location.

"I'm calling an ambulance. Is there anyone with you?"

"Couple of runners. They already rang."

"Stay put until I get there. Do you understand?"

He thought he heard her mutter the word 'bossy,' but she agreed. He disconnected the call, then called Bridget, grateful the nurse had given him her contact details, and put her on speaker as he took off up the road. Asher was a ten-minute drive away. She would be fine. The ambulance would be there. Bridget, too. She was closer. *Stick to the speed limit*. His foot pressed harder on the accelerator. It seemed like forever before he pulled into the small parking lot at the lookout.

He flung the door open and ran toward the ambulance before he realized what he was doing. She sat in the back of the ambulance, huddled next to Bridget, her face as pale as the gash on her forehead was ugly.

Her striking cobalt eyes were enormous in her ashen face.

"Hi." She smiled. "Thanks for calling. You interrupted him," she croaked.

Him who? Interrupted what? Not the time or place for an interrogation though. "You're welcome." He turned to Bridget. "How is she?"

"She needs stitches." Bridget pursed her lips, then continued. "The bruising round her throat will fade."

I am going to find who did this and I'm going to pummel him into the ground. "Is she going to be okay?"

"The medics want to take her to emergency but she's refusing." Bridget threw her arms up. "Typical."

"Hello, I'm here. Capable of talking for myself." Even her voice sounded pale.

"Did you see anything, Asher?" He laced his fingers together, stretched, then placed his hands on his head. If he didn't, he was going to drag her into his arms, and he knew that wouldn't go down too well.

"I've told Ethan what I remember."

Mitch nodded. "What about the stitches?"

"I'll call a colleague." Bridget replied and grabbed her phone from her pocket.

"I'll take you." Mitch told Asher.

The paramedic stepped up into the ambulance and Mitch moved away so the man could finish cleaning her wound. Mitch couldn't drag his gaze from the bloodstained gauze.

"You may have a slight concussion." The paramedic informed Asher. "If you won't go to Emergency, when you see the doctor, ask for an x-ray, just as a precaution." With that, he stuck a bandage on the gash. "Take it easy for the rest of the day."

Asher nodded and winced.

Mitch helped her out of the ambulance. "I'll take you where you need to go."

"Good luck with that!" The paramedic grinned. "We should ban doctors and nurses from getting sick. They're lousy patients." He closed the door and a minute later, the ambulance drove away.

The runners who'd been hanging around melted away as well.

Bridget stalked toward Asher and Mitch. "I've called Macie, she's expecting you." She handed Mitch a slip of paper. "Here's the address."

"Thanks" Asher said.

Bridget hugged her. "I'll see you later. Rest up." Then she, too, left.

Mitch looked at the bruising round Asher's throat and shook his head. *The bastards will pay.* "Get in the car."

"Don't yell at me." Her voice wavered.

He gave himself a mental kick and met her gaze. "I'm sorry. I didn't mean to yell."

Tears pooled beneath her dark lashes, before spilling down her cheeks.

He cursed softly and moved to wrap her in a hug. But she stepped away, anxiety flashing in her eyes. He didn't leave her side. "I didn't mean to frighten you," he kept his tone gentle, "And I'm sorry that asshole hurt you. But you're safe now. With me." A few minutes after her sobs subsided, he offered her his hand. She gripped it tightly. The heat of her touch, the softness of her skin, stunned him. *Focus on the job, Buchanan.*

"I couldn't believe it was happening," she said in a small voice. "All those self-defense classes I've taken went straight out of my head. Every time I tried to get away, he tightened his hold around my throat. I haven't felt so weak and pathetic in years." She twisted her pinky ring round and round.

"You did the right thing, not retaliating. He could've killed you. You needed to keep your cool. And that's what you did." He fought the urge to hug her. He smiled. "Let's get you to the doc, doc."

The slight twist of her lips rewarded him. When he'd heard her voice, small and scared on the phone, his imagination had warped into overdrive.

Somehow, she'd become important to him, filling the hollowness of his soul. *Get real, Buchanan, she's a job, that's all.*

He placed his hand on the small of her back and guided her toward the truck. He opened the door and helped her inside.

Color tinged her cheeks now, and the hollow, haunted look dimming her eyes had lifted.

"How's your head?"

She winced.

"Bridget gave me the address." He climbed in beside her. "Let's get you sorted."

She stared out the window.

"Do you want to break some rules?"

"Like what?" She turned to face him.

He patted the seat beside him. "Sit closer. There's a seat belt."

"I didn't think anyone had bench seats in private cars anymore."

He smiled. "This truck was my dad's pride and joy. We spent hours restoring it. We rebuilt it from a shell. It was the last truck we restored together. It's special to me."

She slid over, buckling up.

"If your head hurts, you can rest against my shoulder."

"Dream on."

He smiled. "Worth the ask."

She shook her head, closed her eyes, and leaned back against the leather.

"Don't you go to sleep."

"I don't think that would be possible."

He started the big truck and reversed out of the parking lot.

"Mitch?" Her voice was hardly above a murmur.

He shot her a quick glance. "What?"

"I'm frightened."

"Understandable."

"He's after my brother."

Mitch dragged in a breath, focused on the road. *If you'd found him, she'd be safe.* "He said that?"

She nodded. "He told me to find him. Or..."

Mitch turned his head, held her gaze. "I'll help you find him." *Or die trying.* He tightened his grip on the wheel until his fingers ached.

CHAPTER 7

After a frantic drive down the highway to the doctor's office, Mitch parked in the lot outside the small suburban practice and assisted a ghostly pale Asher from the truck. He escorted her inside to the reception desk and gave Asher's name, then they took a seat. A few minutes later, a tiny, dark-haired woman called her.

"That's Macie. She's my doctor," Asher whispered.

Mitch helped her stand then ushered her toward the doctor. "I'll wait here."

She gave him a brief nod before disappearing through a door.

Waiting for Asher gave him time to think. He tapped his fingers against his aching thigh, as he visualized the faces of Jones's gang. How in hell did they find Asher? Had Jones talked about her? It didn't matter. They'd found her. Mitch sucked a breath through clenched teeth. Damn it, I should've found that bastard by now.

Half an hour later, Mitch rose and strode toward Asher as she reentered the waiting room. Her face had regained some color. It wasn't as white as the bandage covering the stitches.

He held out his hand and she clasped it as they walked toward the car park. He opened the truck door. She slid in, pulled the seatbelt over her shoulder, and stared at him through the open door. Her eyes were wide.

"How are you feeling?"

"I have a stinking headache and six stitches. How do you think I feel?"

"Happy to be alive?"

She raised her brows and winced as though pain had shot through her head wound. "Whatever."

He shut the door, strode round the bonnet, and climbed in, started the car, and drove out of the parking lot. He glanced at Asher, who rested her head back against the seat. The beginning of a bruise darkened her temple, and she'd closed her eyes. He turned the music down, and a few minutes later, her head lolled to the side, and he realized she'd fallen asleep. With her face relaxed and her lips parted, she looked even more beautiful without her usual scowl. He didn't want to wake her, but the paramedic said she may have a concussion, so as much as he hated to wake her, he said. "Asher." No response. Then louder. "Asher."

She woke with a start, stretched, then wriggled back against the seat. "What's the time?"

He checked his watch. "Eleven-thirty."

"Damn. Lily's expecting me at eleven." She leaned her head against the head rest.

"Lily?"

"My friend. She looks after my girls."

"Maybe you should cancel?" Mitch indicated and switched lanes.

"No." Asher glared at him then turned away to look out the window.

"Didn't your doctor tell you to take it easy for the rest of the day?"

"Were you listening at the door?" She huffed out a breath. "I'm only doing observations nothing strenuous. They need to be done today."

"Do you need me to take you?" Mitch gave her a quick glance.

"If you could, I've promised Macie I wouldn't drive for twenty-four hours."

"No worries. Did you get my message about driving for you?" He shot her a quick glance.

Her lips curved. "Thank you. I'm grateful. Although after what happened earlier, I think I need a bodyguard more than a driver."

He focused on the road ahead and music flowed through the cabin. Uselessness roiled in his gut. *You need to find Jones. Fast.*

"We need to talk about your brother," Mitch said.

"I feel sick enough without thinking about him. Can we leave it until later?"

Mitch shrugged. "Sure." After a pause, he added, "Maybe you should change your clothes first."

She looked down at herself and nodded. "I look like I've been on the losing side of a fight with a pit bull." She turned her head to stare out the window. A sigh escaped as she bowed her head. "A shower and change of clothes are exactly what I need."

"Bridget gave me your address earlier."

"Why?"

"I told her I'd drive you home when they'd finished stitching you up." When she didn't respond he asked, "Do you want to call your friend and tell her you're held up?"

She nodded and fished her phone from the pocket of her running pants. As he drove, he listened to her filling in Lily about the earlier incident. And she played it down. *Why? Why would she not share the horror of what she'd been through? Did she play it down so as not to frighten the other woman? Or did she not want to revisit the nightmare yet?*

He followed the navigator's directions that took them to a suburb close to the Street Doctor Hub. He didn't know what he expected from her home. She didn't seem to care about material things, so this ultra-modern brick and glass dwelling sitting at the end of the cement driveway was interesting.

"Come on in." She unlocked and opened the heavy wooden door.

He followed her, noting she had no alarm system. He'd have to figure out a way to change that. This woman didn't know the danger surrounding her. He couldn't tell her because of his orders, but somehow, he'd keep her safe.

"Coffee?" Asher wandered into the opulent, gray-and-white kitchen and opened the overhead cupboard to grab some pods.

"Thanks."

She turned on the machine, then crossed to the fridge, grabbed the milk, and poured some into the warmer. Placing the re-usable cups under the dispenser, she pushed a button, and the coffee dripped through. "When the light turns red, the milk will be ready. Just pour it over the coffee in the red cup." She looked at him across the stone island.

"I'm sure I can handle that."

"This coffee won't have you grimacing. It's delicious." As she strolled past him, she give him a small smile. "I'll be quick."

"Remember to keep those stitches dry."

She turned to face him. "You were listening at the door, weren't you?"

He laughed. "I've had my fair share of stitches. I know the drill."

Once the coffee dispensed, he filled the red cup with warm milk, then grabbed the other and sipped. She was right, it was delicious. When he heard the plumbing kick in, he focused on the ticking of the clock above the window to drown out the sound of the running shower.

It didn't work.

He visualized her, naked in the shower, with little rivers of water and soap bubbles running all over her naked, lushness hitting all those spots he'd imagined touching with his hands, his mouth. Instant hard on. He drained the coffee in one swallow then put the empty coffee cup in the sink and blew out a breath.

Put it away, Buchanan. Focus on your job. He'd told Asher he'd help her find her brother. He would. She didn't need to know anything else. They were only business acquaintances. *That's right, Buchanan, you keep telling yourself that.*

"Asher, Asher, you're here," Nikki called as they entered the living room of Lily's home.

Asher pushed the trolley into the room and smiled as she looked at the gaggle of gorgeous, healthy, almost full term, fifteen-and sixteen-year-olds.

"Sorry I'm late."

They fell silent when Mitch strolled in behind her. She'd filled him in a little on Charli's story, but not the other girls. He'd accompanied her here as her bodyguard, and she'd asked him to use his experience as an investigator to ask some questions. Charli's boyfriend intended to sell her baby. Asher hoped Mitch could help her figure out how.

Asher performed the introductions.

"Ladies. You look radiant." He met the eyes of each of the young girls as he acknowledged every one of them.

"We know." Nikki waddled toward the communal lounge and settled into the leather recliner.

Asher laughed at the confident, purple-headed teen as she worked through Nikki's obstetric observations. After she finished with Nikki, there were three others. They were so different from when she'd first met them, frightened, vulnerable, and without a plan. With Lily's care, they'd blossomed. When they had come to Asher, she'd encouraged them to get off the street and move into a "live in" home, for their babies' sakes.

For girls to live in this house, they had to sign an agreement stipulating they would continue their schooling. For them to provide for a child, they needed a decent education.

Some girls adopted their babies out. Some kept them, some didn't stay. Asher couldn't let that get her down. She had to look at the success her program had achieved. There were plans to open another home, but not soon.

"So, Nikki, how did you do in that English exam?"

"Aced it." Nikki lounged back on the chair, shirt up, eyes fastened on her belly as Asher ran the Doppler across it. The baby's racing heartbeat brought tears to Nicki's eyes. "I've decided I'll give her up."

Asher took a deep breath. "Okay. What changed your mind?"

"I'm fifteen. I can't look after myself, let alone a baby. There are heaps of people out there who would buy her."

Asher almost dropped the Doppler. "Sorry?"

"Some guy approached me yesterday at the shops. I recognized him from central. He said he could get me quite a few thousand for her."

Asher straightened, struggling to keep her jaw clamped.

Nikki carried on. "Yeah, it's a house like this. We go there, sign the forms, and they take the babies after they're born. I get a few thousand to get me back on my feet. Sounds good, huh?"

"Did you get any details from this guy?" Asher kept her tone casual and managed not to scowl.

"No, but he said he'd be around."

Asher's blood froze. *This wasn't good.*

"Nikki don't do anything rash. Discuss it with your social worker first."

The teen shrugged.

As Asher examined the other girls, she dropped what Nikki had said into the conversations. No other girl had been approached. These girls were keeping their babies. Until now, so was Nikki. How quickly things change.

Did this nameless guy approach Nikki because he recognized her? Asher sighed. Nikki said she'd remembered his face from her time at Homeless Central. The other girls weren't from there. Maybe he only worked on girls he knew. That Nikki thought she could give up her baby so easily showed how vulnerable she really was.

"Where's Charli?" Asher asked Lily.

"In her room. She rarely comes out."

"I'll go see her." Asher glanced into the other room. Mitch rested on the couch, flanked by young girls, laughing, and asking questions about his time overseas. Asher didn't hear him mention military police, just a soldier. They were young girls with baby bellies. They'd never be young again but seeing them relaxed and happy gave Asher hope they'd be okay.

"Mitch, I'd like you to come with me."

"Sorry ladies, duty calls." He levered himself up off the couch and limped after Asher as the girls said goodbye.

Asher knocked on the blue door and pushed it open. "Hi, Charli."

The young girl roused herself from the recliner, turned to face Asher. Her smile widened when she saw Mitch at the door. She must have recognized him.

"Time for obs." Asher said, pushing the trolley into the room. Asher felt Mitch's heat as he followed her. "Do you remember Mitch from the other night?"

Charli nodded.

"You're looking better." Mitch told her in that sexy voice.

Charli nodded again.

"Are you happy for Mitch to stay while I examine you?"

"He's ok to stay because he helped me the other night." Charli gave Mitch a shy smile.

Asher worked through the obs, jotted them on the chart, then pulled up a chair and sat next to Charli. "Everything looks great. Baby's heartbeat is strong. Another few days' rest and you'll be ready to go home."

Charli turned her head and looked out the window.

"What's wrong?"

"I don't have a home. I've nowhere to go."

Asher held Charli's hand. "What about your mum?"

Charli shook her head vehemently.

"Would you like to stay here?"

Charli turned to face her; tears hovering on her lashes. "Could I stay?"

Asher nodded. "Okay, I'll talk to Lily, and she can set the paperwork in motion. Over the next few days, social workers, and people within my group will help you. For now, just rest and eat. You can get up and about, maybe go for a walk in the garden. I'd prefer you not to go outside the yard, but if you do, go with one of the other girls."

Charli nodded and patted her stomach. "Thank you."

"Have you heard from Travis?" Asher replaced the doppler onto the trolley.

She shook her head, not meeting Asher's gaze.

"Charli?" Asher prompted.

"No. And I don't want to."

Mitch crossed over and knelt on the floor by Charli's feet. "I'm glad to hear it." He glanced into the young girl's troubled eyes. "He came looking for you the night after you went to hospital."

Charli shot her gaze to Asher. "You didn't tell him where I am?"

Asher shook her head. "No. I said you were in the hospital. I didn't tell him you were being moved. So, you don't have to worry about him," She gave Charli's arm a slight squeeze.

"Doc's right." Mitch strummed his fingers on the wooden floorboards. "If you don't want him around, don't contact him or any of the others you used to hang with."

"He was the love of my life," Charli whispered.

Asher's chest tightened at the sentiment. "First love is like that. Sometimes it doesn't work out." She gave Charli a brief hug and stood.

"You'll get through." Mitch gave her a smile.

Charli grabbed his hand and tugged him down. "Did Doc tell you what I told her the other day?"

"No. All I know is Doc wants you to get strong before your baby arrives. She doesn't want to stress you by asking too many questions."

Charli nodded and motioned him closer. Mitch stood and bit back the groan as his leg throbbed and settled into the chair Asher had vacated.

"Travis said I have to give the baby up. That I'm too young to bring up a baby."

Mitch kept his expression neutral. *He should have worn a condom.*

"When I told him I wanted to keep my baby, he said he'd already taken some money for it. As an act of good faith." Charli's voice shook.

Mitch gritted his teeth. "Did he hit you?"

She shook her head. "I pushed him. I yelled and swore. He tried to grab me, and I twisted away. Then I fell. He stormed out, screaming at me they would kill him if I wouldn't give my baby up."

"Travis is a lot older than you, isn't he?"

"He's twenty-four."

And you're fifteen. He clamped his mouth shut. "Did he say where these people were located?"

"No, but he seemed scared, pacing around, looking out the window." Charli sighed. "I can't believe he thought I'd just give the baby up. He doesn't love me at all." Tears thickened her voice.

"Don't think about him. Just focus on you and your baby."

"I'm not giving my baby up."

"Good for you." Mitch withdrew his hand from hers and followed Asher outside.

Asher stored the trolley away, and Mitch leaned against the door jamb as he waited.

Lily strode toward them. "Coffee before you go?"

"Thanks, I could use one," Mitch said.

"Me too." Asher turned and faced her young patients. "Girls, look after yourselves. Take care of each other."

When the three of them sat around Lily's circular table, Asher filled her in.

"Such a co-incidence. Charli and Nikki." Lily sipped the black brew. "Have you spoken to Ethan to see if he can help?"

"Sorry, what did you say?" Asher queried, sounding confused. "I seem to have lost the plot somewhere."

"Time to get you home," Mitch said. "You're wincing and massaging your temple. How's the headache?"

"Coming back like a steam train. The pills Macie gave me were strong. I thought they'd last longer."

Mitch looked at Lily. "Asher said you have someone you can talk to about this situation with the girls?"

"I called her. I'm waiting for her to get back to me."

"Please let me know what she says."

"I will." Lily nodded and helped Asher stand. "Take care of you. No more running by yourself."

"Trust me. I'll stick to the treadmill for a while."

Mitch stood and ushered Asher toward the door. "Are you working tonight?"

Asher massaged her scalp and nodded.

"How about I drop you at your place, and you can grab a few hours' sleep. I'll pick up Bridget, and we can come back and collect you."

"I'm not incapacitated. It's only a headache."

"The paramedic said concussion."

Asher stared at Mitch. "One, I have no blurred vision. Two," She emphasized her words by holding up her fingers, "No pressure in the head, just an ache. Three," she practically waved her fingers under his nose, "no dizziness. No ringing in my ears. It's only a headache. I'm a doctor, I'm not going to risk my life by working with a concussion. So, let's get it straight. I've got a headache. A nasty skull splitting headache. Understand?"

"Yes, ma-am." He gave a mock salute and followed her to his truck.

CHAPTER 8

*H*is lips nibbled the skin at the junction of her neck and *jaw. A shiver travelled the length of her spine as she traced her fingers down the corded length of his arm. His mouth inched nearer to her chin, his breath hot on her throat.*

She eased deeper into the pillow.

The buzzing in her ear intensified as he drew closer. *She inhaled his citrus scent and reached for his broad shoulders to pull him closer. His kissable lips were millimeters from hers. Would he taste as good as he smelled?*

That buzzing insisted.

Asher groaned, rolled over, and patted the bed. Nobody. She sighed. How had Mitch found his way into her dreams? Thank heavens the buzzing had interrupted her subconscious fantasy. Mitch challenged her sensible self and unsettled her thoughts. Reaching over the bed, she picked up the phone, grateful it had awakened her before her mind could take her to the next level.

"This had better—"

"Ash, it's Bridge. Mitch's on his way to pick you up." Her voice wobbled. What's the matter?" Asher sat up, fully awake, years of middle-of-the-night emergency training kicking into gear. "What's wrong?"

"There's a fire."

Asher leapt out of bed before her next heartbeat. "Oh no."

"He'll be there soon. I'm sorry." Bridget sobbed as she disconnected.

Which squat? How bad is it? She dragged on her clothes from earlier in the night before and grabbed a heavy jacket from her closet. She glanced at the clock. Two a.m. She lifted her doctor's bag, pocketed her keys, and bolted out of the house. *Please don't let it be too bad.* Some of those squats housed dozens of kids.

Mitch pulled up at the curb just as she sprinted up the driveway. He took off the minute Asher climbed inside.

"Where? What?" Her words were hardly coherent. She sucked in a breath. "Which squat?"

Mitch's attention didn't leave the road as they sped through the quiet streets. "Didn't she tell you?"

"I just heard, fire."

"It's not a squat." It sounded as if he was speaking through a clenched jaw.

Relief washed through her, and she sank back against the seat. "Oh, thank God." She reached over and squeezed his hand as it gripped the steering wheel.

He didn't say a word. Asher looked at him. His lips were a long, stern line. His features stamped with harshness, and his fingers on the wheel were so tight his knuckles were white.

Asher's belly churned as she dared to ask. "Where's the fire?"

He kept his focus on the road. "Street Doctor Headquarters."

"No!" Asher wrapped her arms around her middle, trying to hold in the pain clawing at her. She rocked back and forth as anger and disbelief battled for attention. Her lifelong dream, up in flames. It had to be a mistake. Had to be. Life couldn't be this cruel. Could it? Tears stung her eyes, and she bit down hard on her tongue to stop herself from crying out loud. Then sucked in one deep breath. Then another. This couldn't be happening. "How bad?" Her voice trembled.

He shrugged. "Not sure. We'll find out."

Don't cry. "Anyone hurt?"

Another shrug.

Chaos, absolute chaos, greeted them as they pulled up outside the building. Strobing lights, fire trucks, firefighters shouting, noise, hoses, water.

Asher jumped out of the truck and made her way to Bridget and Ethan, watching helplessly from their vantage point on the fringe. They stood rooted to the spot behind the official tape, as the carnage unfolded.

"We have to stay here." Bridget encased Asher into a hug when she tried to lunge past the barrier.

Mitch arrived after parking the truck and paced back and forth like a caged panther.

Asher could do nothing but stand and stare at the destruction unfolding. *I'm going to heave. My work. My ambulance. Destroyed, a smoldering mess.* They'd doused the flames, but what the flames hadn't destroyed, the water had. Tears stung her eyes. She'd locked the ambulance inside the garage after the shift. So how did it get outside? She sniffed, but smoke irritated her nose and watered her eyes. *It's the smoke, not tears.* The street doctor didn't cry.

Ever.

At least not in public.

She glanced around. Firefighters hosed the smoldering shell of her dream. How in hell am I going to help all those people now? They wouldn't come to a clinic. Dammit. What am I going to do? With every thought, tears choked her. *Don't cry, Asher.* She sniffed. She couldn't help it. *Hold it together.* Her thoughts raced. *Just breathe.* Her breathing slowed.

She caught the attention of a firefighter as he dragged a hose. "I'm Doctor Jardine. This is my business. I need to get inside."

"Sorry, ma'am. Too dangerous. You need to stay where you are."

"But…"

He turned away and kept dragging the hose. Asher couldn't believe they wouldn't let her any closer then gaped as Mitch ducked under the tape.

"Behind the tape," someone else shouted.

Mitch either didn't hear or ignored him and picked up his pace. He stopped before a bearded older man with more official looking patches on his oversized jacket who seemed to give orders and pulled his wallet from his back pocket. The bearded guy nodded and called over another officer, who led Mitch inside the garage. Seeing this, Asher ducked beneath the tape and headed in Mitch's direction, only to be stopped by another firefighter, a female this time, who wouldn't take no for an answer. She escorted Asher back to the taped off area. So much for the sisterhood. How could they let him in when he wasn't even the owner? And what did he show them? Or did he bribe someone to get inside? She could see enough to know he'd opened his wallet, but his body had blocked her view of what else happened.

Eventually, Mitch strode toward them, his face streaked with black like the water now pouring from her ambulance. A giant of a man, wearing the full safety garb, accompanied him.

"I'm Captain Scott." He looked at the group before him. "Doctor Jardine?"

"I'm Doctor Jardine. How did this happen?" She sucked in a breath, almost choking on the acrid smoke still thick in the air.

"Call came in from a passerby who noticed the burning vehicle. When we arrived, the fire had taken hold."

"We'd locked the ambulance in the garage," Mitch stated. "How did they get it out?"

"Initial observation? They smashed the side door to get inside the building, then jimmied the lock on the roller door before maneuvering the vehicle outside."

Asher stared at the scene. Sickness welled in her throat. She bit her lip. "Is the office destroyed?"

Captain Scott shook his head. "No fire damage. Just turned over and graffitied. I'd have expected them to be after drugs, but it just looks trashed, more deliberate." He spread his hands and shrugged. "It's repairable." With that, he turned and strode back toward the other firefighters, shouting orders as he did.

Her legs threatened to give out. Mitch's solid presence beckoned her to rest against him. And she so wanted to feel the strength of him against her. But she didn't. She did what she always did. She planted her feet against the ground, determined to stand strong. Alone.

Asher looked at her sturdy work anywhere boots. "Not having an ambulance is going to make my job more difficult. But I'll be back at Mates and Eats for next shift."

"Are you kidding?" Mitch must have overheard her.

She looked up at him. "What?"

A scowl marred his brow, and his eyes blazed. "You're going back out there?"

"Of course. Those people need me."

He held his hand out in front of him, palms up. "Is it worth your life?"

Asher gasped as his quiet tone slashed her. "They're just trying to intimidate me."

"Who? Tell me who? Street kids? The homeless? Who?"

"I don't know." She pushed the quiet words out past the lump in her throat.

"Damn right you don't know." Mitch's gaze pinned her to the spot. "Because it could be anyone." This time he flung his arms side-ways, clearly frustrated. "Over the past couple of days, you've been a verbal punching bag for scum. And earlier today, some creep hit you, and you're still choosing to go back out there."

"Mitch." She grabbed his arm, his warmth seeping into her skin.

He pulled away. "Get in the truck, I'll take you home."

Asher pulled herself to full height. "No. I've got stuff to do here."

He leaned forward and fisted his hands on his hips. "You have got to be joking."

"I don't joke." She tipped her chin and stared into his chocolate eyes. He looked at her as though she was some airhead. "It's my business being threatened, not me."

"That's crap and you know it. You've got that young punk hunting down his girlfriend, and the creep threatened you twice."

Asher crossed her arms and straightened her shoulders. "That's all he is—a creep. He wouldn't do something like this."

"How do you know? Are you psychic? I told you the night he came to you looking for his girlfriend. That guy was trouble. And now this." He waved his hand in the building's direction. "When will you listen? Tell me, Doc, when?"

She stared at him.

His eyes blazed like hot coals. He stood ramrod straight and held her gaze. "Forget it. The all-important Doctor Asher Jardine listens to no one. No one." He turned on his heel.

She shook her head and looked around. Nobody seemed to pay them any attention. Why would they? It wasn't like he'd raised his voice. But the intensity of his words showed his anger, bubbling just under the surface. Why?

He started walking. "I'm out of here."

"Mitch. Listen to me." Her voice sounded harsh, even to her.

Ignoring her, he turned and stalked toward his truck, wrenched open the door, and jumped in. A few seconds later, the beast roared away. She'd obviously pissed him off. *Understatement of the year.*

Asher shook her head and strode back toward Bridge and Ethan. Could it be Charli's boyfriend? She didn't think he was capable of something like this. He was small time-scum. But really, she didn't know. She wrapped her arms around her waist.

That guy who'd threatened her earlier, could he have something to do with his? He'd told her to find her brother. And what had Greg involved himself in? Was it something that could cause her business, maybe even herself, to suffer? And why would he do that? Asher shook her head. If she didn't sort this out, she'd go nuts. But first things first. Time to check the damage. As they stepped over hoses, Asher listened to Mitch's F250 tear off down the street and sighed.

Mitch jammed the truck into third gear, accelerated briefly, then dropped the clutch and shoved it into fourth. *What is it going to take for that woman to realize she's in danger?* How would he get it through her head that she was a target without revealing his mission? He glanced at the speedometer and eased off the accelerator. No point wrecking his truck because he'd allowed her to get under his skin.

All week at Mates and Eats, he'd watched her work with the street kids. And the old and the homeless. And the drunks. Her unique personality delighted everyone involved with her.

She fought to keep others safe, to ensure they received the best medical attention to treat their conditions. From behind the scenes, she spent nearly as much time contacting specialists by phone to get help for some of her people pro bono.

Doctor Asher Jardine did everything for everyone, but didn't look after herself, didn't care about herself. Did she not believe in her own self-worth? The thought made him sick. Couldn't she see, unless she put herself first, her enterprise wouldn't continue? Or didn't she care?

Mitch turned onto a side street and pulled over. Staring out of the windscreen into the black night, he shoved his fingers through his hair and battled to bring his thoughts into order.

His primary assignment was to find Corporal Greg Jones before gang members found him. Frustration roiled in his gut with the realization he'd failed.

Jones had proved elusive. First up tomorrow, Mitch would go back to headquarters and do another computer search to doublecheck he had missed nothing.

Asher's ambulance being torched heightened the need to find him, especially if gang members were behind the destruction of Asher's property. But why? A warning? To prove to Jones that they would use her to draw him out of hiding?

What if it wasn't the gang but that creep boyfriend? Could it be payback for Asher not giving Charli's location to him? If he'd taken money for the unborn child, he couldn't afford not to deliver Charli's kid.

Mitch rested his head on the steering wheel. *Just do your job, Buchanan. Find Jones.* It would be so much easier to do his job if he weren't so hooked on Jones's sister. She had no interest in Mitch, but that didn't stop his awareness of her. Asher Jardine had wormed her way under his skin.

The other night, when that young bloke grabbed her, he wanted to throttle the guy. It rattled him, and he didn't like it. Didn't understand it. In Afghanistan, he'd worked with female soldiers. He enjoyed being around intelligent, powerful women.

He thrived on their intellect, their humor. They wouldn't have appreciated him coming on all super protective because some guy had laid a hand on them. They were more than comfortable looking after themselves. Just like Asher. Why did it feel different? He didn't have feelings for those other women. And this was an entirely different war zone with its own rules of engagement.

Mitch refused to allow this attraction for Asher to interfere with protecting her. He'd committed to driving for her, so he'd be by her side, keeping her safe while hunting her brother.

But he wouldn't be the only one.

Jones's gang members were home now, out of uniform, all blending into the scenery. Usually, ex-military was easy to spot if you knew what you were looking for. The way they stood and moved, how they spoke. Unless someone trained them not to be found. And Mitch suspected that was the case. They could turn up anywhere looking for their target.

Mitch vowed to find Jones first. Then after he'd turned him over to the Army, he'd decide what to do regarding his attraction to Asher.

Asher stood in the center of the trashed office and looked around at the destruction. She had no tears, just anger and a determination not to be beaten.

Where to start?

Because no fire damage had occurred inside the garage, just smoke and water, the fire chief allowed her to enter. She dipped her head and sniffed. Her ambulance. Her life goal. Gone. She wrapped her arms around her middle. Oh God, she didn't know how much longer she could hold it together.

Graffiti, dark and nasty, like a cancer, tagged every wall. Trails of red and blue paint, like bruises, patterned the glass partition, so it resembled a spider's web. Bile clogged her throat.

The vandalism of her stuff made her want to puke. She moved to her comfy scarlet couch with its million-colored scatter cushions. She lifted one, turned it over in her hands, and dropped it to the floor. *Doubt I'll get that clean.* Paint had soaked right through. The others were just as bad.

She trudged to her vision wall and picked up what remained of her goal chart from the floor. Thoughts stampeded her. *I can't believe someone could do this.* Her eyes drifted around the devastation. And Mitch, who did he think he was, dictating to her? Didn't he realize she refused to be controlled by anyone? She'd worked too damn hard to overcome her abusive father's tyranny to give in to another man's dictates, and to be completely independent. *Pull yourself together.* She walked outside, dragging in deep, smoky breaths before the freezing wind picked up, forcing her back inside.

The firefighter proved right about the lock...someone had smashed it beyond repair. Asher needed a locksmith. Now. She grabbed her mobile, moved outside for fresh air, and tapped her screen for contacts and pushed the call button for Mac. She apologized to the locksmith for the late call and explained the urgency. Thankfully, he committed to be out within the hour.

This damage had to be a random act and not payback. Mitch had to be wrong. But what if he wasn't? What if Charli's boyfriend had done it for revenge? Did he think threatening her business would make her give up Charli's whereabouts? No way. Living with Lily ensured Charli's safety, at least until her baby arrived. Then she could decide to keep or adopt out her child and not have it ripped from her just because the boyfriend made other plans. Who else could it be?

Asher returned to the office and watched Bridge wipe filth from the computers. "Go home, there's nothing you can do for now."

"I can make sure these still work."

"I'll call our tech guy later. That's his job." Asher managed a wobbly smile. "As soon as the locksmith goes, I'll head home too."

"How? You came with Mitch." Bridget continued scrubbing the computers. "Ethan and I aren't leaving you by yourself."

"I adore you two, but once Ethan helps me get this door shut, no-one's getting in."

"We're not leaving you." Ethan stalked into the office and crossed to Bridget's side. A united front.

"Honestly, I'll be fine. No one can get in." Asher threw her arms around their shoulders and gathered them into a hug.

"They did before." Bridget whispered.

Gooseflesh crimped Asher's skin. She shoved her fear back into its box. "Go home."

"We will not leave you alone." Bridget shoved her hands onto her hips and glowered at Asher.

"You won't have to. I'll be here." Mitch's deep, gorgeous voice slid over her like caramel sauce over ice cream.

Asher screwed her eyes shut tight for a second as she reconciled how just hearing his voice tied her stomach in knots and made her want him. Gathering her wits, she turned to face him. "You can go too. I don't need anyone."

"Never said you did."

She met his steady gaze.

"I brought coffee to apologize." Mitch held out a to-go cup.

"For what? Being a pompous prick?" Asher didn't reach for the cup.

Mitch cocked his head to the side and smiled. "That's about it." He turned to Bridget and Ethan. "I won't let her scare me away. Okay?"

Ethan dropped his arm across his wife's shoulders and pulled her to his side. "He's got her. She'll be fine."

"Night Asher. We'll organize some help to get this mess sorted." Bridget stepped away from Ethan and hugged Asher.

They all walked outside together. "See you." Asher waved her friends goodnight and headed back toward the entrance.

"You want this coffee?" Mitch proffered the takeaway mug.

"Thanks." She took the cup, careful not to touch him in case the connection would somehow break her resolve to stand alone. But looking at his strong welcoming presence, she acknowledged she didn't want to stand alone. She just didn't say it out loud. Back inside, Asher looked at the files strewn all over the place.

Mitch moved behind her and looked inside. "Somebody really doesn't want you out there."

"Maybe not." She took a sip of the coffee and continued slowly. "But they don't know me if they think this is going to stop me."

CHAPTER 9

"Drink." Mitch pointed toward the coffee cup in her hand. "Then we'll get something done while we wait for the locksmith."

"He shouldn't be too far away." Asher took a sip of cooled beverage. "How did they know I parked here?"

He looked deeply into her eyes and gave a slight smile. "You've been doing this deal for a year. I'm sure it's no secret where you park. Plus, there's been a lot about your service in the papers. If they named the business here, maybe whoever did this just put two and two together."

"I suppose that's a possibility." She shrugged.

"Anything taken? Drugs?"

"I don't keep any drugs here."

"Where's the storeroom?"

She pointed toward a cupboard set against the wall and watched as his long strides carried him quietly across the cement expanse. For such a large man, he was incredibly light on his feet.

He was back a few minutes later with a big broom. "Might as well get some of this mess sorted." He stepped into the office.

Asher dragged her body slowly behind him. Exhaustion filled her bones, and she wanted to curl up in a ball and cry. She gnawed her lip. *Wallowing fixes nothing.* Her beloved foster mother, Riva Jardine's voice filled her head. And as usual, it perked her up. A bit.

"Twelve months it's taken me to get this service up and running, and I've never missed a shift," she muttered, more to herself than Mitch. She squared her shoulders. "Those lost people depended on me for some type of normality, even if it is just turning up at the same place, same time, week after week. I should be there tonight." She huffed out a breath. "What am I going to do?"

Mitch shook his head. "Whatever needs to be done."

She took another sip of the lukewarm coffee and stared into his tough face, noticing the tiny scar near his temple and the laugh lines fanning out from his eyes. "I know, it's just..." She stretched her arms above her head then let them drop by her sides. She bit her lip. "I'm so tired, and I can't think straight to save myself."

She looked properly at the mess. The shards of glass that had once been a coffee pot. Sure, it was ancient, but it still worked and didn't deserve to be smashed into pieces on the concrete. Invoices and bills were strewn over the floor. God, she hated filing at the best of times—but doing it twice! And her gorgeous scarlet couch, painted and slashed beyond repair.

She turned slowly and looked at her vision board. Although barely recognizable beneath the paint smears, Asher saw it clearly in her mind. Newspaper cuttings—from when she purchased her ambulance, when she'd picked it up, and after she'd revamped and stocked it to suit her work on the streets. It resembled confetti. The photos of her and Bridge and a few of the volunteers celebrating the launch of "Health for the Homeless" lay wadded up on the floor. She clamped her lip between her teeth to stop them from trembling. Those magazine photos of plans for the refuge for teenage girls and all the other hopes and dreams built up over the years.

Destroyed.

She inhaled deeply. They were mere physical mementos.

In her head, her heart, she saw that board as clearly as she had last night. Those memories lived in her head, and nobody could take them away from her.

Street Doctor was only part one of her projects. And someone was trying to ruin it. At the sound of Mitch sweeping shards of glass, her chest tightened, and her jaw set as anger slowly devoured the pity consuming her. She welcomed the heat and the strength it brought but knew while a little rage would fuel her determination, too much would just waste precious energy and create wrong decisions.

She swallowed back the defeat that threatened to consume her, reached behind her head, and pulled her ponytail tighter. "You're right, Mitch. I'll sort something."

"You're insured?" He swept the strewn files into a pile.

She nodded.

"I'll take some photos for your insurance company. They're going to need them."

"Good thinking." She reached over and touched his arm. "Thanks."

Lights arced across the front of the garage as a large vehicle pulled up outside. Not long after, the locksmith entered the garage.

Asher left the office and crossed the space to meet him. Mitch shadowed her as she explained her needs to the older man. As much as she hated to admit it, Mitch's presence eased her fear and made her feel safe.

Asher watched Mitch beat the framework for the roller door into shape and admired his strength as he swung the hammer as effortlessly as a stick. When he finished, the locksmith worked his magic. Together, they hauled the big metal door down, then the locksmith slapped on the deadbolt and lock.

"Thanks Mac, I appreciate you coming out this late. Just send the bill to my work email."

The locksmith handed Asher the key. "No charge, Doctor Jardine. My way of saying thanks for helping the people others don't acknowledge." With a wave, he climbed into his van and drove off.

"There are some truly wonderful people in this world." She strolled back toward the office.

Mitch's footsteps sounded behind her, following her. "And you're one of them."

She stopped and turned to face him. Tears, more tears. God, she thought they'd all gone, but no, here they were again, threatening to spill over her cheeks at Mitch's quiet praise. All those tears and her pity party were giving her a headache. "Thanks." She met his gaze, "I've never thought of myself as one of life's wonderful people."

"Lady, the work you do for others amazes me. Here you are, your ambulance a shell, you're under threat, and all you worry about is taking care of others. How could you not see yourself in the same light as you see Mac?" He shrugged his big, square shoulders. "Doc, no matter what it takes, next shift, Asher Jardine, Street Doctor will be back on her turf. While you fuss over your people, I'll watch out for you, making sure you're safe. Okay?"

They'd moved closer to each other. His heat reached Asher, tempting her to step into the warmth of his body. It would be so easy. Too easy. She clenched her fist hard to stop her fingers from moving to stroke his jaw.

She nodded. More emotion to fuel her headache.

"And doc, when I find out who's responsible for doing this to you, they're going to suffer."

Asher pushed her fingers through her hair, dislodging her scrunchie. She tightened it before dropping her hands to her side. On her next breath, she stepped back from Mitch. And his warmth. "We might as well head off. I've had enough for one day." She massaged her temples.

"Headache back?"

"Like a steam train."

He draped his arm across her shoulder. "Do you have your doctor's bag?"

"I think I left it in your truck."

"Okay. I'll take you home."

They crossed the garage and stood at the door, looking toward the yard and the burnt-out shell of the ambulance. Asher gulped back a sob, and Mitch flicked the switch, flooding the garage with darkness. He locked the side door, and together they edged past the police tape toward the parking lot.

He opened the truck door and helped her into the cabin before shutting it behind her. He strolled around the other side, hauled himself up inside, started the engine, and turned on the heater.

Ten minutes later, he pulled the big truck in behind Asher's car and turned to face her. "What are your plans for later today?"

"The guy from the fire department mentioned an arson investigation. For the ambulance." She shoved her teeth against her lip to stop tears from falling. "But there was no mention of how long it will take." A sigh escaped her, and she blinked furiously to stop the tears. "I'll talk to the authorities later this morning, get some sort of time frame. Hopefully sooner rather than later. Then I can start sorting my office." She pulled the handle and when the door opened, she climbed out, grabbed her doctor's bag, then placed it at her feet. "Then I guess the clean-up begins."

"Insurance should cover cleaning." Mitch said as he crossed to stand beside her.

Asher lips twitched at his words. "Probably, but I worked to set it up. I'll need to be involved in the clean-up to make sure it feels like mine. My filing system is a tad unique. Thank heavens for Bridget." A sigh escaped, and she looked at him. "You think I'm nuts, don't you? After all, it's only a building. It's only an ambulance." The sob escaped, almost deteriorated to tears. She shook her head, straightened her back, and turned away.

A big warm hand clasped her wrist. She turned and looked up at Mitch, glimpsing compassion in his gorgeous eyes. Her heart thumped harder.

"Whatever happens, wherever you work from, you'll stamp your personality all over it."

She smiled. "Thank you."

He smiled back. "I have business to take care of early. I'll come by later to see how you're doing."

"Not necessary."

"I know." He held her gaze. "I'll see you around mid-morning."

"Thanks." She yawned, and her lips twisted. "It's been a rough day."

Mitch released her wrist and stepped back. "It will get better." He picked up her bag and walked beside her. "Go inside, take some pain killers, and hit the sheets. If you need anything, call. Okay?"

"I will. Night.".

"Night Doc."

She unlocked the door, stepped inside, and closed it behind her before crossing to the front window, watching Mitch climb into his truck. Asher didn't drop her gaze. He gave a salute and reversed up the drive. She stood motionless until he turned his truck onto the road.

The annoying ache inside her skull refused to abate. Negative talk slid in, filling every synaptic space with issues she couldn't deal with. Not now. Her mind flashed back to when the man hunting her brother had grabbed her. She didn't fight. She'd have to accept that. But it didn't make her a coward. It meant she was a darn sight smarter than she thought.

Maybe all the breathing and counting techniques were working. After the time she'd been practicing, she hoped so. Learning to control her emotions made her way of looking at life a lot easier. But sometimes, just sometimes, the old Asher reared her head. And that rarely ended well. The new Asher hated it when that happened. Hated when she lost control. And the negative effect it had on her.

At the kitchen entry, she flicked on the light, opened the cupboard door. With still so much to do before bed, she'd make do with over-the-counter meds with some herbal tea. Surely that would get rid of her headache.

Flicking the switch on the kettle, she drew a deep breath. What was that scent? She sniffed again. Musk? She shook her head. Never in her house. That scent curled her stomach, fed fear through her veins. Resurrected memories of a man she despised. And feared. She froze. *Run Asher. Get out.* She fled across the polished wooden floors toward the front door and hauled it open, only to have a big hand reach over her shoulder and slam it shut jarring her whole body. She trembled with rage. She would not be at anyone's mercy, not again. Sucking in another lungful of the disgusting musk scent, she turned, fists clenched, teeth bared. And swung blindly. Hard. Her fist connected with bone.

She turned back toward escape.

"Who taught you to punch like that?"

At the sound of a familiar voice, air whooshed out of her. Her legs wobbled as she turned and faced him. Her throat closed. He'd changed. Hollow cheekbones, pale skin, dark circles surrounding his eyes. Not her father, but the next worse person in her life.

Greg. Her brother. With eyes so like hers, but sharper and almost slitted. The five o'clock shadow he favored looked like midnight. He looked hard. Mean. Even as he rubbed his cheek where her fist connected with it, didn't soften him. If there were any gentler emotions inside him, he'd hidden them well.

She didn't know what he'd done to become involved with the guy who assaulted her earlier, but from his icy demeanor, she guessed, it wasn't anything positive.

A red graze marked the bone beneath his eye. "Hello, Asher."

The siblings glared at each other.

"Goodbye, Greg. You're not welcome here."

His empty stare unsettled her gut. He was on something. She could guess a dozen names. None of them good. She tipped her chin and refused to drop her gaze.

"I need to talk to you." His tone was somewhere between whine and threat.

She assumed he was trying to be nice. It wasn't working. "Why?" She shook her head, ready to battle. But her training kicked in. *Be calm and give him nothing.* "What do you want?"

He raked his gaze over her. "You've changed."

She shrugged. "Again, what do you want, Greg?" Asher pushed past him and went back to the kitchen. Her head pounded. With trembling fingers, she broke the blister pack of pain killers, popped the pills into her mouth, and swallowed them. An irrational thought lurched through her brain. Is this how he started his drug dependence? Whatever it was—or wasn't—he'd followed her into the kitchen as she hit the switch to reheat the kettle. *Breathe, Asher.*

"I need to talk to you. I'm in trouble." More whine this time, less bluster.

"With whom? The same guy who caused this?" She touched the bandage on her head. "The same guy who threatened me?"

She shook her head, wincing as the pain jabbed. "Are you involved with him?"

"No."

Of course not! "So why are they chasing you?"

"I know stuff. They want to shut me up."

"So, you *are* involved." *Please pain pills, kick in soon.*

"I told you no." His voice ascended to a chilling shrillness. He took a couple of breaths before turning away.

In those few seconds, Asher observed him and noticed the sporadic movement of his head and the wildness in his eyes. He looked primed to explode. Asher shivered. No point talking to him in this state. "Do you want something to drink?"

He nodded. "Coffee." He paused. "Please."

Asher made herself a cup of herbal tea and Greg, his strong, black, no-sugar coffee. When she pulled out a seat at the kitchen table, he drifted across the room, sat opposite her, picked up the mug, and sipped.

Ignoring her earlier advice to herself she asked. "So, you have no involvement with someone who wants to shut you up. Permanently, I assume. What do you expect me to do? Beat them up with my stethoscope? Tell them to play in some other sandpit? Kick sand in their faces?"

Her macabre humor obviously made no impact on him in his drug-addled state as he sat staring at his coffee.

Time for a different tack. She sighed. "Is there anyone you can contact to help you? Someone in your unit maybe?"

He thumped the timber topped table so hard her tea sloshed. "No. If you can't help, there's no one."

"So, I repeat. What in hell do you want me to do? Maybe I could contact someone." She almost said Mitch but changed her mind.

"You honestly believe that would work?" He scoffed. "Obviously, you still think you're the world's number one fixer."

"That's not such a bad thing when you want me to fix something." Asher lifted her cup, sniffed the chamomile, and sipped the tea.

"It is when you put your career on hold to look after street people." He made it sound like a disease.

"We're not discussing me." She met his gaze and held it.

"You took her name. Why?"

She hadn't expected that! Asher sucked in a breath and shut her eyes. *Because Riva Jardine took me into her home after my stinking, drunken father dumped me into foster care. Because she saved my life.* "That's none of your business." She took another sip of tea. "Greg, what sort of trouble are you in?" She kept her voice gentle.

"None of your business," he snarled.

"Well, actually, yes, it is. You want me to fix something for you but won't tell me what. Not to mention that someone looking for you physically assaulted me. They said they'd be watching. Tell me how you think I can help you, or get out. I don't want your problems."

"I need the letters I sent you from Afghanistan."

What? Another sip. "I don't have any letters."

"What did you do with them?" He slammed his mug down, slopping coffee everywhere.

Fear reared its head. She began silently counting in French. "I received no letters from you."

"Liar." He roared. His face flushed as he rested his fists on the table, stood, and loomed over her.

Asher shoved her fists against her stomach to halt the fear snaking into her gut as she watched Greg morph into their father just before he'd given her a flogging for some trifling offence. Taking a deep breath, she forced her hands apart and lifted them, picking up her cup so he wouldn't see them tremble. Her stomach lurched. Bile welled in her throat. She met Greg's gaze, determined to control her anxiety. "I've heard nothing from you since they deployed you. Nothing. That includes letters. Now, get out."

She refused to drop her gaze and watched as he sat back down. He'd obviously realized bullying wouldn't work. If he reverted to his usual ways of manipulation, pleading would be next.

"Asher, you have to. They're going to kill me."

She rolled her eyes. She'd heard it all before, every time he'd come begging for money to keep his bookie off his back. "That's not my problem."

"I need those letters."

"I. Don't. Have. Them." She considered his blue eyes so like her own, and prayed they'd never look that cold. "Give yourself up, Greg."

"And who will protect you if I do?"

He would protect her! He couldn't protect himself. "I don't need you. I can look after myself. Now get out before I call the cops and report you for breaking and entering." Asher rose, strode to the front door, and tugged it open.

He moved toward her, eyes downcast, shoulders slumped, a pitiful figure. It wasn't working this time. At the door, he faced her. "Asher?"

She shook her head. "Leave, and don't come back. You're not welcome." She slammed the door shut the second he was outside.

With trembling fingers, she dragged the latch across the door. Back in the kitchen, she checked the deadbolts on the windows and door. All still locked. How in hell did he get in? She thought back to earlier when she ran out of the house. Had she locked the door? Or had she only pulled it closed? Her head throbbed. Her throat ached. What was she going to do? Would he come back? What if the guys after him were watching?

Call Mitch. His image swam into her mind. Big. Strong. Warm. She sucked in a breath. *No. It's too late.*

After rinsing the mugs and wiping the coffee spills, she trudged down the hall to her room and switched on the light. Her reflection stared back at her from her dresser mirror. Pale-faced with big eyes. *Is that really me?* "You're okay," she whispered. "You're okay." She flopped onto her bed and buried her head under her pillow. *Your entire world's falling apart, and you hide under a pillow.* She squeezed her eyes shut. "Shut up, Asher."

CHAPTER 10

At the sound of the doorbell, an exhausted Asher dragged herself away from the computer. Passing the window, she saw Mitch outside, and her brow dipped. He said he'd come, but she hadn't expected him to. It had been a rotten night. And now she'd have to tell him about Greg. Jaw clenching at the thought, she decided not today. Tomorrow would be soon enough.

Long, slender fingers tugged the band on her ponytail and smoothed the shirt down over her jeans before reaching to yank the door open.

As always, at the sight of him, all male, all sex on legs, leaning against the door frame, her heart settled into its usual accelerated beat. His dark blue hoodie emphasized broad, muscled shoulders. Her gaze dropped to the jeans. Thigh huggers. *Breathe, Asher. Just breathe.*

"Morning, Doc." He passed her a to-go cup that smelled of something divine.

Accepting the coffee, Asher sipped and sighed. "Mm, nectar. I so need this. Thank you, Mitch." Pulling the door wide open, she gestured for him to enter.

"How are you holding up?".

Asher closed the door gently before turning back to him with lips curled in an attempted smile of reassurance. "I'm getting there. On the phone since eight this morning. Insurance, police... I called Hamish."

"And?"

She headed for the living room, with his solid presence following close behind. "He's organizing a meeting with the local council and the others involved with our charity, to see how we can continue our service. He'll let me know when it's arranged."

"Doc...I need to ask. Can you take some time off? Like now? I've arranged to meet some friends, and I'd like you to come."

"Where?"

"Mt. Tambourine."

She huffed out a breath. "I'm trying to find a van I can use for Street Doctor."

The faint smile that curved his lips and lightened his eyes hinted at secrets. "I've been making calls too, Doc. I might have a solution. But I really need to leave now. I had to rearrange the times, and I don't want to keep the guys waiting."

Asher tried to hide her curiosity behind another sip of coffee, before querying, "Guys?"

Wide shoulders rose and fell in a shrug. "Friends. Please come. The past few days have been beyond stressful. You need some time off."

Unable to look away from those gorgeous shoulders, Asher jotted down a quick mental list of to-dos versus done. Done won. She grinned back at him. "Okay."

"Gotta go." His lips curved into a full smile that reached his eyes this time.

Her stomach lurched. *No feelings,* she reminded herself with a mental shake. But that little voice in her head demanded, *then just have sex.* But she crammed that little voice back into its box while placing the coffee cup on the side table and grabbing her jacket off the couch.

"I'm ready." With that she picked up her cup, bag and phone and headed out the door. Making sure it locked behind her.

At his truck, he held the door open for her, his heat caressing her as she brushed past him to climb up into her seat. With a little shiver and a silent sigh of appreciation, Asher shoved the buckle of her seatbelt into place.

The big V8 under the hood of his truck ate the miles to Mt. Tambourine. Music played softly, while he filled the hour telling stories about his time as an MP.

She laughed. "And you survived that?"

He grinned. "Barely. Those female soldiers outsmart their male counterparts every time. Despite that, they don't see it coming."

"Tell me about your friends," Asher prompted.

"I'll let you make your own mind up about them. But I guarantee you, they'll help get your mind off your troubles for a while. They're great guys."

"Okay then."

They pulled into a parking lot where three men waited—different shapes and sizes—but the common denominator was the smiles that spread across their faces as Mitch ambled toward them.

"Guys, this is Doctor Asher Jardine." Asher stepped towards Mitch. "She's—", he paused, his eyes narrowing, "— my friend."

"Hello gorgeous. I'm Nic." He grasped Asher's hand and raised it to his lips. "My pleasure is your pleasure."

"Back off, Romeo." Another guy jostled him out of the way. "I'm Pete. Don't let him turn you off the male species. He thinks women love him." He flashed a big smile. "We know they just feel sorry for his ugly mug."

"Really?" Asher looked back at the gorgeous, blond Nic. "I can understand that."

Raucous laughter erupted at her comments. Asher's lips twitched.

"I'm Ryan. My friends call me Legs." The third man pulled up his jeans to show her his prosthetics.

"I'll stick with Ryan."

"Don't you want to be my friend?"

Asher met his gaze and saw the devilment in his eyes. "That might be the safer option."

"Safe. Safe? Are you kidding me? You're hanging out with him." He pointed at Mitch. "Man, I'm a sweetheart next to him."

Asher met Mitch's gaze, and all the tension of the past twenty-four hours dissolved.

"Let's get this show on the road," Mitch said.

Asher watched, enthralled, as the group pulled out bags from the back of the van and set up hang-gliders. They worked in unison amidst laughter and taunting.

"Doc, can you give us a hand?" Mitch called.

She strolled to where the men stood and stroked the colorful fabric of the two kites. Mitch's eyes resembled warm chocolate, and a flush tinged his cheeks. He looked like a kid in a candy shop.

"Hang gliding. Really? I never picked you as an adrenalin junkie." Her lips twitched.

"There's nothing like the freedom of floating on air." He fitted a piece of fine metal into a cloth cover and continued to the next one.

"I'll take your word for it." She shook her head. "You needed my help?" She wrapped her arms around herself to ward off the biting wind.

Mitch met her gaze. "You don't fancy floating on air?"

"It's not the floating, it's the crashing into the ground that puts me off."

"Que sera sera." He grinned again. "Will you please drive my truck down to the pickup area? Ryan will drive the van."

"So that's the reason you asked me along, to drive your truck?"

"No. Look if it's…"

She smiled. "Teasing. I really don't mind."

He shook his head. "We're ready guys. Let's go" Mitch said.

Asher stood back and scrutinized Mitch as he carried the kite to the launch position. Her stomach churned as she appreciated his powerful physique. When he laughed at some comment of Nic's, the deep husky sound gave her goosebumps. Her stomach clenched as he prepared to launch. What if he crashed to the ground? What if they collided midair? The thought of not having Mitch around filled her with dread. She shook her head. *Don't think like that.* She changed her focus to the view.

Her breath caught at the beauty of the colors of the earth, blended like a glorious patchwork quilt. Icy wind whipped her face and plastered her clothes to her body.

Nic was solo, with Mitch and Pete in tandem. Helmets, yes. Kites attached. Yes. Heart hammering against her ribs? Yes. Her breathing stalled as they disappeared off the edge of the cliff. She didn't breathe again until they floated above her. Like they were dancing in the stunning azure sky.

Ryan approached her a short time later. "Time to go."

"Already?" They strolled toward the cars.

"They'll probably be waiting for us."

"Hopefully in one piece." Asher frowned.

"Mitch has been doing this for years. He's a qualified instructor. He wouldn't put himself or anyone else at risk."

"Good to know."

"He's one of life's good guys."

Asher turned her head and glanced at the tall bloke beside her. "You don't have to sell him to me. I can see the value of the man." But she believed Mitch was withholding something from her. She'd noticed the look in his eyes as he stared at her. Then he'd say something, stop, and continue on to another subject. She didn't like it.

"Well, let's go get them. I'm starving." Ryan said then stepped up into the driver's seat. She watched ensuring he had no problems then climbed into Mitch's beast.

When they arrived at the pickup point, Mitch, Pete, and Nic had collapsed the kites, ready to pack away. Asher climbed out of the truck as Mitch's wide smile lured her to his side. "Looks like you enjoyed yourself."

"I did. It's been ages." He knelt and packed the kite into its carrier and loaded it into the van. "You guys made a booking?"

"Yup. We'll meet you there. The band starts at three." Nic smiled.

"Here's hoping there's a crowd," Mitch said.

"Adrian reckons they're getting a good following. See you there." Nic pulled the door shut.

Mitch waved as they drove off. "Ready, Doc?"

"Absolutely."

"If you need to go back?"

"No." It sounded harsh. She swallowed, then smiled. "No. As you said, I need a bit of relax time." She stared up into his eyes. "I'm looking forward to having something to eat and listening to music. I haven't had a day off in ages."

He opened the truck door for her. "Let's go have some fun."

They were heading toward the cafe when Mitch's phone rang. He pulled over and picked up the cell and after a few minutes said. "Okay. We'll be there." He disconnected and turned to face Asher. "You and I have an appointment tomorrow to see about buying a baby."

"How?"

"Someone I know made some calls to set it up. Now, we can gather whatever information we can and pass it on to the authorities."

"That's the best news I've had in days."

"Let's go celebrate." He pulled the truck back onto the road. A few miles further up the road he dropped Asher outside the café and went to park the truck. The café enticed her inside with the smell of percolating coffee and spices. Asher's stomach grumbled. She glanced at her watch. Well past lunch. No wonder everything smelled extra delicious.

Mitch held the door open, and she preceded him along the extended corridor and out the back to an enormous deck. PVC blinds held back the brisk breeze.

Tucked against a rail, the three-man band tuned their instruments—one on double bass, one on keyboards, one on drums. Further along, Mitch's friends waited. She waved back. Mitch pulled some tables together as everyone gathered around. Asher settled into a heavy wooden chair facing the view, relaxed her shoulders, and breathed in a huge lungful of peace.

A server placed bottles of water on their table, then handed them menus. "I'll be back to take your orders." She breezed away.

Half an hour later, they had ordered their lunches, and were sitting around the table, sipping drinks, and appreciating the stunning view, when Mitch brought up the subject of her ambulance. The joy filling Asher fizzled out. With a gusty sigh, she gave her attention to the mountains. As, her mind replayed the horror of the fire.

"Asher. Asher..." Mitch's voice broke through her reverie.

"I'm sorry, my mind was elsewhere." She made herself smile.

"We've figured out how we can get you back on the streets." Laughter erupted as the words came out of Pete's mouth.

"Ha. Ha." A lopsided grin twisted Pete's lips.

"I get comments like that all the time. I'm used to it." She rested her chin against her steepled fingers. "So, tell me."

Pete continued. "After Mitch told us why he had rearranged our time this morning, we put our heads together and made some phone calls. We've found you a camper trailer."

Asher straightened and took in the beaming expressions on their faces. "Really? How much?" She could hardly string the words together.

Pete shook his head. "Gratis."

Asher placed her hands on her chest and struggled not to gape, amazed at the generous offer. "Free?"

"Free," Mitch repeated. "It's old, but well maintained." He pointed to the guy with the double bass. "Since Adrian started this place, he doesn't use it. Until you get your new ambulance, it's yours."

Asher's fingers covered her mouth. Tears stung her eyes. She tried to speak, but nothing came.

Mitch continued. "It takes a bit of setting up, so, the guys here"—he waved his arm toward his mates— "are new volunteers for Health for the Homeless. Their primary responsibility will be the setting up and packing up of your new office." He looked at her. "You okay with some injured soldiers on your roster?"

Asher's heartbeat throbbed like bongo drums. "At least they don't look like cops." She held Mitch's gaze and smiled. "Thanks."

"You're welcome."

"Hang on, what about us?" Ryan demanded. "Where's my thank you?" He puckered up.

Asher rose and hugged her newest volunteers. "I'm so grateful. When can you start?"

Mitch looked at her. "We've set up a tentative roster. After we've had lunch, the guys are going to tow the trailer down and set it up. I arranged it with Hamish. There's not a lot of storage, so on the way back, we have to stop at a hardware store and buy some big plastic storage boxes."

Asher walked back to Mitch, leaned over the chair, and wrapped her arms around his shoulders and hugged him. His heat mushroomed through her body. *Damn, he feels good.* Her head rested against the side of his neck, and she battled the urge to press her lips against the pulse beating there. Instead, she inhaled his spicy scent. Mitch's big hands covered hers and held them against his chest. She wanted to burrow into him. Sanity shredded the magical veil shrouding her, and she eased away. It was a much safer choice. "Thank you again."

"It's only a temporary measure. But at least you'll be able to work. That's what's important." He smiled.

After the band finished their set, the musicians placed their instruments against the wooden rail, and Mitch motioned one of them over to the table.

"Asher, meet Adrian."

Adrian took her hand in his firm grip and shook it.

"Your offer of your camper trailer is a godsend. Please, let me compensate you."

Adrian shook his head. "Not necessary. Don't need it anymore, and I'd rather see it being used for a worthwhile cause than sitting in a garage going moldy."

"I'm truly grateful." Asher's voice thickened.

"The service you offer shouldn't be at risk because of what those assholes did to your business. This is my way of sticking it to them, so, you keep it for as long as you need." Adrian met her eyes, with dead seriousness "But, you're going to have your work cut out for you looking after this lot." He nudged Pete in the ribs. "This one never shuts up. Within a couple of days, you'll be begging me to take it back."

Asher laughed and settled back against her chair, listening to their banter. They'd drawn her into their circle of friendship, and for the first time in ages, calmness filled her.

"Hey, Mitch, did you mention a fundraiser?" Nic asked.

Asher groaned aloud. Between Bridge and Mitch, she was sick of hearing about it.

"You don't sound keen, Asher," Pete said.

She shrugged. "It's a brilliant way to raise much-needed funds. And everyone will have a great time. But..."

"But?" Pete asked.

She looked from one curious set of eyes into others. "I hate public speaking. Hate it. But the council is adamant this year that I talk about the service we offer."

"Is there dancing?" Nic asked.

Asher nodded.

"Decent feed?" This from Pete

"Four exquisite courses. And fine wine," Asher replied.

"How many people will attend this soiree?" Ryan threw at her.

"Three hundred."

Nic leaned toward her. "Do you have a date?"

"Um..."

"I'm taking her." Mitch stared into her eyes. "Aren't I?"

Her belly clenched. "Are you? We'll see."

"Do you have a friend?" Nic met her eyes.

The crowd around the table erupted into laughter.

Nic joined in. "You can't hang a bloke for trying, can you?"

• • • • ● ● ● ● ● • •

Asher and Mitch followed behind the lunatics driving the camper trailer down the mountain.

"What did they do in the Army? Drive badly? They're shocking."

Mitch wore a lop-sided grin on his face. "These guys do lots of crazy stuff."

"Like Hang gliding?"

He shot her a quick glance, "Doc, you gotta learn to let go. You could have an accident crossing the street. You can't worry over what might happen."

"Says the adrenaline junkie that I let drive my ambulance." Just saying the word caused her throat to tighten.

"It's going to take time to sort out a new ambulance. Until then, we'll get your little army-type hospital up and running. When we erect the annex, it's an old fashioned, made of heavy canvas, along with the camper van, it will keep many patients warm and dry. It's not great, but it's enough to keep you on the streets and tending to the people who need you."

She twisted her pinky ring. "I know. But."

"No buts, Doc. We'll stop at the hardware shop, buy some containers, and get tonight's surgery up and running. We can get everything else we need tomorrow." He switched on the truck lights. "We're going to have to hustle, or we'll to be late.

"Mitch." She reached over and rested her hand against his knee. "If I haven't said so, I'm so grateful for what you organized."

A smile ghosted his lips. "No worries. Glad to help. We all are."

Mitch concentrated on the road as the twists and turns took his full concentration. And it gave him a chance to think. He was going to catch Jones and give him to the authorities, who, hopefully, wouldn't just put him in a psych ward this time.

They needed to lock Jones up. He hated not telling Asher the whole truth, but orders were orders.

"I received another phone call earlier when you and Adrian went to look at the camper. It's a definite go-ahead for tomorrow. My contacts received a message from the lawyer requesting confirmation they'll attend the three o'clock appointment."

"You never said who your contact is."

Mitch kept his gaze on the road, grateful he didn't have to meet her shrewd eyes. "I have lots of contacts I've met through my role in the Army. I just put it out there. One thing he specified—this is top-end organization. Tomorrow, we will take on new identities. No jeans and Doc Martens. If we are looking at a private adoption, we must play the part of people who can afford to pay."

"Ok, I'll drag something suitable from my daytime wardrobe."

"And I'll wear a suit."

"I'm still not happy about it, Mitch."

"You'll be fine."

"What if I'm not? What if my anger gets the better of me?"

A quick sideways glance. Then he sighed. "That night Charli's boyfriend harassed you. You were livid. How did you calm yourself down after that?"

"Counted in Greek."

"Well, if you feel your emotions getting the better of you, walk away and count."

She nodded.

"We don't have to do it My friend can find someone else. May take a while. But he will find someone."

Asher shook her head. "No, if I can prevent any young girl from being coerced by a threatening partner to sell her baby, I'm in. And if by some chance we can link Charli's boyfriend to some sort of baby-selling scheme, that's a bonus. That guy is a bully. I'll do what needs to be done, and I'll be convincing. Watch me."

"The appointment's set for three. They've asked us to arrive fifteen minutes early to do the introductory paperwork. Then we meet the lawyer who will explain the entire procedure to us."

"What time will you pick me up?"

"Two."

She nodded. "Okay."

Mitch continued. "And they have created a full dossier for us, including names, backgrounds, and jobs. He's supplying me with a new Beamer. Gotta look the part."

Asher smiled. "I used to have a BMW. Sold it a while back."

"What color?" He glanced her way.

"Midnight blue convertible. I miss her sometimes. Especially in the summer. Flying down the M1 heading for the Gold Coast, roof down, wind blowing, singing at the top of my voice."

"Why did you sell it?"

"We needed work done on the ambulance more than I needed my car."

He said nothing. A lump stuck in his throat. He'd read in the dossier someone left her a substantial legacy. For a while, he'd thought her a spoiled rich girl. "Never judge a woman by your mother's standards," his father had told him many times as he grew up.

They stopped at a hardware store, grabbed what they needed, and drove to Street Doctor. As promised, her three new volunteers had set the camper trailer up, but not the annex. That would be a job for tomorrow night when they would have more time.

Mitch opened the door for Asher, noticing the brightness of her eyes as she shook her head and took in the crazy scene before them.

"Life changes in a heartbeat, Doc. The past twenty-four hours proved it. Let's go."

CHAPTER 11

itch reversed the BMW into a vacant space on the street, shut off the ignition, and turned to face Asher. She'd drawn her lush lips into a straight, tight line, and her eyes flashed blue fire. It took a truckload of determination to stop himself from reaching over and easing the frown marring her brow. "Are you alright with how this is going to play out?"

She huffed out a breath. "I am. But I don't like it."

"Doc, more bees with honey, remember?"

She rolled her eyes. "Whatever."

Giving up his internal battle to keep his hands to himself, he reached across the center console of the luxury vehicle and took her hand. "Trust me. This is the best way."

"Going into that office and pretending we're a married, barren couple desperate for a baby...you think that's a good plan? Really?"

He ignored the sarcasm in her voice. "It's the way they work. The emailed report we received last night explained it. We're being interviewed as prospective parents. After the interview, they will run a credit check on the information we've given them. After a few days, they'll call us back in for another interview if we're eligible for their private adoption service. That's what we're finding out about."

"Selling babies is illegal."

"That's not what we're looking at."

She blew out a hard breath. "I know. I know. It's just, I really don't like any of this."

He stroked the back of her hand. "Me neither. But we said we'd do it, so let's go."

They climbed from the car. Mitch couldn't drag his gaze from Asher as she grabbed the light grey jacket that matched her skirt off the back seat and slipped it on over the silky, long-sleeved, high necked, pink blouse. He sucked in a breath. *She's a stunner.* In her usual work gear of Doc Martens, jeans, and sweatshirt, she looked gorgeous. But dressed to the nines, her beauty shone. Shame about the scowl marring her beautiful brow.

He buttoned his jacket, locked the car door, and moved to the footpath to stand beside her.

At this time of the afternoon, the city noise drowned out any conversation as they moved amongst the crowds of people scurrying along the streets. An endless procession of vehicles hummed along the roads, honking horns, and skipping lanes.

He looked around the architectural high-rises dotting the landscape. He stepped closer to Asher. "I much prefer the older buildings."

She shrugged. "Me, too. Although, not all the modern buildings lack character."

"See?" He nudged her with his shoulder. "Something else we agree on besides our enjoyment of coffee."

She shook her head and gave a gentle smile.

They stopped outside the building housing the lawyer's office. Mitch gathered her hand in his. "Let's get this show on the road." An elevator whisked them to the twentieth floor of the chrome and glass building in ten seconds flat.

Mitch kept hold of her hand as they stepped out into the foyer. He told himself it was for show and to make sure she didn't bolt. That it felt right had nothing to do with it. *Yeah, you just keep telling yourself that.* He bent his head toward her. "Doc, your face looks like thunder. We don't want to give them any reason to doubt our application."

"I won't give them reason to doubt us. If I feel my emotions rising, I'll remember the reason why I'm here."

"Good. We're here on a reconnaissance mission to learn what we can and gather evidence, so we can pass the info onto my sources."

The tapping of Asher's heels on the granite tiles echoed along the hallway as they looked for the office.

Outside the frosted glass door with the placard advertising *Cassidy, Swain: Lawyers*, they paused. "Take a breath, Doc."

He pushed open the door and paced toward the ultra-stylish receptionist sitting behind a waist-high wall of polished mahogany. Mitch greeted the receptionist and said, "Mr. and Mrs. Hammersfield. We have an appointment with Ms. Cassidy."

The receptionist smiled. "Ms. Cassidy is on a call. Please take a seat. She shouldn't be long."

Mitch followed Asher as she paced to the window to stare out over Brisbane's cityscape. Her hand trembled in his. He ran his fingers back and forth to ease her nerves. "It'll be fine," he whispered close to her ear, playing the part of supportive husband to the max. "Just do your counting thing. Relax."

"Mr. and Mrs. Hammersfield."

"Showtime," Mitch whispered and dropped his arm across Asher's shoulders.

Together, they followed the older woman into her private lair. The plush office screamed interior designer, from the enormous mahogany desk, and cushioned leather chairs to the top-of-the-line barista coffee machine sitting idly against the far wall.

"I'm Cynthia Cassidy. Please take a seat." She indicated the chairs facing her desk with a sweep of her hand before reclining gracefully in her own leather swivel chair. "Can I offer you refreshment?"

"No. Thank you," Mitch replied. "We have another appointment in an hour. We'd like to get started."

Auburn brows arched. "Of course." She fussed with a stack of papers on her immaculate desk. "I'll explain how our service works. Then you can fill out the paperwork."

"I emailed the completed paperwork to you last night." Mitch stated.

"Thank you for that. I'll have my secretary bring it in after our discussion." She leaned further back into her chair. "We'll do our checks and get back to you about your application within a week." Her monotone didn't change.

Mitch nodded.

Asher remained silent. She hadn't taken her gaze off Ms. Cassidy since they entered the office. *Keep it together, Doc.*

The lawyer droned on for what seemed like an eternity.

"If we pass all your checks, how long until we can have a baby?" Asher finally asked. Her voice wavered, but Mitch knew it was from anger, not from the emotions of a frustrated woman desperate for a child. He hoped the Cassidy woman wouldn't realize the difference.

"There isn't a set time. We try to find a child that will match the adopted family." Again, that cold, passionless tone grated on Mitch's nerves.

"Do we meet the mother?" He asked.

"No. Complete anonymity," Ms. Cassidy replied. "From the time they sign the agreement to give up their child, our company houses the birth mother in one of our exclusive residences and meets their medical expenses. We register them in one of the finest private maternity hospitals in the city. After the birth mother has delivered, pediatricians perform a complete health check on the baby. We return the birth mother to the residence, where she remains under the care of a mid-wife until her final health check. After that's completed, our company lawyer oversees the finalization of the legal matters and the doctor's discharge."

"And then?" Mitch hoped he sounded like an apprehensive future father who wanted things done right and not like an interrogator.

"We pay the last payment into the birth mother's account. She leaves with a substantial amount to start a new life without the drain of a child she can't afford to keep. And our adoptive parents have their baby. It's a win-win situation."

"What age is the birth mother?" Asher asked.

"That's not relevant."

"They're probably young, though. Is a sixteen-year-old's signature legally binding?" Asher demanded.

Shutters fell over Ms. Cassidy's eyes. "I don't believe I mentioned the age of our birth mothers." Her tone changed to match her eyes. Icy.

"Just a figure of speech." He waved his hand, dismissing the subject. "But what occurs if she changes her mind?"

Jacketed shoulders rose and fell. "When the women first approach us, we invite them to a meeting where we explain all aspects of the adoption. Then we put them through a stringent selection criteria, where we explain due process to them. They know what they're doing."

Sure, they do, Mitch silently fumed. Like a frightened fifteen-year-old knew what 'due process' was.

"But can they change their minds?" Mitch pushed.

"They can, until they sign the last document."

And still no mention of the cooling off period, he'd read about in the research he'd done for private adoptions.

Asher's nails dig into his skin. He stroked her wrist, leaned toward her, and kissed her ear. "Count." Asher squeezed his hand back.

Mitch attempted what he hoped was a winning smile at the granite-faced female sitting opposite. "Sorry, we're just so worried that something could go wrong, and our dreams disappear in a cloud of dust, because a young mother changes her mind."

The lawyer inclined her head, her voice emotionless as she replied. "If you have no further questions, I'll have my secretary bring in the prepopulated paperwork for us to sign."

Asher broke into huge, gulping sobs.

"Darling, what's wrong?" Mitch asked.

Asher ducked her head. "I didn't think it would be so complicated. I don't want to wait. I want my baby now." Her voice grew shriller. Mitch kept his gaze averted so the lawyer wouldn't see the grin on his face from Asher's acting abilities.

"I know, but Ms. Cassidy has explained the procedure."

Asher lifted her face and met his eyes. Tears running down her cheeks. "You said there wouldn't be a wait. You promised."

Mitch stroked her arm. "Darling. It's okay. We'll find us a baby." He gave his attention back to Ms. Cassidy. "What can I do to expedite the process?"

"Nothing." Ms. Cassidy squared her shoulders. "We have our procedures. If you desire one of our babies, you need to go through due process."

Asher rose and pushed her chair back. It fell backward and landed soundlessly on the thick-pile carpet. "I have to go. I'm sorry." She turned and dashed from the room.

Mitch met Ms. Cassidy's gaze. "Have those papers brought in, I'll sign them. I'll talk to my wife and call back to set up our next appointment. They led us to believe you could help us get a baby quicker. I apologize for the misunderstanding."

After signing the forms, he rose, shook Ms. Cassidy's cold, limp hand, turned, and left the room.

Asher waited for him at the elevator bank. "So, how did I do? Do you think she believed my performance?"

"I believed it. But she didn't deviate from her original statement. If we want a baby we go through the correct channels."

Asher stabbed the down button. "From what I gathered, we, the professional couple, pay the expenses for the birth mother, who has already given the child up for adoption. We're not paying for the baby. We're just paying for the administration and to help a woman down on her luck. So, it's not illegal from their perspective. Sounds like crap to me."

The ding drew Mitch's attention to the arriving elevator. As the doors slid open, he scanned the people alighting and froze as he recognized a face in the crowd. Mitch turned on his heel to block Asher with his body and eased her backward against a wall. His head swooped, and he covered her mouth with his. His action was intended to keep her from asking questions and maybe drawing attention to herself but ended up becoming something entirely different as the magic of their kiss faded everything around him to background.

Asher wrapped her arms around his neck, drew him closer, and opened her mouth wider. The intensity changed, grew hotter, deeper. He leaned against her body and reveled in the feel of her breasts and her legs against him.

Her scent enticed him closer. He sucked in a breath and shuddered. *Pull away.* Then she sighed, and the sensible thought bolted.

His hands followed the lines of her body, found her hips, and tugged her closer. Her heat swamped him, and those little sighs from her drove him nuts. Asher in his arms, flush against him, felt more than right. Her tongue touched his, and his cock hardened. Damn. He'd never enjoyed kissing a woman as much as he did her.

DING.

It was like a bucket of cold water and the effect, immediate. He eased away, just far enough so he'd remember to breathe. He leaned his forehead against hers. "Where did that come from?"

She shook her head and looked away.

He let her go, turned, and stalked down the corridor.

Asher rushed to his side. "What?" she asked in a husky voice.

"Travis. He got out of the first lift."

"So, that's why you kissed me?"

He shrugged and stared into her steady, cobalt blue gaze. "I acted on impulse. I didn't want him to recognize us."

"Where did he go?"

"Not sure, but I'll hazard a guess."

They hurried down the corridor and stood to the side of the frosted glass door of Ms. Cassidy's office, just in time to see her lead Travis through her private door.

"Due process my butt. I bet we get a phone call real soon," Mitch stated.

"Let's go. As you said, we don't want Travis coming out and recognizing us. And I have to be at a meeting about the security of the Street Doctor." They were quiet as they headed back to the Beamer.

Twenty minutes later, Mitch dropped her at the front door of the local government office complex. "Asher, there's someplace I have to be, but I'll be here to pick you up around five."

"Thanks. The meeting shouldn't take that long."

"Good luck in there."

She grabbed her bags and turned to face him. "I'll see you later. Bye."

He leaned in to kiss her but stopped himself. *Let her go, Buchanan. Let her go.*

Hurrying toward the council building, Asher delved through her handbag for her phone and called Lily. "I'm running late. I'll call in the morning. Is Charli doing, okay?"

"Still resting."

"Okay. I'll fill you in on the meeting tomorrow."

"I'll make you brunch."

"Thanks. I have to go."

Asher disconnected, raced through the sliding glass doors and into the foyer, and stopped at reception. "Hello, I'm Doctor Jardine. I'm attending a meeting here."

"Yes, Doctor Jardine. They're expecting you. Third door down the hall on the right."

"Is there somewhere I can charge my phone?"

The young woman gave a smile. "There are charging ports on each table inside.

"Thanks." Asher placed her bags at her feet as she tidied her hair and straightened the pencil skirt. With a smile at the young receptionist, she picked up her bags and dashed down the hall and into the meeting. "I apologize for being late. My last meeting ran into overtime." She smiled at the suits and hurried around the table to sit by Bridget and Hamish. And plugged her phone in.

"Doctor Jardine," Councilor Jordan Anderson called from his position at the front of the room. "I want to say how sorry we are to hear about your ambulance being destroyed in the fire at your office complex."

Asher looked toward the authoritative voice. "Thank you." She smiled briefly.

"Are you going to be able to operate without your ambulance?" Councilor Anderson questioned.

She nodded. "We sure are. A little old fire won't stop us. Some friends have gifted Health for the Homeless a camper trailer for as long as we need it." She smiled. "And some extra volunteers to set it up and take it down. But we will only use it at Ridgeleigh. St. Joeys has set aside a room for us to work from, so yes, Street Doctor is still out working in the community."

Applause broke out around the room.

Then Councilor Anderson continued. "There have been some security issues at the Street Doctor site. Is there a reason for concern?"

Maybe if you got out from behind your desks and come out to the site, you'd find out for yourselves. She fixed a smile on her lips. "There have been a few issues. There's a drug gang, or should I say Ice gang, seeing as that's their drug of choice. They've caused a bit of trouble. I've notified the local police, and they're going to do extra drive bys. I have a full-time driver now for myself and my nurse. He also doubles as security. I can't foresee any problems he couldn't handle."

"Good to know. Your safety is paramount to us."

"Thank you." She took a deep breath. "Councilor, there are so many people out there that desperately need our help. We need more donations."

Another member of the local council stated, "After the Gala on Saturday, with all the positive publicity it will garner, companies will fall over themselves to become involved."

"I hope so. The patients need us." Asher poured herself a glass of water. Her mouth felt like cotton.

"This gala is vital to the growth of this service you created, Doctor Jardine. We don't want any trouble. I'll speak to the venue regarding extra security. We will make sure security is visible." He smiled and looked around the table. "Thank you all for coming, I'll see you all Saturday night." He looked back at Asher. "Save me a dance, Doctor."

Asher smiled. Again. "Of course."

Suits exited the room. Asher dashed to a side table and grabbed a coffee and a sandwich. Hamish and Bridget joined her.

"That wasn't as bad as I thought. I was terrified they were going to close us down," Asher said.

"Not going to happen." Hamish draped his arm over her shoulder. "And how in heaven's name did you score a camper trailer?" Bridget demanded.

"One of Mitch's mates." She didn't go into details. "So, Health for the Homeless survives another night. Mitch is coming to pick us up around five."

"Ethan's here already. I'll see you a little later. Hamish, we'll drop you home if you like?" With that, Bridget dropped a kiss on Asher's cheek as she passed.

"Bye." Asher grabbed her carryall and headed for the bathroom set to the side of the room. It was way more comfortable out on the streets wearing jeans and a sweatshirt, rather than her pencil skirt and sheer blouse.

She changed quickly, wiped the make-up off and tidied her ponytail. She recalled Mitch's fingers combing her hair back from her face as he kissed her earlier. She shivered as the heat of that memory filled her. Her lips still tingled from his mouth on hers. Sweet heavens, even just thinking about it, made her breath hitch. Did he want to kiss her again? Did she want him to? She shook her head. *No point fantasizing, Asher, you've got work to do.*

After they finished up at Street Doctor last night, they towed the camper trailer and parked it at her place. But tonight, she would be working in a fully functioning mobile clinic, with a collapsible table and bed and folding chairs.

Not perfect, but she'd have walked to the Street Doctor quadrangle towing a suitcase with supplies if she'd had to. She smiled as she pondered Mitch's reaction to that suggestion.

They'd bought a camp cupboard to hold dressings and utensils. It had a military hospital feeling, but for now, she'd make do. As excitement surged through her, she wrapped her arms around herself and laughed out loud. It didn't matter that it would take longer to set up. She was back working on the streets, where people needed her.

She shoved her clothes into her carry bag, hitched it over her shoulder and pulled on the door.

Nothing.

She tugged harder. Still, it didn't budge.

"Are you kidding me?" She heaved as hard as she could and still nothing. Her breathing quickened as she rattled the door. She went to grab her phone out of her bag and mentally saw herself plugging it into the port at the table. She peered at her watch. After five, Mitch would probably be outside waiting. *You will be fine.*

Then the lights went out.

Asher's breath lodged in her throat. What's happened? Power failure? Just here, or the entire building? *Stay calm.* She pounded her fists against the door and screamed at the top of her lungs.

Nothing.

Nobody.

She leaned back against the wall to work out what to do next. Chair legs screeched across the floor outside the door. An electrician? A cleaner? "Hello. Hello. I'm locked in here." She rattled the door to give emphasis to her yelling. *Are they deaf?* Nothing. Only footsteps and the sound of furniture being moved. And they were right outside the door. *Why won't they let me out?*

Somebody whistled softly. The tune resurrected memories. Dank, ugly fear gripped her throat, and her thoughts went dark, spiraling back to childhood when her father had flogged her before locking her away in a dark closet for tiny mistakes like spilling a cup of tea on the dining room table or not washing the dishes properly. Or for any other reason that took his fancy.

Tears burned behind her eyes. She tried to get a breath. *Don't go there, you're not that little girl anymore.* Still, she battled for calm. Knowing there was someone outside who was ignoring her plea was too much. She sank down and leaned against the door. *Breathe Asher, breathe. Be brave. Be brave.*

"Hey doc, where are you? I've been waiting outside."

Asher slammed her fists against the door. "In here. I can't get out."

Footsteps drew closer. The door opened a fraction. She scrambled to her feet, and it swung open. Mitch stood there. She launched herself against him and hung on for dear life. Tears held in so long escaped and poured down her cheeks.

"Doc. Doc. Settle." He ran his hand up and down her spine. "Asher."

She clung to him. "I couldn't get out. I couldn't get the door open. Someone locked me in. Nobody would help me. I heard someone." Her thoughts, her words, spilled out of control.

Mitch gathered her close and continually ran his hand along her spine, as though comforting a sad child. Which was exactly how she felt. After a few minutes of his gentle petting and soothing words, she stepped back.

He bent his head to stare into her eyes. "I've got you. You're okay."

She sucked in a breath. "I couldn't get out. The door wouldn't budge. Then the lights went out."

"Asher, I pushed it open."

"I'm not lying." She dragged in a breath.

"I'm not doubting you."

"Honest, I couldn't get out. I tried."

"It's okay. Let's go."

She nodded.

"Where's your other bag?" he asked as he half carried, half steered her toward the exit.

"Next to the food table. My phone's charging beside it."

"Wait here, I'll get it."

"No." She latched onto him tighter as fear snaked along her spine. "Don't leave me."

"Okay." He tucked her under his arm and crossed to the table. He bent and scooped up her mobile. When he grabbed her bag, a piece of paper fluttered to the desk. He lifted it and scanned the scrawl. "Asher, you're right, someone purposely locked you in there."

"How do you know?"

He handed her the paper.

Her hand trembled as she read the words aloud. "Bring your brother to us. Or next time you don't get out."

CHAPTER 12

Ten minutes later, they were travelling down the highway toward Mates and Eats. As Mitch turned his big truck into the parking area, the headlights hit the camper trailer and illuminated the Street Doctor logo emblazoned across the side. Someone had even painted a big red cross on the front flap. Asher smiled. Now it really looked like a mobile hospital.

When Mitch switched off the engine, Asher just sat and stared out into the hub.

"Are you going to be okay?" His velvet voice slid over her.

"Yes. No. I hope so." She pressed her lips together and pushed the heels of her hands against her eyes. "Please say nothing to Bridge about my melt down. I don't want to upset her."

It had taken Mitch a while to calm her. He hadn't asked questions as he held her against his strong chest, just ran his fingers up and down her spine, and murmured gently. It's okay, you're safe. Still now, her heart pounded way too hard. A panic attack? She hadn't suffered an episode like that in years and prayed she never would again. Hopelessness and weakness would never again define her.

So why now? Stress maybe? The last few days had been hellish.

She let out a heartfelt sigh and met Mitch's gaze. Her heart skipped a beat as the memory of that kiss, of being flush against his body earlier today, stampeded through her mind. Her body heated as the event replayed. She swiped her damp palms down the sides of her jeans. She should have pulled away, or at least not have responded so intensely to his curious mouth. She already believed he would be potent. Now she had the proof. All she had to do was figure out how to keep her hands off him. And that little voice deep down inside asked, *Why? And why hadn't she resisted?*

"When you're ready to talk, I'll listen." He stroked her arm from elbow to wrist.

A shiver followed the trail of heat from his touch. "I will." She nodded and turned away from the concern in his eyes and climbed from the truck.

Strains of "Rudolf, The Red Nosed Reindeer," rang out across the quadrangle as Asher dashed toward her temporary clinic, desperate to get out of the cutting wind. She shivered and pushed on, finally walking into the canvas waiting room of Health for the Homeless.

The tent held out the wind, making it a haven of relative warmth. Ryan, Pete, and Nic had done an outstanding job setting it up. They'd partitioned two of the walls off, one section for consults, the other as a waiting room. In the consultation room, there was a large fold-out table, stacked with heaps of huge plastic containers filled to bursting with every item a doctor would need. A big black chair sat behind another collapsible table holding a laptop, printer, and a blood pressure monitor. A couple of chairs stood before the desk.

The waiting room was empty, but they had set the chairs out, along with clip boards and patient forms. Everyone who came to see her had to fill out a form, but the end results varied. Not everyone used their legal name. Some signed, some didn't, it didn't matter. She turned no one away, except the Ice gang.

When Asher headed back outside, Legs sat in his wheelchair, by the table laden with food. Asher heard the banter between the group he was with and smiled.

"Man, this food is exceptional. "Christmas in July. I could get used to this. Wonder who came up with the idea?" Ryan looked around the small group.

"An advertising executive," Nic said, examining the roast potato on the disposable wooden fork. "Sell Christmas twice." He bit into the potato.

Bridget rolled her eyes. "My guess, an exceptionally smart woman. I mean, really, who'd want to cook a full hot Christmas lunch in the middle of a Queensland summer? The heat would be suffocating. Nobody should have to toil away, cooking a hot meal in stifling heat. Ever."

"That makes more sense than Nic's concept," chimed Ryan before forking another mouthful of roasted meat into his mouth. "Damn good thinking, I reckon."

Asher smiled. "So, you've eaten?"

"I have, but I left some for you and for him." He jabbed his thumb toward Mitch, who ambled in their direction.

Mitch slapped him on the shoulder. "Thanks, man. I'll grab some."

Jace maneuvered his chair around. "I'm heading over to the other table, there's cake for dessert."

Asher smiled. "I'm going over there now. Hamish is waving trying to get my attention." She moved to follow Jace, then turned back to face Mitch and placed her hand against his broad chest. The slow thud against her fingertips enticed her closer. And she so wanted to feel his entire length against her. Instead, she said, "Remember, please. Say nothing to Bridget." Hearing her own unwavering tone gave her the courage to smile before turning away.

"Asher."

Mitch's voice halted her. She looked over her shoulder.

His strong, steady gaze held hers. "I meant what I said. I'll listen when you're ready to talk."

A quick nod, then she hurried across the quadrangle to join Hamish.

Mitch watched Asher scurry away, disappointed that her long sweatshirt hid her butt. He trailed behind at a much more sedate pace and joined Asher, Bridget, and Hamish, standing at the end of the table weighed down with the feast, laughing. Someone playing a guitar and singing softly replaced the recorded music.

"Mitch. What do you think of our celebrations?" Hamish asked.

Mitch looked around. There were people everywhere, some wearing Christmas hats, others wore Christmas T-shirts over the top of their sweatshirts. Little kids ran around, laughing. Their runny noses and no shoes didn't seem to bother them. *Resilient creatures.* Mitch watched as two scampered past him, dropping food as they played.

Tonight, the homeless mingled together, as they sat around eating the roast meals piled onto their plates, listening to the young man with the guitar and joining him in song. They gave murmurs of thanks to the volunteers who meandered around offering juice or soft drinks.

Mitch smiled as Asher handed him a plate of food. "Thanks."

"Least I could do."

"I can't believe how different it is here tonight." Mitch forked some baked potato into his mouth.

"This is how it used to be. It's only been this past couple of weeks that it's gone a bit nuts."

"Why do you think that is?"

She shrugged. Then met his gaze. "You showed up."

He almost choked as the food he was about to swallow lodged in his windpipe. "You think I have something to do with the escalation of violence?"

Another shrug. "Maybe not you personally. When you first rocked up here, I thought you were looking for someone. I still feel that. But then maybe you just expect trouble. You are a cop, after all."

He didn't reply. He just shoved more food into his mouth. What could he say? *Yeah, you're right, your brother is a danger to you because he won't come forward. If I spent more time looking for him than watching you, I may have found him by now and we wouldn't be having this conversation.*

Then Asher reached out and rested her hand against him. Her heat seeped into him. "I'm sorry, I'm just thinking aloud."

"Whatever." He put his plate on the table and strode away.

The rest of the night crawled past. Mitch, bent against the wind, strode the perimeter of the parking lot, doing his last check for the night. He'd turned back toward the food truck, saw Asher talking to one of the homeless men, then pointing toward him. The big, bearded bloke approached Mitch and stepped right into his personal space.

"You're Doc's driver?"

Although framed as a question, Mitch knew the man asking already knew the answer, so merely nodded.

"You doing security as well? Yeah?"

Another nod. "Yup."

"I'm Rick. I've been squatting at Homeless Central for the past couple of nights. There's talk. Someone's trying to get to Doc. Something about using her to draw someone out."

"Got a description?"

Rick shook his head. "I'll keep my ears and eyes open. If I hear anything, I'll let you know. From what I've heard, they're mean sons of bitches. Keep Doc safe." With that, he drifted onto the road. With every streetlight blown, he melted into the darkness.

Homeless Central. They'd driven past there many times. A massive, abandoned building, surrounded by a ten-foot-high fence topped with barbed wire. Asher mentioned she'd stopped there a few times to offer her service, but both the local city Council and police had deemed it too dangerous, and they had advised her to stay away.

For once, she'd listened.

Mitch chatted to a few kids as he did his last security check for the night, then helped his mates pull down and pack up the makeshift clinic.

He'd stayed away from Asher. Better that way. No more tough conversations. When she came to stand by him, for the first time since meeting her, he couldn't find anything to say.

He drove her home, and together they strolled toward Asher's house. The uncomfortable silence stretched between them, and he realized he'd hardly spoken since she'd basically accused him of being the source of all the trouble happening around her.

He huffed out a breath.

A brushing against his legs stalled him.

Asher looked down. "Peaches, how did you get out?"

Mitch crouched and scratched the cat under the chin. "Problem?"

"He was inside when I left."

"You sure?"

She nodded.

"Then that's a problem." He scooped the big ginger cat into his arms.

They approached her closed door, and Mitch twisted the doorknob. Locked tight.

"You positive?" He queried.

Another nod.

"I'll come in, look around."

"Thanks." Her fingers were shaking as she took the keys from her bag. With a gusty sigh, she fitted it in the lock, twisted and pushed the door open.

Mitch stepped into the foyer before her, flicked the light switch, and put the cat on the floor, and closed the front door. "Anything out of place?" He took in the magazines and books cascading from the couch to the coffee table to the polished floor.

She shook her head. "Just the usual chaos."

"I'll have a look around. Wait here." He checked the pristine kitchen and twisted the handle on the back door. Locked. He heard her footsteps as she followed him down the hallway.

He stopped and turned to face her. "I asked you to stay put."

"And I choose not to." She stepped in front of him and moved to the first door and flung it open. "Spare junk room. Looks the same as it did last time I was in here."

"My room." She opened the door.

He strolled in, and her familiar scent bombarded him. Her bed was big and white, with a slatted headboard, the gaps just wide enough to thread some soft rope through to hold her to the bed. He sucked in a breath as an image of her with arms tied loosely above her head as her naked body writhed beneath him filled his head. Instant hard on, damn it, *Buchanan, put those thoughts away.*

He shook his head, eased past the jumble of cushions on the floor and into the ensuite bathroom. Floor to ceiling cupboards.

He pulled open the doors. Nothing. A red claw foot bath took pride in place alongside a shelf laden with a multitude of bottles. He kicked away the temptation to open one and sniff the contents.

"The office is through here." She opened the last door and froze.

Mitch stopped behind her and glanced over her shoulder into the room. Whoever had been through here didn't give a shit about stealth. They'd upturned her desk, her chair, and the laptop lay on the floor, smashed. They'd pulled the filing cabinet open, and paper files were strewn everywhere.

"What in the hell were they looking for?" Mitch asked, placing his hands on her shoulders, and turning her to face him.

Her complexion resembled the color of milk. Her blue eyes blazed. And if she bit that lip any harder, it would bleed.

"Doc?"

"Letters maybe?" She gnawed on her lip, then continued. "The other night when my ambulance got torched..."

"Go on." Mitch encouraged. His eyes fixed on hers.

"When I got home, my brother was inside my house, waiting for me."

"How in the hell did he get inside?"

Asher shrugged. "I've asked myself the same thing."

"Did he hurt you?" Mitch straightened. Squared his shoulders. Anger pulsed through him at her not telling him. And at himself for just letting her go inside alone in the early hours.

"No." She reached around and tightened her ponytail. "Apparently, he sent some letters home. I told him I had received nothing. He obviously didn't believe me."

"Obviously." Mitch's pulse kicked up a notch. "So, you believe your brother's responsible for this?" He gestured toward the upturned room.

"Who else?"

"The guys looking for him. Maybe even the same guy that grabbed you the other morning."

The little color she had in her face drained and he wished he'd kept his big mouth shut. "Why didn't you tell me your brother had been here? You asked me to help you find him. You should have told me."

"I know, but honestly, I don't want to talk about him. He makes me..." She shrugged, looked at the timber floor, and scuffed her toe. "He makes me doubt myself. My choices. I know I need to talk about him but, I can't."

Their gazes locked.

Pain etched the depths of her eyes. "Okay, I'll let it go. For now. I'll call Ethan and get some of his boys over to check for prints."

She stood there, shaking her head. "Will you still help me find my brother?"

Mitch nodded. "I will." He turned away and spoke into his phone.

"Ethan's on the way and bringing Bridget."

"I'll brew some coffee." She straightened her shoulders. "I need to calm my mind. If I think about what they messed up in there, I'll scream."

"Doc. I said I'd help you find your brother. And I will. But you need to let me know if he comes anywhere near you. Or if he calls. And we need to have a conversation about what went down the other night. Okay?"

Within half an hour, someone hammered at the front door.

"I'll get it." Mitch strode along the hallway, past the clinical gray and white kitchen and through the living room. He side-stepped Peaches intent on massaging a big purple ottoman.

Two police officers stood at the door next to Bridget and Ethan.

Before he even had time to say hello, Bridge shoved past and headed straight to Asher and wrapped her in a hug. "Are you all right?"

The color had returned to Asher's face, but she spoke through gritted teeth. "I'm so pissed. We just completed all those files for the accountant."

Bridget chuckled and ushered Asher into the living room. "At least you still have your priorities straight."

"You'd think those two knew each other in a past life the way they get on," There was a touch of awe in Ethan's voice as he waved the other officers in.

I know how that feels, Mitch thought. "Funny that."

"Where to?" The cops asked.

Mitch led them to the office. They seemed to know what they were doing, so he didn't go in after them, instead went back to the kitchen. He grabbed the filled coffeepot, right beside the mugs, and everything else needed to make any sort of beverage. Like her ambulance, the kitchen was micro-organized to make the most efficient use of every inch of the modest space. Of course, a tray was nearby, so he loaded it up and carried it through to the lounge room. He laid the tray onto the coffee table, poured himself a mug, then moved out of the way to lean against the window.

"So, you're sure you had locked the door?" Ethan asked, looking directly at Asher from the seat opposite. as he pulled out a notebook and pencil from his jacket pocket.

"Definitely. I used my key to open it."

"I can vouch for that." Mitch took a swig from the mug. Ethan nodded his acknowledgment of Mitch's comment.

In a formal 'cop' mode, Ethan continued, "Why did you believe there could be someone inside?"

"Peaches was outside. Somebody must have let him out. I never leave him outside when I'm not home." Asher leaned forward and poured herself a coffee. Her hands trembled.

"Mitch offered to come inside and look around." She glanced at Mitch for confirmation, so he nodded and moved to sit on the arm of the couch she was sharing with Bridget. "Nothing out-of-place till I opened the office door." Asher looked toward the hallway. "How long do you think they'll be down there?"

As if they'd heard the question, the officers strode into the lounge room. "We checked the other rooms, the back door, and every window. No sign of forced entry."

The creased face of the older officer looked at Asher. "And you're sure you locked up before you left the premises?"

Asher nodded, apparently unfazed by the repeated question.

The older officer continued. "We've taken photos of fingerprints and uploaded them to the national database. If anything shows up on the search, the experts will have an ID within an hour or so."

Ethan rose and escorted the officers to the door.

"If we get a positive ID, one of the fingerprint team will let you know."

A chorus of goodnights followed. After they'd drunk the coffee pot dry, Bridget yawned. Ethan stood and pulled his wife to her feet.

"Goodnight you two." Bridget leaned down and gave Asher a hug. "Try to get some sleep."

Mitch was right behind Asher as she followed them to the street, obviously trying not to be obvious about nervously looking around. She needn't have worried. The minute the door had opened, every sense he owned, and some that weren't even on any list, were on alert for any movement, any hiding place and anything even slightly out of the ordinary. Nothing was - which didn't stop him worrying, anyway.

Bridget turned as they reached the car. "And don't you dare clean that room. I'll come by with some helpers to sort the mess."

"No, you won't," Ethan added, looking sternly at his wife. "You'll wait till you get the okay from us before you touch anything."

Bridge rolled her eyes at Asher as she got into the car. Asher waved, then hurried back to the house, firmly shutting, and locking the front door as soon as Mitch had followed her in.

Mitch stood at the office door and watched Asher straighten some furniture.

She sighed. "First my ambulance and my office, now my home. I'm so over this crap."

Mitch uncrossed his arms and wandered into the room. "Asher, you heard Ethan, please leave this mess till you hear back from the cops. You look exhausted." He shouldn't still be here consoling her. He should be out looking for her brother. "If you'd told me the other morning that your brother visited, we wouldn't be standing here trying to figure out how to clear this mess." He waved his arms toward the spilled files. "It could've been a much different result." He shook his head, wishing he'd kept his mouth shut rather than allow that patronizing tone to escape. But it still jarred that she thought he may be responsible for what was happening around her.

She twisted her pinky ring. "I know. I know, but..." She turned to stare out the window. Her shoulders rose and fell in a deep breath before she lifted her head.

"I should leave...."

After a few seconds, she turned back to face him, a sad smile distorting her lips. She opened and closed her mouth as if wanting to ask something. Instead, she said, "Thanks again for everything."

"But I don't like you being here by yourself. It's not safe, so I'm staying." He continued as if she hadn't spoken.

Asher took a deep breath and blinked furiously.

"Go to bed, Doc."

"I wanted to ask you to stay." She bit her lip. "I didn't in case you had other plans."

He had plans. He had planned to spend another night scouring the dank holes in this area, looking for scum. "Nothing important. I'll sleep on the couch."

"Thanks." She exhaled loudly and laced and relaced her fingers. "I just don't want to be here by myself."

He reached out to touch her but dropped his hand to his side. "That's understandable. It's fine. I'll stay here as long as you need me."

"Thank you. I'll see you in the morning."

They walked from the office toward her bedroom.

"Night." Asher pushed open her bedroom door and stepped inside. Mitch continued up the hallway and checked around the kitchen and living room, trying to figure out how in hell someone had gotten in. Even with every door locked and no windows broken, somebody had gotten in here. Tomorrow, Mitch would talk to her about arranging an alarm system. He had to ensure her safety, especially in her own home.

"You might need these."

Her deep, throaty voice turned his thoughts carnal as he slowly turned to face her. *Does she ever let her hair down?* One day, he'd get her to let it down for him. *Yeah, right.* "Thanks." He accepted the sheets, a pillow, and quilt from her outstretched arms.

"Couldn't have you being cold. Night." She turned and bolted back down the hall.

Not a hope. Not with you two doors away. He threw a sheet on the huge leather couch and stripped off his shirt but left the jeans on. He stretched out and pulled up the puffy quilt.

Sleep had just about seduced him when a soft thud sounded by his side. He turned his head and stared at the feline eyeballing him. Peaches was checking him out.

"She's safe," Mitch whispered.

The cat stared at him for a few more seconds then moved onto Mitch's stomach and started kneading the quilt covering his belly. Seemingly satisfied with the mess he'd created, Peaches curled up and went to sleep.

Mitch stroked the cat's ears and listened to the purr as he drifted into the half-doze that was enough to refresh his mind and body without dimming his awareness of his surrounds. Military training came in handy sometimes.

The sound of footsteps snapped him into full consciousness, but training kept his body inert until he could assess the situation. His gaze scoured the darkened room. And stopped on Asher wandering around the kitchen.

With her hair out and mussed, a fluffy bathrobe covering her from neck to toe, she tiptoed around the kitchen area. He lost sight of her as she opened the fridge, coming back to view holding a carton.

She switched on the kettle and settled against the cupboard, staring out the window into the darkness. What thoughts were going through her head? Obviously not good ones, by the way her shoulders sagged, and her head bowed.

The lost demeanor didn't suit her. And he didn't enjoy witnessing it. Standing strong and arguing suited her, suited him. Mitch reached over and turned on the lamp beside him. Every nerve in his body told him to go to her, to talk to her.

He stayed under the quilt. But Peaches took off to investigate.

"Sorry, I didn't mean to wake you." Her voice soft.

"I sleep light. Training."

"I'm having warm Milo. Want one?" She held up the container.

Mitch raised up on an elbow, wishing she'd offered herself rather than a crunchy, chocolaty-malty beverage. "I haven't had Milo in years."

"So, that's yes?" She smiled.

That tug in his belly for her pulled harder. *Let it go*. He swung his legs off the couch and pushed to his feet. When he felt the pressure against his fly, he was glad he'd left his jeans on. No point bringing her attention to his physical attraction for her. He doubted she'd appreciate it.

CHAPTER 13

Asher hit the light switch, and the fluorescent bulbs brightened the room. Being with him in the near dark was too intimate for her sanity. "I really didn't mean to wake you."

He strolled toward her. Shirtless. She sucked in a breath. *Lordy that chest.* Her mouth dried, and her heart rate soared. To lay her head against that chest would be... She clamped her lips together to smother a groan. She didn't even want to think about it. *Dare she touch?* Just to see if the skin was as smooth as it looked. She shook her head and turned away, busying herself spooning the malty grains into the mugs and adding sugar.

The frother turned itself off. She poured the milk into the mugs and stirred. Taking a deep breath, she squared her shoulders, fixed a smile on her lips, and faced him, mugs in hand. "Here you go."

He took the cup from her fingers. "Thanks." He sipped the drink, then licked at the milk moustache on his top lip. "Delicious. I'd forgotten how good this tastes."

Asher couldn't drag her gaze from him. Watching his tongue had her thoughts running in all directions...very carnal directions. She counted in her head, in Greek, until her heartbeat slowed and the heat in her face eased. Hopefully, he was so busy drinking, he hadn't noticed the peaks in her robe where her nipples had hardened.

"We can have this in the other room."

He nodded, turned, and headed back to the living area.

His denim-clad butt flexed as he walked. Her heartbeat accelerated. *Focus, Asher.* "Sit." She motioned to the couch. "Seeing as you're awake anyway, I need to talk to you." She sat on a chair opposite him. "I need to clarify something."

Another nod. He was a man of few words this morning.

"You said you'd help me find my brother. And that you have permission to drive for me."

"I spoke with my physio. She's fine with it." He bent his head and sipped his drink.

"So, when do you have time to do your own job?"

He lifted his head and smiled at her. "Doc, Trust me. It's covered. I'm currently on medical absence. Me helping you find Greg won't interfere with my rehab."

Asher looked straight into his eyes. "How did you know my brother's name?"

He held her gaze. "There's a photo of a guy in army gear on your cabinet. It's got, my brother Greg, written underneath it."

"Of course. I'm sorry, I'm overthinking everything." She sucked in a deep breath, gathered her thoughts. For a minute, she almost wondered if she or Greg was the focus of Mitch's investigation. "He scared the shit out of me the other night."

"Why was he here?"

"Asking for help."

"What sort of help?"

She blew out a breath. "He says if he doesn't find what he sent me from overseas, this gang he's involved with is going to kill him."

"Do you believe him?"

She shrugged. "I told him they're threatening me. He didn't seem to care." She rose and paced the room. "He's scared. He swore he never mentioned me to anyone. But I sensed he was more worried about himself."

"Did you give him what he was looking for?"

"I would have." She held out her arms in frustration. "But I don't know what he's talking about."

"How'd that go down?" Mitch still sat on the couch, expressionless, calmly asking questions as if he did it every day.

Get real, Ash, he does! For once, she was glad she was a victim and not a perpetrator. It would be an unsettling experience being interrogated by him. "You've seen the office. That guy that attacked me told me to find my brother. Then a couple of nights later, my brother turns up. What I'm trying to understand is why doesn't he come forward?"

"Self-preservation is a potent motivator."

"Do you think these guys chasing my brother will hurt my people to get to me?" She eased back down into her chair, picked up her mug and sipped her drink.

"I expect they're not interested in your people. They want your brother, and they'll do what they can to get him."

"Earlier, one of my patients told me there's someone after me because I'm sticking my nose in where it's not needed. Looks like there are two separate lots of people out to get me." She stared into her almost empty mug, wishing she could figure out what in hell was happening in her life.

Mitch stood and stepped around the coffee table, knelt in front of her chair, and placed his hand over hers. "We'll sort it."

She looked down. Such big hands, yet such a gentle touch. He turned her hand over and traced the fine veins on her wrists. She gasped but didn't pull away.

"What else happened when your brother was here? I need details."

"Nothing. We argued. I told him I wouldn't help him. I threw him out."

"Did he say where he's staying?"

She shook her head. "Nothing. I've been racking my brain, but I really can't remember. We've never been close, flooded waters under a bridge. But I don't want him hurt." She gnawed her lip. "I just don't want him around. Too many memories. And not good ones."

"I will find him."

Asher smiled. "I hope so, because I believe he's losing it." She rubbed at her head.

"Headache?"

"No."

"I think you need to change your bandage."

"In the morning." She yawned.

"How about I do it for you before you go back to bed. Where's your medicine kit?"

Asher sighed. She wasn't used to being pampered. Wasn't sure how to handle it. "If you insist. It's in the cupboard above the stove." Asher rested her head on the back of the chair and listened. His footsteps tapped on the timber floors as he moved toward the kitchen. The cupboard hinge squeaked. She visualized him reaching up, saw the movement of the muscles in his arm as he grabbed the kit, and shut the door.

Then he stood behind her. His body heat enticing and jarring her from her fantasy. "Head back."

She tilted back. He eased the gauze from her forehead, swiped a cool alcohol swab across the stitches, and replaced the bandage. It took no time at all. Then he threaded his fingers through her hair and eased it away from her forehead.

She groaned deep in her throat, almost a purr. *Omg, I sound like Peaches when I scratch his ears.*

"Am I hurting? Do you want me to stop?"

"If you did, I'd probably kill you." Her laugh was light.

He directed her head back until it rested against his warm, solid stomach. Oh, she could sit like this forever, regardless of her inner battle against turning her head and pressing her mouth to his bare skin to taste him. A heavy sigh escaped.

Now was not the time.

As much as Mitch attracted her, she would not break her vow of abstinence. Not for a one-night stand. *Why not? You want to feel him pressing that long hard body against you as he kisses you deep and wet.* She bit back a groan, and reluctantly eased away from his heat. She stood and turned to face him.

Dark chocolate eyes watched her from where he stood behind her vacated chair.

Asher's tongue swiped across her lips. She wanted to kiss him again. To feel his lips come to life beneath hers. No, she needed to kiss him. That brief interlude earlier, his mouth on hers. The heat, the passion demanded an encore. If she didn't, she'd go nuts wondering. And it might be the catalyst to remove this stupid craving for him out of her system.

Except she didn't want the complications of a man in her life. *Asher, it's a kiss, not a commitment.* She huffed out a breath. No! She would not kiss him! That was the safe option.

And she always chose the safest path. Didn't she? She picked up the mugs from the coffee table, crossed to the kitchen and rinsed them in the sink. On her next breath, she turned back to face him to say goodnight.

But his bare chest drew her gaze like a magnet. Unable to resist, her gaze drifted over him. She marveled at his shape. The way his shoulders, so square, tapered down to those sculpted arms. Even relaxed, the muscled definition was delicious. She'd love to see them flexed. *Stop staring at him.* Her gaze rose. Heat flooded her cheeks when she recognized the gleam in his eyes. *How do I get out of this? Do I want to?*

He was honorable. She already knew that. All she had to do was say goodnight. She tried, she really did. Her mouth opened, but nothing came out. His gaze never left hers.

Her breathing hitched. She realized he was leaving the next step up to her. *Dare she? Just one kiss. But would one be enough?* Her belly churned. *No. She would want more.* But she'd chosen abstinence. And no one had even remotely tempted her. So why now? And why this man standing before her, looking like a feast of delicious candy? She closed her eyes, sucked in a breath, opened her eyes, and smiled. "Night, Mitch."

"Night, Doc." A noise from outside froze her mid breath and mid stride.

"Just a branch." His smooth, unfazed voice thawed her instantly. "Nothing to worry about."

She looked back, and he was still standing there, looking toward the window behind her, but still the epitome of relaxed attention.

She was a street doctor who faced drug addicts and violent street thugs on some shifts. On her own. So why did a simple branch scraping a window have her stepping toward the only man to upset her equilibrium in ages?

Slightly reassured, she stared at him. He made no move, decent man that he was. How much easier if he just jumped her bones? Then she could blame him instead of her own stupid, rebellious body. Even better if he ignored her. Except she'd still want him.

Her smile in place, Asher strolled toward him. Up close, his scent shattered common sense. Her fingers snaked around his forearm.

His warm skin invited further exploration.

"Mitch, I'm... Oh, God..." He'd reduced her to babbling. "Not worried." Words just wouldn't come in logical order. "Not about what's outside." She couldn't look up at him. "I'm torn between going back to my bed and shutting the door or...or staying here and devouring you." Her gaze finally lifted and met his. *Melting chocolate!* "I want to taste you," she whispered on a breath. "I want your mouth on mine. This feeling, it's driving me nuts. I know we've—"

"Doc."

Her heart hammered. "What?"

"Shut up and come here." He captured her hand and rested it on his chest.

Mesmerized by his gentleness, her gaze followed her fingers as he carried them from his chest, up to that full bottom lip she'd fantasized about nibbling.

Ever. So. Slowly. He turned her hand and kissed the pulse spot on her wrist and stroked his tongue over the sensitized point. Asher forgot to breathe.

"One kiss," she whispered. *Was she asking or telling?*

He grinned. "We're adults. We can control ourselves."

He might, but could she? She nodded anyway and leaned into his powerful body. It was like being wrapped in a cozy, warm blanket in the middle of a snowstorm.

Necessary.

Her hands, resting against his chest, felt the solid thudding of his heart before inching up to his neck to cradle his head. His short hair tickled her palms. On her toes, she leaned closer.

"We're a good fit." His deep, velvet voice flowed through her, escalating her heart rate. Still, he didn't move. Didn't embrace her.

Did he not want this? Was this attraction one sided?

Without warning, muscular arms looped around her waist, and she sighed. Despite the looseness of his embrace, his eyes betrayed desire. But she knew if she stopped this madness and pulled away, he'd let her go. That made her want him more.

She pressed her lips to his. The heat of his muscled frame spread through her, and she slanted her mouth against his, settling into the kiss, sucking his bottom lip into her mouth, and biting gently down on it.

Breath hissed from him, and he dragged her flush against him. The fingers of one hand circled their way up and down her spine as the other hand pushed her hair off her face. She shuddered.

Then he upped the ante by touching her tongue with his. Her breath lodged in her throat.

Fire raged. Heated blood flowed like warm honey through her veins. Nerves twitched. She wanted more. His lean hips now rested against the kitchen table, and she nestled within the vee of his thighs.

She sucked a breath into her searing lungs. Their lips drew apart, but that was all. His lightly bristled cheek came to rest against hers, and his fingers splayed through her hair.

"Your hair's like silk. I love your hair." His warm breath huffed against her ear, his voice deep and hypnotic, stirring her senses.

Asher's fingers trailed across his wide shoulders, and she reveled when he shuddered beneath the light caress. As if not wanting to betray what her touch did to him, he gently urged her back, creating a small space between them. Enough to reveal her robe had fallen open, exposing camisole and knickers and plenty of bare skin.

At his sharp intake of breath, her gaze flew up to meet his again. His eyes betrayed, he wanted this as much as she did. If he was trying to hide what she did to him, he was failing.

"I've imagined you in my arms. So gorgeous. So lush." The tips of his fingers brushed across the swell of her breasts. "Like velvet." His lips curled into a small smile. "Hair like silk, skin like velvet."

His head turned, and he brushed his lips against her neck, his tongue licking across her frantically beating pulse. He met her gaze, through the tightening grip of his fingers, she sensed his restraint and knew it was still up to her how much further this went. The man was a saint. But she didn't want a saint.

She groaned. Hands on either side of his head, she forced it back so she could reach his lips. "Kiss me, Mitch."

The sensual assault on her parted lips stirred embers of desire she'd believed doused, igniting fire deep in her belly. Her breasts, crushed against his chest, felt every breath he drew, every shudder that traveled through his hard-muscled body.

His generous mouth created so much pleasure. She moaned deep in her throat and leaned even further into him. Then froze as the hardness of his erection nudged the apex of her thighs.

The erotic haze shattered.

She was on the other side of the kitchen before her next breath. Guilt bit her hard. Resting her elbows on the island, she buried her face in her hands. Just a *kiss. One little kiss. Not an out-of-control brush fire.* She shoved her fingers through her hair.

"Guess I was wrong." His deep voice broke through her musings.

She met his gaze.

His eyes still smoldered with want.

"What?"

"Thinking I could control the situation." A smile quirked his lips. "But looking at you, who could blame me for losing it?"

She stared at him.

"Night, Asher." He turned and walked away.

And she let him go. Even though, deep down, it was the last thing she wanted to do.

CHAPTER 14

Mitch rested his shoulder against the timber window frame and gazed out into the darkness. When Asher had broken the kiss and bolted to the other side of the room to stare at him with wide, horror-filled eyes and her lush lips quivering, her emotions were palpable. And they twisted his gut.

Despite his rock-hard cock, he accepted her calling quits to the hottest kiss he'd experienced, because if she hadn't, God knew she'd have ended up flat on her back on the kitchen floor, with her legs wrapped around his waist. A ragged groan erupted from deep inside him as his cock twitched.

And a quickie wasn't how he envisioned his first time with Asher. No, his imagination led him down a longer, slower path to pleasure. She was worth more than a quick bang on the floor.

The sensations of her long, lush body crushed against his created a buzz deep inside. He gloried that her breast fit his hands, that her mouth fit his. He groaned. Her taste could bring a man to his knees. He didn't want to let her out of his arms. She belonged there.

She had the same effect on him as a double Johnnie on the rocks. Straight to his head. He'd never enjoyed kissing a woman so much. Leaning forward, he rested his forehead against the cold pane of glass.

How could he have lost control like a schoolboy? Especially after the dramas she'd been through the past couple of days. From being assaulted by a man who was still on the loose, to having to deal with her stinking brother. He rested his mouth against his fist. *Man, you were all over her like a rash.* He shook his head and battled the urge to punch his reflection in the window.

He sucked in a deep breath. *Get back in the game. Put her out of your mind. Find her brother.* Then maybe he could move forward. *Stay away from her.*

Yeah, right.

He sensed her hesitancy as she eased into his peripheral. Her heat radiated toward him. Drew him. He looked down into her eyes and smiled. "You kiss amazingly."

She touched a finger to his lips. "You're not too bad yourself."

"But?" He quirked his brow, pulled her robe together, and tied the belt at the waist. Tightly.

"I...I didn't intend to kiss you like that." She stared up at him.

"I'm so glad you did."

"Really?" Her eyes widened.

"Since the night I first saw you, I've wondered what you were like beneath your all powerful, all strong doctor persona. I wondered what Asher was like."

"And?" she asked, her voice soft and vulnerable.

"She's all powerful and all strong, with a huge dash of lush, gorgeous and sexy as hell."

"And abstaining."

Mitch tucked a strand of hair behind her ear and wondered why had she chosen to abstain from sex? Or was it relationships she backed away from? Had someone hurt her? And if yes, why? Why would someone hurt such a strong, beautiful woman? Hopefully, she'd tell him sooner rather than later. But she obviously didn't want to rush.

He stroked her cheek. "Look, Doc. I can't deny the attraction I have for you." He laughed. "I think you've figured that out for yourself. But I'm patient. I'll wait. You'll eventually realize I'm a good guy."

"I've believed that since before I got to know you. And yeah, there is a definite connection between us. But I'm not ready to travel that path."

"What path?" He took her hand and tugged her close. "Look at me, Asher." When she lifted her eyes to meet his, he smiled. "I will never pressure you into anything you don't want to do." He leaned forward and pressed his lips to her forehead. "Ever. Okay?"

She nodded and pulled back. "I'm going to bed."

"Okay." Clasping her hand, he escorted her down the hall and opened her bedroom door. He bent his head, pressed his lips gently against her temple. And backed out of the room, shutting the door behind him. Locking her away from him, or vice versa. Either way, that was the way it had to be.

For now.

He moved back to the big comfy lounge and lay down.

From that first night at Mates and Eats, she drew him like a magnet. He'd watched the way she treated everyone around her, patients, volunteers on the various food trucks, her friends. She radiated warmth. People responded to her. Now she was under threat. Keeping her safe was the number one priority. It meant one hundred percent job focus. To do that, he had to bury the soul stirring passion, for her, gnawing deep down inside himself.

He went through his mental notes. Was she being used to draw Greg Jones out of hiding? The gang he'd turned on was back in Australia being questioned. They denied everything, of course. The only lead the Sentinel Bureau had was Corporal Jones, and he was missing.

There was no way Mitch was going to allow anything to happen to Asher. The supposed information her brother, Jones, had would put these guys behind bars. All he had to do was keep her out of harm's way. Without telling her why. Pummeling the pillow into shape, he shut his eyes, but sleep proved elusive.

Was that why Jones rocked up here the other night, looking for the information he'd sent? For all they knew, he could've sent it anywhere. And now all this crap was happening to Asher's business. Was it related to the gang of miscreant soldiers?

Or the sale of babies? Or the warning by her patient to watch her back? There were too many possible suspects.

Then tonight, with her in my arms, I almost lost it. Didn't matter that she instigated it. And like a starving man, he'd feasted on what she'd offered. At the memory of her wound around him, flush against him, his maleness twitched to life. Seeing that silly little tank top outlining those breasts, his control fled.

He'd cupped one breast briefly, felt the weight, but had controlled the desire to bend his head and suck the nipple into his mouth through that top. Just as he controlled the urge to sink into her dampness, her core, and feel her legs wrapped tightly around him. He shoved the fantasy aside.

He needed to find Corporal Jones. And soon. Mitch still believed the best way to do that was to stay close to his sister and grab him before Asher got hurt. *How's that worked out so far?* He screwed his eyes shut. They'd hurt her already. And destroyed her ambulance. His gut burned, and he realized it would not get any better. Eventually, sleep slowed his thinking. As his eyes closed, he whispered, "I'll keep you safe, Asher."

A few hours later, Mitch's phone buzzed. He reached over the side of the couch, picked it up, read the message, and huffed out a breath. Standing, he folded the quilt, laid it on the cushions, and grabbed his shirt, slipped it over his head and turned.

Asher stood at the doorway. Hair tied back. Her T-shirt clinging to her breasts. His heartbeat kicked up. Hard.

"Morning. You want coffee?"

He shook his head. "No, but thanks. I've been called into a meeting. I need to go home, grab a shower, and change my clothes."

"You can shower here if you like."

He pushed away the image of her naked under the pelting water, snug against him "Thanks, but I don't have spare clothes."

"Okay."

He followed her into the kitchen and struggled, big time, to drag his gaze from the sway of her jeans-clad butt. *Put it away.*

"I got a message too. The council has hired extra security for the fundraiser."

"Good move."

"I have to meet with them again today, as if yesterday wasn't enough. Then more calls to the insurance. I'm going to Lily's to check on the girls. Might spend a few hours there."

"Just don't be by yourself."

She rolled her eyes. "Really, Mitch, I'm fine. I'm a big girl used to looking after myself."

He crossed his arms over his chest. "I know that. It just makes sense to stay around others."

"Mitch, go to your meeting. I managed perfectly fine before you arrived on the scene. I'll keep looking after myself."

This morning, with her armor back in place, she sounded like her normal tough self. He hoped it was just a front. After all the dramas over the past few days, she couldn't really be so stubborn that she would ignore advice to stay safe. Could she? He remembered her whispered admission from last night. *I'm scared.*

Her strength, her independence, kept her grounded. She'd be fine.

He should have paid more attention to how actual people behave, instead of focusing on bad guys and what they might do. Maybe he should have looked more into her background as well as her brother's. Normally, he wouldn't hesitate. But he already knew, in the back of his brain he'd never check Asher's past, because he'd never invade her privacy. Ever.

Not being able to find the divide between his job and his crazy mixed emotions for the woman before him, irritated him. He refused to allow his frustration to get the better of him. "Asher, remember, you are under threat. But you do what you want. I'll see you tonight. You've got my number if you need me." He turned away.

"Mitch."

He faced her, his jaw tight.

She met his gaze, gave him a crooked smile. "What I should have said is, I'll ask the security guard at the council building to escort me to my car, then I'll stay with Lily and make my calls from there. I'll make sure I'm not ever by myself."

He relaxed his jaw.

"And Mitch," Another silly little smile played on her lips. "If you hear anything from Ms. Whatever-her-name-is about the baby, you'll call me?"

"Of course." With that, he left, deliberately shutting the door quietly behind him even though he wanted to slam it. It took a concentrated effort not to remind her to make sure she locked the doors.

Last night, when she'd accused him of being the instigator of all the garbage going on around her venture, he'd felt useless. If he'd found Jones, maybe there wouldn't have been the hassles, but he believed most of the crap going down around her was from Charli's boyfriend. And the Ice gang. He shook his head.

How did they fit into it? Was it coincidence? Were they trying to intimidate her into getting out of the area? He didn't know, but he'd figure it out.

And he didn't believe in coincidence. It seemed choreographed to him. Too well set up. He was going to find out who was buying those babies. Maybe it was just a money-making scheme, tailored to the rich who were too frustrated with the lengthy wait in the adoption system, or toward desperate infertile couples who believed, after years of disappointment, this was their only option. But his mind went to a darker, more sinister place. He shook his head. No, he'd get the info, give it to the right government department. At least that was one problem he could sort. He hoped.

He checked his watch as he pulled into his apartment block. Just enough time for a quick shower and a change of clothes. Under the hot spray, he closed his eyes and imagined Asher, lush and wet, pressed against him. When she'd offered him the chance to shower at her home, he struggled against the urge to say yes, then inviting her to join him. With a groan, he flicked the tap off and stepped from the cubicle. He dressed in record time. Back in his truck he realized she hadn't mentioned kissing in the kitchen. *Neither did you.* He huffed out his frustration. So, it looked like they were just going to ignore it.

• • • • • • • • •

Mitch rolled his chair toward the computer, clicked the keys, and brought up Corporal Gregory Jones's file. *Don't know why I bothered. I've got nothing to add.* He thumped the desk.

He believed in his ability to do his job. But he'd never actually had to find a missing person before. And this guy, it seemed, had disappeared into vapor. He tapped a few more buttons. Jones's photo filled the screen. He scrutinized his face, the shape of it, visualized it with a beard, darker hair. The photo on the screen looked nothing like the photo Asher had of him at her house.

Mitch exited the file and pulled up the soldiers Jones associated with in Afghanistan. He looked at the faces, recognizing the names. Military Police hauled them in for brawling, insubordination, and a couple of them on theft. But regarding the smuggling ring Jones had accused them of being involved in? Nothing. The military had no concrete evidence. Making those charges stick relied on Jones offering the proof.

He turned when the door behind him opened. Colonel Llewellyn Mason stood in the doorway, his civilian clothing neat and tidy, his grey hair still cut with military precision.

"Morning, you got something for me?"

Mitch rose, and even though the colonel had retired, saluted.

"I've told you, that's not required." The Colonel shook his head.

Mitch shrugged. "Habit."

"So, what have you got?"

Mitch followed the Colonel across the sparsely furnished room to his large timber desk. "Jones visited his sister the other night. Looking for something he sent her from overseas."

"Did she give it to him?"

"No. She reckons she had received nothing from him since his deployment, and from what else she's indicated, not from a long time before that. They're not close."

"You haven't told her you're looking for her brother?"

"No, sir. As ordered. Last night," Mitch continued, "someone broke into Doctor Jardine's home and trashed her office."

"You think it was Jones?"

"Yes, sir. He was adamant he'd sent her something. He obviously didn't believe she didn't have it, so decided to look for himself.

"In your email, you said someone assaulted Doctor Jardine. Was that before or after her brother showed up?"

"Before."

"Thoughts?" As always, Mason was curt and to the point and much like an interrogator.

"They're using her to draw him out."

"What's her reaction to all this?"

Mitch shrugged. "She's royally pissed. Wants to know what's really going on."

"You can't actually want to tell this doctor, who's out on the streets looking after homeless, of her brother's involvement with a notorious gang who has committed atrocities that would give most people nightmares. That they steal precious stones from traders in Afghanistan and smuggle them into Australia?"

Mitch nodded. "These guys are violent. We know what they're capable of. If Doctor Jardine knows the truth, she may be more amicable about being offered protection."

"You're already protecting her. There's no need to tell her anything more."

"Yes, sir."

"Okay. Keep in touch." The colonel strode from the room.

Mitch moved back to his partitioned part of the office and flung himself onto the chair. He cut and pasted some information into another file and printed it. He'd put it with the rest of the document stored at his place.

Mitch checked his watch. He would not find Jones while sitting here. There were a few more places to check out and more people to talk to. *He was going to find Corporal Jones. He had to.*

Asher's life depended on it.

Later that night, Mitch prowled the perimeter at Mates and Eats. As he approached the parking lot, a bloke resembling Jones opened the door to a white Holden Commodore and slipped inside the car. The interior light illuminated the driver's face. *It is Jones.* Mitch broke into a run heading toward the car as it reversed at high speed out onto the road. He upped his pace as the car drove away, hoping for a glimpse of the license plate. But he was too slow, and the car screamed off down the road. Mitch's confidence deteriorated as he stood and watched Jones's car disappear into the night. Fuck this injury. *I should have found him by now.*

Mitch's leg throbbed to the marrow with every step he took as he moved toward Asher, Bridget, and Hamish, standing together, chatting at the opposite end of the quadrangle.

"All packed up for the night," he ground out against the pain.

Asher nodded. "Great. I'm just filling Hamish in about extra security for the gala."

"Good. I have something to add."

They looked at him. He crossed his arms and rocked back on his heels. "I've spoken to our newest volunteers." He pointed toward the ex-soldiers driving out of the parking lot. "We're going to work alongside security."

"Isn't that overkill?" Asher asked.

Mitch shook his head. "No. The rent-a-cop the council is hiring doesn't have the skills to defuse difficult situations. We do."

Hamish pulled keys out of his pocket. "I agree with Mitch. Can't have too much security, not with all the drama that's been happening around you."

Asher nodded reluctantly. "Okay."

Mitch slapped Hamish on the back "Good. I'm glad you agree. I'll talk to Ethan. Let him know what we've arranged." Then he faced Asher. "Ready to leave?"

"Sure."

After dropping Bridget off, he pulled up outside Asher's place and turned off the ignition. Even though she'd scooted to the far side of the truck the minute Bridget got out, Asher's scent teased him, resurrecting memories of her wrapped in his arms. Still, she hadn't mentioned last night. Obviously, it meant nothing.

She didn't make a move to get out. Just sat and stared out the window.

"I've always loved coming home to my little house. But tonight?" She shrugged. "I don't want to go in. They have violated my private space." Her voice dipped. "And I'm terrified."

Mitch turned to face her. "I'll come in, check it out."

She smiled. "I'd appreciate it."

He jumped from his truck and his knee gave out from under him as he landed on the footpath. "Damn it." Burning pain wracked through his joint and travelled up his thigh. Is *this injury ever going to heal enough for me to get back to work?* Frustration gnawed his psyche.

"Mitch." Asher was out of the vehicle and beside him in a flash. "Let me help you up." She crouched by his side, maneuvered her shoulder under his armpit, and pushed to her feet. "I've noticed you've been limping more."

"I know and it's doing my head in. This injury was supposed to be healed by now. I'm doing the recommended physical therapy, sometimes more, if it feels strong. But times like this, it just gives out for no reason."

Asher shifted closer, supporting him to ease his discomfort. "I can make you an appointment with a friend of mine who's an orthopedic specialist. He can check you out."

He grimaced as he put his full weight onto his leg. "It's okay, I'm still under the Army specialist. I'll make an appointment with him, and he will check it out for me." He couldn't afford this injury to interfere with keeping her safe. He smiled down at her. "Thanks for helping."

"No problem. I like to help." She stared into his eyes.

Mitch eased away from her.

"Will you stay with me?"

"Why?" His stomach lurched, and his breathing stalled. As he prayed, she'd say the words he wanted to hear.

"I'd feel safer if you stayed."

"Sure." He swallowed the disappointment.

"Just for a couple of nights."

Could he, do it? Just sleep on her couch when his body ached to hold her? "Sure, Doc." *Heaven help me.*

CHAPTER 15

He'd been her bodyguard since that night she'd asked him to stay. He told her he didn't need a bed because he was happy to share the couch with Peaches. But she'd insisted. So, for the past week he'd been living in her home, sleeping in her spare room, and using her main bathroom as his.

That was the hardest part about sharing her home with him—imagining him naked and wet every time he showered. His presence in her home sent her senses soaring, imagining all sorts of scenarios. Everywhere she looked, Mitch filled up the space. And she liked it. Way too much.

Every night he drove her and Bridge to wherever they had to be, did his volunteer role with the patrons of Mates & Eats, and when they arrived back at the house, he'd search every nook and cranny before allowing her inside. On the days she had to see the girls at Lily's, he accompanied her, talked with the girls, and shared his views of life, the whole-time ensuring Asher wasn't far away.

He took his protector role seriously. And being the honorable man he was, he never stepped over the 'protector role boundary'. She wondered, what if he did? And then wondered how she'd respond.

She discovered a few things while living with him. His sense of humor was wicked, and when he laughed, she laughed with him. He was as addictive as chocolate.

And she loved chocolate.

Now he was shaving in the bathroom, his hips wrapped in a bath towel. Wide shoulders flexed with each swipe of the blade. The length of his spine drew her gaze to the nasty, puckered scar halfway down his back. Bullet wound? That close to the spine could have left him paraplegic. She shuddered and sucked in a huge breath, as reality hit her like a sledgehammer. It would make no difference in her feelings for Mitch if he were confined to a wheelchair. He'd still be the strongest man who'd ever graced her life.

His honor, determination, and sheer strength showed through all he did, from helping at Mates and Eats to working with the ex-soldiers, who now volunteered for her.

She wanted to walk into the bathroom, wrap her arms around his waist, and lay her chin against his back. To feel his warmth seep into her and hear the solid thudding of his heart.

She was a right royal mess for him. She was torn between keeping this thing between them professional and friendly, or allowing the deeper emotional pull between them to develop. Her mind jumped and in her next heartbeat, she had the urge to wrap her legs around his waist and feel him deep inside her, thrust after thrust. Would she scream? Sex had never been the be all end all, probably why abstaining for the past couple of years hadn't been a hardship. Now, if he even showed the slightest interest, she'd have him.

Who are you kidding? Every time he looks at you, you bolt. She didn't question the reaction, knowing it was self-preservation, because she knew she could—if she allowed herself to—develop serious emotions for him. He wasn't even trying to influence her. He was just being Mitch.

She met his gaze in the mirror.

"Did you need something, Doc?"

His voice slid over her like Bailey's over ice cubes. *Oh yeah.* She swallowed. *But not right now.* She shook the crazy thoughts aside. "This dress, I can't do the clip at the back."

"No problem." He rinsed his face, wiped his hands on the hand towel, and moved toward her. Big, strong, dependable. Sexy. His chest went on for miles.

"Turn around."

She did. One of his hands rested on the curve of her back as he tugged the zipper up that last bit. Heat branded wherever he touched, and she struggled to gather her senses.

"Done."

"Thanks." She gave him a smile and stepped away.

"Have you memorized your speech?"

Asher shrugged. "Sort of. It's precise and factual. Boring."

He raised his brow and grinned. "What's the real problem?"

"I should print it out, throw it in front of a fan so they get blown a copy each, bow, and run away. Probably be more interesting that way."

"C'mere." He reached out his hand.

She wrapped her fingers around his, and he gave a slight tug and pulled her flush against his chest. His spicy scent filled her nostrils, and a sigh whispered softly from her lips.

"Those people attending tonight don't care about what you're talking about. They've read about the Street Doctor and are coming to meet you. You *are* the business. You're the one they'll donate to, so you're going to get on that podium, and you're going to dazzle them with your wit."

"They'll be waiting for me to mess up." She lifted her head and stared into his eyes.

"If you do, laugh about it. You take yourself way too seriously, Doc. Have fun with it."

She stepped back out of his light embrace. "You see me so differently than how I see myself."

"I see the real you. The fighter, the compassionate woman. Tiger, Tiger. That's what the homeless and the sick who visit your service say about you."

"But?"

"Doc, you'll be among friends. I'll be guarding you, along with my buddies. I'll be prowling around looking for who shouldn't be there to make sure whoever is threating you can't get to you." He tipped her chin and gazed into her eyes.

Asher's belly flopped.

"When you're giving your speech, I'll stand and look only at you. You will have my full attention. I'm wearing a red bow tie to match your dress, so I'll stick out. When you're up on that podium, find me. Look at me, talk to me, Doc. You'll be fine."

"You reckon you can take my fear of public speaking away?"

"No, but I can help take your mind off the people."

"We'll see. You'd better get dressed or I won't be the only one looking at you."

"Not going to take long. All I have to wear is my bow tie."

She gaped.

He grinned.

"See, change your focus. So, when you look at me at the back of that hall, all you'll visualize is me wearing nothing but a bow tie and a grin."

She'd be lucky if a coherent word passed between her lips, but she smiled. "That could work. I'll meet you in the lounge in ten."

"Hey, Doc?"

"What?" She turned to face him.

He stepped closer, reached up behind her hair and pulled the pins. "Leave it loose. I dare you."

With her heart thudding twice its normal pace, she nodded and moved out of the bathroom.

She stared at her reflection in her bathroom mirror. "Leave it out indeed." A pink hue stained her cheeks, and her eyes sparkled brightly. Dare she? "I'll do it, Mr. I Dare You! I'll show you I can be a free-spirited woman." She scrounged around the cabinet and found a tube of product, squeezed some into her hands, and scrunched handfuls of her hair. It looked blonder with the curls.

Asher gnawed on her lips wondering if she should wear the gorgeous, provocative red lipstick Bridge had given her when she'd stopped by earlier to give her a pep talk. Trouble with that was whenever she wore red, she usually ended up in trouble. Oh well. She shrugged and swiped the color across her lips. No mouse tonight. She rubbed her lips together and smiled. "Brave and bold," she whispered to her vibrant reflection.

Asher strode into her bedroom. Her fingers wrapped around the softness of the pashmina on her bed, and she whisked it around her shoulders and strolled to the lounge to wait for Mitch.

Naked in a bow tie.

Yes, please. The image seared into her brain during the never-ending but all-too-short drive to the event venue.

Mitch pulled the truck into the car park of the venue and turned off the ignition, then turned to face Asher. "If I haven't mentioned it, you look beautiful."

"And you look," she almost said, hot, but pushed out, "Handsome."

His brow shot up. "Handsome, really? Handsome? I was hoping for something not so generic." With that, his phone rang. He grabbed it from his pocket, checked the screen and hit accept. "Blaine. What's happening?"

Asher met his gaze and raised a brow. He gave her a smile and her heart picked up its pace.

"I'm going to put you on speaker, so Dr Jardine can listen." He pushed another button, and a light feminine voice filled the interior of the truck.

"I've been following up on that information on the lawyer, Cynthia Cassidy, regarding private adoptions."

"What did you find out?" This from Asher.

"Her names come up in some other private adoption companies. And there's been numerous serious complaints lodged against her."

"So, what's the next step?" Mitch reached across the seat and squeezed Asher's fingers.

"A unit attached to child protection spoke with the directors from the companies Ms Cassidy worked for and presented the evidence gathered against her. After speaking with them, they went to her office to discuss the complaints against her."

"And?" Asher practically yelled into the phone.

"As of today, Ms Cassidy has been stood down from her position, until all allegations and complaints against her are investigated."

Asher sighed and leaned her head against the truck seat. "That's great news."

"It's a positive outcome. Your help is appreciated. Thank you both." With that, the connection was cut.

Asher lifted her head, leaned in, and kissed his cheek. "This night just keeps getting better. "

As they entered the building, Mitch bent toward her. "I'll catch you up, I want to meet with the head of security."

Asher reached up and stroked his jaw. "I'll see you inside." As Mitch strode away, Bridget rushed to greet her, wearing a stunning sea green chiffon number.

"Not a spare seat." Bridget hugged Asher and danced in happy circles with her. "Three-hundred-dollar-a-plate banquet, and a silent art auction."

A knot twisted in Asher's gut. She looked around and took in all the beautifully dressed people milling around, glasses in hand, smiles on faces. Wait staff scurried, carrying trays laden with hors d'oeuvres. Black tablecloths contrasted with white drapery, and candles cast the room in a warm glow. It was stunning. She smiled.

They would make a decent, much needed profit.

Ryan, splendid in a tux, sat in his wheelchair by the door, checking names against invitations, and handing out name tags. Nic and Pete meandered through the crowd, smiling, and chatting. Asher's nerves settled. These men would help keep everyone safe. Hopefully, there would be no need for the extra security, but she had to admit she was pleased they'd arranged it.

She'd helped herself to a cracker piled with pâté when Mitch came into view. Although, dressed in a tux like most of the men, he stood out. Bigger, broader, and sexy as hell. She smiled. He must have sensed her perusal because his gaze zeroed in on her. He gave her a salute. Heat travelled through her body as she stared at him. *Sexy beast*. Her belly clenched.

Bridge continued. "They've pledged heaps already. Checks are being placed in the donation basket." Bridge pointed toward the back of the room. "And there are new sponsors looking to come on board, which means, hopefully another twelve months of funding for us, and maybe another ambulance in another community." She hugged Asher close. "You should be so proud of yourself."

Asher seized a breath and squared her shoulders. "I am. But I couldn't do it without you and the rest of the team. I'm proud of you all."

"Okay, here's the program. You get to eat before you speak." Bridget handed her a cream-colored card.

"Good." She found the dais at the front of the room. Maybe she could get the band to play and drown out her speech.

Asher nibbled at the glorious meal, constantly checking her watch. Almost time. "Excuse me. I won't be long." She snatched up her purse, shoved away from the table and rose so quickly she almost twisted her ankle in her stupid heels. She smiled at those around her as she headed toward the exit.

At the ladies' room door, a deep spicy voice asked. "Freaking out, are you?"

"That obvious?"

"Only to me." Mitch smiled. "Maybe Bridge."

"I'll be a minute." Asher turned and pushed the door open. When she entered, she confronted her reflection. *Damn it, Asher. Get back out there.* Instead, she cradled her head in her hands and screwed her eyes shut.

"I'm coming in." After a brief knock, Mitch pushed the door open and stepped inside. "You're not hiding, are you?"

Opening her eyes, she turned to face him. She couldn't drag her gaze from the snow-white shirt and the splash of red around his neck. She wrung her hands together and sighed. The master of ceremonies announced her, his faint voice echoing through a speaker in the hallway. Panic clawed her consciousness.

"Doc, you'll be great. Remember, focus on me, talk to me. He bent forward and touched his firm lips to hers in a gentle kiss. It was like an electric shock. Asher's hands separated and crept to his neck. A low moan escaped her throat as he leaned in and ratcheted up the chaste kiss until her blood boiled.

Her name being called pushed through the haze of passion engulfing her, and she gave him a gentle push. He leaned his forehead against hers. "Remember. Focus on me."

She stepped out of his embrace. "I will. Head up, eyes straight, smile. I will do this. But first," She opened her purse and pulled out the dare me red lipstick. And reapplied it to her trembling lips. Then she turned away and strode back to the function.

On the dais, she smiled at the faces peering up at her. Then extended her gaze, and true to his word, Mitch stood at the back of the room watching her with those heavily lidded eyes. Even across the distance, his vibe touched her. He tapped his fingers on his bow tie and grinned. Asher's smile broadened in return. And calmness filled her.

Once she started, the words fell from her mouth. She must be doing okay. The audience laughed when she said something humorous and gasped in dismay when she recited the dismal facts of life on the streets.

Applause thundered when she finished her speech. As she descended the stairs, a throng of well-wishers gathered around. Bridge and Mitch were right. The attendees came to see her and listen to her story. Joy swelled in her soul as she shook hands and chatted with her supporters

Moving around the room, conversing with different people—some she knew, others were strangers—she hummed along with the band as they gave a rousing rendition of Rod Stewart's classic "Tonight's the Night." And for Asher, it was. Two years ago, she'd vowed to abstain from men after yet another bad experience. But Mitch was changing that. Scanning the room, she spotted him in a group, laughing, head thrown back and humor coloring his glorious face. Her insides throbbed. Somehow, he'd snuck into her heart, and she wanted him.

Bad.

So badly, she wanted to drag him away from this event to have her wicked way with him. A flush of heat infused every part of her body as she visualized them, naked, flush against each other. But not yet. She could wait a few more hours. She smiled.

The rest of the night flew by on festive wings.

She'd danced with anyone who asked her and had had a few glasses of rosé champagne. Mitch stayed close to her side, and she clutched his arm. "I love this song. Let's dance."

"Sure." His deep voice washed over her, filled her pores with heat, and seeped inside to stoke the ember of need for him.

Clasping her hand, he led her to the overcrowded dance floor and gathered her tightly against him. They moved well together, no awkwardness. They fit snug against each other, shoulder to thigh, his muscled body pressed against her breasts, although his embrace hung loosely around her waist and hers around his neck.

His fingers danced their way up and down her spine. "You did well."

"I know. And I'm so happy I've conquered that fear. Yay for me." She pressed her lips to his cheek. "Thank you. You were the best focal point."

"You're welcome." He brushed his lips against her hair.

She snuggled in closer as they moved in unison to the seductive beat. "I could get very used to being in your arms."

"I could get very used to having you there. We're a good fit."

"We are." She smiled as his words echoed her earlier thoughts.

"So where to from here?" He tightened his arms around her.

Does he sense the change in me? Asher thought as she met his sexy brown eyes. "Let's just enjoy tonight. Don't worry about what ifs and buts, rights or wrongs, just tonight."

"You and me. Just tonight?"

What's he really asking? Does he want more than just tonight?

Asher thought he wanted more as much as she did, but he seemed happy to let her set the pace for the evening. He probably didn't want to scare her off. Good move. Slow suited her, except for the times she wanted it fast and furious.

When the music stopped, he escorted her back to her seat. "Be right back." He kissed her neck.

Asher trembled. *Tonight's going to be a good night*. She picked up the bottle of champagne from the ice bucket, poured herself a glass, and sipped the icy delight.

At the evening's end, she shook hands, had her cheek kissed, and smiled politely, listening to comments like "great organization," "fabulous cause," and "happy to help."

She smiled, glad she had an accountant to sort through the financial side of Health for the Homeless. She would know within a week if there was enough funding for another twelve months. The way the politicians were talking, another ambulance in another community could happen, just like Bridget said. God, she hoped so.

Asher and Bridge sat sipping coffee when Mitch strolled toward them. When he took Asher's hand, Bridge raised a brow and gave Asher a knowing smile.

Leaning toward Asher, Bridget whispered. "Remember condoms. Oh, and drink heaps of cranberry juice."

Asher rolled her eyes, then laughed. "Oh, Shut up."

Mitch looked at her with a question in his eyes. She smiled. *Please let me be doing the right thing*. She shoved that thought away. It was the right thing. One night at a time, that was it.

No tomorrow.

No next week.

Just tonight.

She picked up a bottle of still corked champagne, the manager of the facility gifted her and followed Mitch outside.

CHAPTER 16

I n his truck, Mitch glanced at Asher. "You're very quiet." At the ball, she'd sparkled. Now, away from the buzz and excitement of the gala, her mind seemed to be elsewhere.

"Just thinking."

"About?" *Second thoughts, probably.* Which wouldn't be a problem. She could change her mind any time. She was probably nervous. *Please let it be nerves.*

She shrugged.

He grinned. "Asher. You think too much."

"Okay."

He heard the question in that one brief word. "There is nothing I want more than you naked beside me, but there's no rush, no expectation. Just tonight. Just us. What happens, happens. Okay?"

"If we were to play, what then?" Her tone was velvety soft and questioning.

He turned the radio down. And tapped the seat beside him. "Shimmy over here."

She did. Every movement of her delectable body had him seeing her naked against him. It was fantasy he'd been fighting against since that first night. She wore her overly independent, and wary of any sort of emotional ties persona like armor, but he'd seen through it, seen the woman beneath.

Tonight, maybe he'd get to show her how she affected him, how she made his heart thump. He glimpsed down at her tucked up beside him, her hair gold and shiny like delicate threads against the darkness of his jacket. She could be as gentle as a summer breeze or as cold as the westerlies howling through Brisbane in August.

But he'd take her any way he could get her. It was part and parcel of who she was. He'd been single for a long time. No ties ever, he'd never really wanted them. Until now, his job meant personal relationships were hazardous at best. He'd rarely thought about falling in love, but believed if he ever did, it would be a gradual thing. Not being blindsided at the first meeting, but now, Asher could tie him up any way she wanted, and he'd be happy.

"Let's go to your place."

He glanced at her. "Not as comfortable as yours."

"Does it have a bed?"

He smiled. "King size."

"Coffee maker?"

"Yup."

"Protection in your bedside table drawer?"

His heart thudded hard against his ribs, hearing those words from her mouth. "There is." That he managed to get the words out surprised him.

"I think that's about all we need." She leaned over and pressed her lips to his jaw, then rested her head on his shoulder. That gentle touch and sweet tease talk lightened his heart.

He thought, tonight might be better at his place anyway. Depending on what happened., They could always go back to the way things had been at her place. It would probably kill him, but it would be possible. He switched on the ignition and as he reversed out of the car park. "I have a pack of cards. We could always play strip poker."

"Really? I'm an excellent poker player." She let loose a wicked laugh. "Poor you, sitting all naked, and me fully clothed, just teasing you."

Good, she was coming out of the funk. "Sounds like fun. What makes you think you'd be the one fully clothed?"

"I never lose." She lifted her head from his shoulder and looked up at him. "Never."

He laughed. "Sounds like a challenge."

"Could be if that's the road we're travelling down. Or?" She plucked his jacket sleeve. "We could just be sipping coffee and chatting all night."

"Either's good for me." *Liar.* "As long as I'm with you, I'll be happy."

"Alright, so we can talk and drink coffee while we play strip poker. What about sex?"

"If sex is on offer, I'm sure we can work something out."

She laughed—long, sexy, and husky.

By the time they pulled into his driveway, Asher had to admit, as far as tease talk went, it was working. Her nervousness had dissolved, changed into a sense of anticipation. Strip poker. She smiled. She was competitive, but she wouldn't mind losing this one.

He opened the door, stretched around her, and flicked the switch, and light flooded into the room.

"Coffee."

She nodded and looked around. A definite bachelor pad but occupied by a neat freak. Not a thing out of place. Maybe it was military training. A couple of photos, one of him in military gear. He looked so incredibly sexy. In another, he was with an older man, same size, and build. His dad? The smell of percolated coffee filled her nostrils.

She followed it through to the kitchen. Again, neat. No wonder he shook his head at her place. One thing he had that she didn't was leafy green plants thriving in every corner.

If he could teach her to grow plants, she'd love him forever. *Whoa. No way.* Where did that come from? *Love? Mitch?*

He placed a mug on the island in front of her and added two sugars. "Strong, black, and sweet, just the way you like it."

She stared at him, long and hard. Saw the man inside the honed body. There was no denying her physical attraction to him. But it went deeper, more organic than that. He attracted the woman she'd frozen inside herself a long time ago. No wonder she fought it. Would he release her after one night? Or something more? Was she ready for that?

"Mitch to Asher."

His teasing tone brought her back to the now, and she focused her attention on his coffee-dampened lips. He still had the jacket on, although he'd unfastened the buttons. The white shirt hinted at the muscles beneath it. But it was the red bow tie that was her focal point. She lifted the cup, sipped, and set the mug down.

She edged around the island to him, put her hand on his shoulder, raised herself on tip toe, and pressed her lips to his. The taste of strong coffee and man flooded her senses, and she savored him. "Want to get naked?"

He pulled her against him and devoured her lips with his. There was no gentleness, no shyness, just warmth. A sigh spilled from her lips as his touch warmed her from her insides out. It morphed into a groan as her body melted against his.

Asher's lips parted, encouraging his exploration of her mouth. The texture of his lips melted her, and she groaned deep in her throat as his tongue trailed to the spot behind her ear and nipped it.

"I know, I know. I'm feeling it too." His voice trembled and her body shuddered.

The zip on the back of her dress slid down. Breath stuck in her throat, and she rested her head against his shoulder.

CHAPTER 17

Mitch trailed his fingers down her back as he unzipped her. With each bump his fingers touched her spine and she shivered. Her skin was as soft as he'd known it would be. Asher tucked her head against his chest, almost as though she didn't want him to hear her groan.

He tipped her chin. Red tinged her cheeks, and her wide eyes sparkled. She swiped her tongue across her mouth, and he moaned as he replaced it with his lips. This woman was electric, sending shocks through him. *Nice and slow, Buchanan. No rushing. It wasn't a race.*

He pulled back and slipped the dress from her shoulders, and it pooled around her ankles in a shimmering red circle. She stepped out, kicked it away, and stood proudly before him wearing a red bra and matching lace thong.

He trailed his fingers along her collarbone and down her arms, across her breasts. "Your breasts are perfect," he whispered, surprising himself with how husky his voice sounded. "How about we get rid of this." His fingers traced the shape of the bra against her breast.

"Why don't we." Asher reached behind her, unclasped the bra, and let it fall.

Mitch feasted his eyes on her bared breasts. "You are glorious." He bent forward, dipped his head, and suckled one nipple then the other. She whimpered as he continued his exploration of her lushness. His fingertips explored her back and hips as he bent his head and ran his tongue over the pulse throbbing in her neck. Cupping her backside, he lifted her against him so she could feel his arousal, and know he burned for her.

He looked into her eyes. They were bright, filled with want. He pulled her closer and covered her mouth with his. It was more potent than a double Johnnie Walker. "Doc, you are everything I've ever wanted." He nibbled her neck. "You give, you give, and you give. How about just for tonight, you take?" He pinned her with his gaze. "Take everything I'm offering, no questions."

"Just lay back and do nothing?"

"Or not." *Or you can touch me. Anywhere. Everywhere.*

"I have one request."

"Just one?" He trailed his tongue down the column of her throat and sucked on the pulse beating there.

"Mmm, leave the bow tie on."

"Okay. Would you like me to dance for you?"

She laughed then. A deep, throaty growl. "I watched you all night, in that silly, sexy tie, and I talked in public, but all I could think about was you wearing that sexy bow and nothing else."

"Not even a smile?"

"Oh, you were smiling."

His cock hardened and strained against the zipper of his pants. "Your wish is my command. And maybe I'll dance just for the hell of it."

"If you play your cards right, I'll dance for you."

"Or maybe we just make up a dance just for us to do together?"

"Sounds good."

"I knew your breasts would be magnificent." He dropped to one knee, dipped his head, and swiped his tongue across her engorged nipple. When she moaned, he did it again, this time sucking the pebble deep into his mouth. She grabbed his head and held and pulled him closer.

"Damn that feels so good." She muttered as he continued licking and kissing her breast.

Mitch stood, picked her up, and she wrapped her legs around his waist. His lips found hers again, and the kiss changed. Heat surged through him as her legs wound tighter. She clung to him as if she'd never let go. And he didn't want her to. He wanted, no, needed, to be this close to her. If they travelled this sensual journey to its climax, or if it ended right now, he'd be happy.

Every part of her lushness pressed against him. Heat pulsed from her.

"Not fair," she muttered.

"What's not fair."

"You've still got clothes on."

He was grateful for that. He doubted he'd have lasted this long if he were naked. "It's okay."

"No. No, it's not. I want to see your body. I want to feel your skin against mine. To watch you after I've stroked you. Your chest feels fantastic though your frilly shirt, but..." She kissed along his jawline. He groaned. "I want to do that all over your naked body, so I can taste your skin."

He carried her through the apartment, his gut tightening when she wrapped herself tighter around him. He lowered her to the bed and followed her down.

She pushed him back. "Shirt off." It was a demand. "Leave the bow tie on."

He stood, unbuttoned the shirt buttons one by one, then pulled at the collar and somehow left the tie in place. He stood before her, naked to the waist.

"Now the trousers."

Her gaze riveted on him as he deliberately slowly untied his laces and toed the shoes off, then the socks, rolling each one into a tube and slowly sliding it into the shoe. Her eyes darkened with every movement, and he wasn't sure she even breathed during the show.

He hooked his thumbs in the waistband of his trousers near the button, shucking them, and his boxers off in two seconds flat. Her eyes feasted on his naked flesh. She raised herself to her elbows and drank in every single inch of him.

"Come closer."

He placed one knee on the bed.

"How did you get that?" She pointed to the jagged scar that ran across the top of his hip.

"Unsatisfied lover."

She raised her brow.

"Knife wound, breaking up a brawl."

She crooked her finger. "Closer."

He did. When she leaned in and pressed a kiss to the scar, he gasped.

"You liked that?" Her smile widened. "Good to know. Come, lay beside me." Asher rolled onto her side, bent her elbow, and rested her head on her hand.

He lowered himself next to her. She trailed her hand down his spine,

"That one's from a bullet." There were better things to talk about than his scars. He moved closer, kissed her neck, and raised himself onto one elbow, gazing into her gorgeous blue eyes.

She cupped his face, her liquid eyes full of passion...and something else.

He saw the hesitation, as minute as it was. "We can stop this. No pressure."

"I don't want to stop." She swiped her tongue across her lips. "I'm just out of practice."

His pent-up passion burst free, and he kissed her, drowning in her, drinking her in until she was his only reality. At Asher's deep-throated moan, he tore his mouth from hers to ease her back against the pillows, pulling her with him and cradling her at his side. "Breathe, Asher, just breathe. Let me take care of you."

So, she did. And closed her eyes. Pleasure spread from the feel of his hands, but sweet heavens, when he followed the touch of his fingers with his tongue, her body sighed. As his tongue forged its path down her belly and dipped into her navel, her core tightened as the slither of an orgasm teased with a promise of what lay in store.

His maleness filled her senses as he continued the sensual trail down the length of her body with hands and tongue. When he slid to the end of the bed and rolled away, her body screamed for his heat. "Don't go."

"I'm not going anywhere."

His spicy scent floated around her. He lifted one of her feet, and massaged the instep, then the calf before moving to the other. Slowly, methodically, his powerful hands massaged her, taking away her ability to think, to move, to do anything but exist in the moment.

Tremors of sensation rippled over her skin, then traveled deep inside, and she pushed aside her fears. There was no rush, no demands, just pleasure. She stretched her arms above her head, her belly clenched.

"Roll over."

She did and, the soft material of the sheets brushed erotically against her aroused nipples. The bed shifted, and she turned her head on the pillow to watch him. He sat beside her, reached into the bedside drawer, and pulled out a bottle and opened it. The scent of lavender mixed with something she didn't recognize filled the room. Then he drizzled the oil down her spine, and he massaged it into her skin in sensual circles.

A deep, guttural groan escaped her.

He teased, rubbed, stroked her spine, expanding to her waist and hips. Dampness settled between her legs as again he traveled down past her moist core to work his magic on her legs and thighs.

"You doing okay, Doc?"

She rolled onto her back and met his gaze. "Oh yeah. You?"

"Hell yeah." His fingers trembled as he stroked her jaw.

Asher reached up, pulled him down, so he landed half on, half off her, and covered his mouth with a deep, passionate kiss. She wrapped her arms around his shoulders, determined to show him how he affected her. His heart thudded in unison with hers, his breathing as erratic as her own.

"I love the way you kiss me, Asher."

She moaned long and hard as his tongue swiped back and forth, teasing.

He reached for the scrap of red lace. "Time for this to make an exit. Lift for me."

Asher raised her bottom, and he peeled the thong from her body. He kissed her belly, her inner thighs, her curls sodden with her own juices.

Asher's fingers combed through his spiky hair, then clung tightly to his head. She had to hold on to something, or she'd float off the bed. Her body writhed as waves of bliss crashed through her leaving her mindless to all but the intensity of pleasure. With one more cry of pleasure, she melted into the mattress.

He lay with his head on her belly, his heat pushing through her core as his ragged panting shouted his battle between need and restraint. "You taste like magic."

Want pulsed as heat speared her entire body. She reached for him, urging him to lie beside her, solid and warm. She slid her hand down his chest, past his hard stomach, and wrapped her fingers around his erection. His body trembled, but he lay still, waiting for her to move.

A sigh spilled from her lips. She eased herself down the bed, dipped her head, and swiped her tongue across the tip of his cock, once, twice before taking him deep into her mouth.

"Sweet hell. No more. I'm not going to last long if you keep that up." He stroked her back. "Come here."

She shimmied up the bed and covered his mouth in hot kisses then whispered. "Mitch, I want you inside me." Her hoarse command urged him into action. He grabbed a condom, ripped off the wrap and sheathed himself.

She rolled to her back, pulling him with her, and spread her legs. He settled between her thighs. His mouth crashed against hers, his tongue pressing against her as his cock slid into her core. Her body contracted around him. His lips moved to her neck, and heat flashed over her as he sucked at the skin before moving back to her mouth.

His thrusts were slow, measured. She shoved her heels into the mattress and met each, of his smooth hard plunges, then wrapped her legs around his waist. One hand gripped her buttocks as he drove deeper and deeper inside her. His breathing sawed in and out in time with each thrust. He pushed the hair back from her face as he thrust into her again. He met her eyes as he traced her lips with his finger. She nipped it before licking the length and pulling it into her mouth.

A gruff groan spilled from him, and the pace escalated.

"Asher," he whispered against her neck as he thrust deeper and harder.

Never, never had sex been like this before. No, she thought with the few brain cells not obliterated by pleasure, this wasn't just sex, or sex of any sort, this was way beyond anything she'd ever experienced before, it was. Her thoughts disintegrated as she spiraled into oblivion. "Mitch. Oh God. That feels so... So good." She turned her head, pressed her lips against his neck, and sucked in his scent. "I've never been... Oh Mitch, I'm... I'm going to come." Her muscles convulsed. "Mitch." She screamed as an orgasm ripped through her, and she fell into the abyss of long denied pleasure as Mitch surged into her, following her into oblivion.

They lay, breaths ragged, hearts pounding, bodies trembling, until Mitch rolled to his side and pulled her close. His fingers pushed the tangle of hair off her face. "You, okay?"

"Oh yes," she whispered as her breath began to return. "My 'girly bits' are a tad sore." She gave him a smile. "But I guess that's to be expected after a two-year abstinence." She stroked his strong jaw. "You?"

"Never better." They lay tangled together for what felt like hours but must have only been minutes before he moved. Soft lips grazed her cheek. "I'll be back."

"Mmm." She pried her eyes open, grabbed his hand, then pressed her lips to his fingers. "

He climbed from the bed and strode buck naked to the bathroom. *Damn, his butt is fine.*

She yawned and stretched her body, the whole time keeping one eye on the bathroom. There was no way she was going to miss the front of his honed body as he came back to bed. Heat surged through her as he approached.

"What's that?" she pointed toward the bundle in his hand as he settled at the foot of the bed.

"A warm washcloth." He eased closer to her.

A nervous laugh fell from her. "Why?" It took ages for the word to find its way out.

"I'm going to bathe your girly bits."

"You have to be kidding?" She edged further up the pillows.

"Why would you think that?" His deep velvet voice slid over her. "I said earlier I wanted to take care of you." His intent brown gaze held her motionless.

She nodded.

"You said you're sore, so I'm going to soothe your discomfort away."

She bit her lip. Wary. "Nobody's ever offered to ease my pain." Her voice sounded raw. "Nobody's ever cared enough." Tears blurred her vision.

"You honoured me with your body." His damn voice was drugging. "So please, let me do this for you."

She nodded because, for her life, she couldn't articulate a response.

His lips pressed gently against her brow. "Close your eyes."

She did. And held her breath as he parted her legs. The warmth from the cloth against her inner thigh eased her tension.

"I believe in giving back." His voice was as soft as she'd ever heard. "What we shared was more than sex." His big hand continued to shape the cloth against her. "It was my intention to give you pleasure."

"You did that." She whispered. Her body softened against the mattress as he soothed every single inch of her ache.

"Feeling better?"

She managed a nod.

"Good." he placed the cloth on the bedside table, climbed into bed, and eased her close. He drew the sheet over their cooling bodies and tucked her tight up against his side.

"Mitch, that was something else. Thank you." She closed her eyes as the sleep of total satisfaction drew her into its warm embrace.

CHAPTER 18

"**M**orning, Asher." He watched her stretch, long and elegant, like a golden cat.

"Morning." She smiled and snuggled into the pillow.

He leaned in and pressed his lips to her temple.

She rolled over to her back and blinked three times. "I could get used to this. Gorgeous, hunky man bringing me coffee after a night of great sex." She winced. "No wonder I ache." She eased herself up to sitting and wound the sheet around herself to cover her breasts. Then finger-combed the tangles out of her hair. "Morning. Again."

He passed her one mug and rested on the side of the bed sipping from his. He battled his urge to haul her back into his arms and go back down the path they'd travelled together last night, but she wasn't meeting his eyes. She placed her mug on the bedside table.

Why? Was she nervous? He hoped not. He wanted to continue this fragile relationship they'd created. Asher Jardine was an enigma. Stern to outsiders, but those around her saw a different side to her, and the patients she tended saw yet another facet. Last night she'd allowed him to see her feminine, sensual, passionate side, a side she kept well hidden. And he hoped like hell she'd want to share it again with him.

"Mitch."

He met her gaze. "Asher."

She rose to her knees. The sheet fell away, exposing her beautiful breasts. He sucked in a breath as the memory of their taste wiped the coffee from his mind. She took the cup from him and put it beside hers. Then she wrapped her arms tightly around his chest. Her hair tickled his cheek as she kissed his neck. A tremor travelled through his body.

"I enjoyed last night. I just wanted you to know."

"What part?"

She smiled. "Do you need to be told how good it was?"

"Only if you mean it."

She laughed, all throaty and wicked. "Last night, everything about last night, the fundraiser, your company, you being so protective and gentle. You reminded me I'm worthy of being cared for. That I don't have to do everything by myself. That it's okay to ask for help."

So, it wasn't just the sex. "Good."

"And the sex was the icing on a perfect night."

"That's even better."

"Mitch." she trailed her fingers down his belly and slipped beneath the band of his shorts. "I'd like some more."

He gathered her into his arms, held her tight against him as he covered her mouth with hot, wet kisses and burrowed his fingers through her hair. "Me too, Doc." He laid her back against the pillows. "Me too."

She met his mouth halfway to hers and kissed him hard, then whispered, "You're not working today, are you?"

"No. It's Sunday."

"Oh, good." The satisfied smile that accompanied those few words held the promise that today would be even better than last night. And it was, not just the sex, but also spending the day together.

He cooked, she ate, and together they did dishes. Like a couple.

What was she thinking as she wandered about, touching stuff, and sniffing the plants? Sniffing? The indoor greenery had no smell at all. He grinned. Obviously, she knew nothing about plants.

She ran her finger across the top of a wooden photo frame. "Who's the man in the photo?"

"My dad."

She picked the photo up for a better look. "You look like him. Is he still around.?"

"Nope." He came to stand behind her, so he could look over her shoulder—and breathe in her scent. "He died after my first tour. He didn't want me to join the Army, but I wanted a change. I'd been a cop for a few years. I thought life as an MP would be the way for me to go. I enjoyed it, worked hard and, ended up an investigator."

"Did he come around?"

"Eventually. I think he was proud of me." He sighed. "Dad was only sixty, massive aneurism. Just keeled over at the beach while he was fishing." Mitch dragged in a deep breath. "At least he died doing something he loved."

She put the photo back and gave him a hug. "What about your mum?"

He shrugged. "Never knew her. She was a pampered rich girl slumming for a while, got pregnant, they got married, but she always wanted him to work within her daddy's empire. My dad was his own man. Eventually, when she couldn't get what she wanted, she divorced him and married the man her daddy had originally picked for her."

"Did she bring you up?"

"Hell no." That part of his life was mostly relief, tinged with a little childish sadness. "Part of the separation deal. I stayed with my dad. She died a few years later. Doesn't matter. I didn't know her. Some women aren't cut out for motherhood."

"Tell me about it."

The harshness in her tone prompted him to ask, "Did your mum abandon you?" Of course, she had. That her mother was deceased was in Jones's file. But he'd like to know she trusted him enough to tell him herself.

"Eventually." She turned and moved to the sink.

"Doc, you don't have to tell if you don't want to." He followed her and stopped by her side.

"It's okay." She was quiet for a few seconds. "My mother committed suicide when I was fourteen."

Damn, that wasn't in Greg's file.

"For as long as I can remember my father brutalized us. As I grew, I begged my mum to take us, to leave him." Tears welled in her eyes.

He took her hand and stroked her wrist.

"On the night she—" she swallowed and shuddered "—killed herself, I'd told my father no. He'd flogged me. When he was dragging me downstairs to lock me in the cupboard, I begged her to help. She didn't. I screamed at her that she was gutless, and I hated her." She dragged in a huge breath. "I told her I wished she was dead."

"Come here." He pulled her into his arms, drawing circles on her back, hoping to soothe her pain. He swore if he ever met her excuse for a father, he'd pummel him into the ground.

With her voice barely above a whisper, she continued. "My father took up with another woman within a month of my mum dying. I guess I became uncontrollable. But the more he beat me, the more I wanted to get back at him, so the worse I got. I hated him and told him often."

"What happened?"

"He arranged for me to go into foster care. Told the social worker I was uncontrollable. So, I took off and was homeless for a while."

"How old were you?"

"Just turned fifteen."

"That must have been so damn hard." Mitch remembered the love and support his father had given him his whole life. His heart ached for the pain young Asher felt, and for how it still haunted the beautiful woman by his side.

"In one squat I stayed at, I got beaten up badly by a group of girls because their boyfriends looked at me." She shook her head. "I ended up in the hospital. One day, I heard the staff talking about what they were going to do with me. They mentioned foster care. I'd run away from that possibility before, and I knew other girls my age who had escaped from foster care. Their stories terrified me. Then they discussed giving me back to my old man. That thought made me sick. I knew I'd be better off homeless. So, I left. That night, as I was sneaking out, a nurse caught me. Her name was Riva Jardine. She was the best thing that ever happened to me." Then Asher burst into tears.

He held her close, as tremors racked her body. He crooned as he rocked her gently, stroking her back in a slow, steady motion.

As her sobs turned into hiccups, he pulled a chair out from the table, sat, and pulled her into his lap. He held her close, kissed her hair as tremors racked her body. He crooned as he rocked her gently, stroking her back in a slow steady motion. He wished he could do something to ease her heartache. As her sobs turned into hiccups he whispered, "Asher, you've come a long way from that frightened little girl. You're inspirational. You're the woman other women aspire to be like."

"So why am I sitting here blubbering like a six-year-old?" she mumbled.

"Because you're human, like the rest of us." When he tipped her chin up, she looked surprised, as if the thought had never occurred to her. He took the opportunity to drop a quick kiss on her lips.   "Well maybe not all of us, you're better than most, but you're allowed to be human. You're allowed to hurt. Everyone hurts about something."

She seemed to think about that for a moment. "Even you?"

'Yup, even me, and... damn it, you're sitting on my bad leg."

She looked at him for a second before the realization dawned. "Oh! Oh, sorry."

Asher quickly slid from his lap and strode across the kitchen to pull a paper towel from the roll, blotting her face and blowing her nose.

So, his banged-up knee was finally useful for something. It seemed to have brought her back to thinking about others instead of herself. Not that she put herself first very often, but he needed to break the past's spell.

Mitch stepped beside her, squeezing her shoulder as he turned her to face him. "You are an amazing woman who survived what would have broken many." *And you'll never be in that position again as long as I breathe.*

She smiled a watery smile and pitched the makeshift tissue into the trashcan at the end of the counter. "It's all water under the bridge now."

Sensing the subject was closed, he tipped her chin and stared into her blotchy eyes. "Let me introduce you to my girls."

"Your girls?"

"Yup. Come and meet Lucy and Marie." He led her towards his Madonna Lily, glad to see a smile replace the tears as he introduced his plants by name, letting her inside his world, and stifling a chuckle when she touched the leaves and whispered hello.

Asher asked questions, seemingly interested in what he loved, what was important to him.

"I adore indoor plants. I wish I could grow them. Whenever I'm gifted a plant and Bridget sees it, she leans and whispers. "Pick up your roots and flee." She leaned in to sniff the last plant on the tour.

"On the way back to your place, we'll stop at a nursery. I'll buy you a couple of well-established babies, and I'll help you place them and give you instructions on how to help them grow. Within a few months you will have a house full of lush, thriving plants. I just need to ask, can you follow instruction, Doc?"

"Depends on who's instructing."

He leaned over and whispered in her ear.

"Yes, sir." She undid the buttons on the shirt and let it slide to the floor.

CHAPTER 19

I f Asher had any more sex with Mitch, she doubted she'd be capable of moving or thinking. He'd invaded her marrow. He warmed her, softened her. Not that she didn't enjoy being hard and decisive, but this was different. Being kind to herself wasn't something she did. He encouraged her to accept she was worth it.

Slipping quietly from the bed, she strolled into his kitchen, wearing nothing but his oversized shirt that covered her from neck to knee. It was soft and comfy and smelled of him. She sighed. It felt good being here, in his house, in his shirt.

In his bed.

She opened the fridge, grabbed a bottle of water, twisted the top off, and swallowed half the contents. She didn't know if she was more hungry or thirsty. Deciding thirsty, she swallowed another few mouthfuls. She replaced the bottle, closed the fridge, then walked to stop in front of his cupboards.

I wonder if Mitch's hungry. Asher opened the cupboard and found a box of savory crackers. She'd noticed cheese in the fridge. She'd put together a sharing platter. Decision made, Asher reached into the cupboard and knocked a folder down onto the countertop. *Who keeps folders in their snacks cupboard?*

As she picked up the folder, she glanced at the label on the front *Dr. Asher Jardine.*

She froze.

Put it back, her polite voice insisted. She shook her head. Shoving the polite voice to the back of her mind, she opened the folder and read the neatly typed sentences of a report.

On her brother.

And her.

Inhaling deeply, Asher leafed through a few more pages and shook her head. It couldn't be right. Mitch wouldn't do this. He wouldn't. She kept reading. Her breath stuck in her throat as the words reverberated in her head. *Keep sister under surveillance. Corporal Jones will contact her. Check Dr. Jardine's financial statements.* A few more pages into the report, she wished she'd listened to her polite voice.

Sickness welled in her gut. Mitch had been looking for her brother since the day he'd strolled into Mates and Eats.

Asher clenched her fists.

He lied.

Rage, pain, and despair roiled in her belly. She was going to heave. Memories wrapped in emotions vied for attention as they played inside her mind. Memories of her twisted around him, kissing him. Him pushing her hair off her face. Meeting his mouth halfway and sharing a kiss that stirred her soul.

That will teach you to abstain for so long. You forgot how good sex could be and didn't require feeling anything for anyone. That it's just a bodily function that two healthy people share. No emotion. No kindness. No tenderness.

Just sex.

The writing on the page smudged as she scrubbed the tears away. He wasn't worth it. *You are so stupid, Asher Louise Jardine.*

She'd allowed him to sneak into her heart, but he'd only been using her. Her heart tried to deny it, but her mind forced the truth down into her soul. *Stupid, stupid, stupid.* She shook her head as tears fell harder.

At this moment, she didn't know if she was angrier at Mitch for using her. Or at herself letting her barriers down and allowing herself to be used. *Stupid, stupid, stupid.*

No. You're not. Just go get dressed, thank him for the good night and half a day, and leave. A groan slipped past her lips. Not only had she had great sex with him, but she'd also spent the day with him, finding out how he ticked. *Boy, did he suck you in.* A harsh laugh ripped from her throat. She battled herself for an even thought process. It didn't work. Pain and all that went with it had her in its vise.

Just put the file back and leave. She picked up the folder, put the papers back inside, closed it, and lifted it toward the cupboard as a huge breath gushed from her.

Then he called her name.

She stiffened and shook her head. *Just put it back.*

Instead, she turned on her heel and strode into the bedroom, folder clutched tightly in her grasp. *Breathe Asher, there's a perfectly reasonable explanation.* Yeah, he used you to get information. She picked up her pace. The bedroom door stood open, and she looked at him resting against the pillows propped against the bed, his broad sculpted chest bare, and the sheet covering his lower half. She shook her head. Don't think about last night. It meant nothing. She dragged in a breath. He must have heard her stomping because he opened his eyes to stare at her. Those sleepy chocolate eyes encouraged her closer. The smile on his lips was warm, genuine.

Lying deceitful, bastard.

"Hello, gorgeous." He met her gaze, and a frown marred his brow. "What's wrong?"

Asher ignored the drugging tone of his voice and marched toward the bed. He reached out to her, but she slammed the folder against his chest. Then stood back to watch his face, hopeful he wouldn't recognize the papers fanned across his chest.

He shut his eyes and shook his head. "I can explain."

Her belly crashed to her toes. Tears burned, and she ground her teeth. No way was he going to see her cry. "I'm waiting."

"Asher." He reached for her.

She stepped away.

His lips tightened.

"Still waiting." She crossed her arms over her chest.

"I wanted to tell you."

"Bullshit."

"I did."

She arched her brow. "So why didn't you?"

"I'm under orders."

"Not good enough." She stepped into her underwear.

"I hated not being able to tell you the reason."

She met his eyes. "I trusted you. I asked you to help me find my brother. You said yes. You had the perfect opportunity then. Yet, you said nothing."

"Look." He wrapped the sheet tighter around him.

"I read the first few pages." She cocked her head to the side. "So glad that you figured out I was clean," she sneered. "I can't believe I was under investigation. Such bullshit. Then your boss agrees to you keeping me under surveillance, hoping Greg would come to me." She lifted her chin. "Well, he did, and you still didn't catch him. Not that good an investigator, are you?"

He slid across the bed, the folder, and its spilled papers apparently unnoticed. "It wasn't like that."

She held up her hand and stepped further away. "Yes. It. Was." She bit her lip, hard. "And building a friendship, getting me into bed, that was part of catching my brother?"

"Hell no. Look, Asher."

"No, I see just fine. You were under orders to find my brother, who, according to your notes, is wanted for questioning regarding members of a gang, and whether or not he's a member of said gang, so you can gather information that will confirm if they are guilty of theft and murder."

He continued to plead with those gorgeous brown eyes. How could she ever have thought them soft and warm? More like flint.

She stepped forward, picked up a few pages of the scattered paperwork, making sure she didn't touch him, and pretended to read. "I don't see, get his sister into bed. Was that an order? Or was that just something you did for a bit of fun?"

"You're being overly dramatic."

"Good, over dramatic suits me. Do you believe my brother is guilty of the supposed charges?" She shoved her fists on her hips and glared.

"It doesn't matter what I think. What I know is he's suffering from PTSD. We believe he discharged his gun purposely to get away from them. I have been under orders to stay close to you in case he showed up, so I could detain him, and to keep you safe.

"You used me."

"It's not like that." He looked as if he was going to stand but seemed to change his mind and tucked the sheet tighter around his hips.

"It is. Dress it up as much as you want. You used me. And you sucked me in with your kindness and support." Tears threatened to choke her. She shook her head. He wouldn't see her weak. Not again. "I've told you stuff about me I've never shared with anyone. You know what I feel about life, and you pretended like you cared."

"I do care."

She waved the sheaths of paper in the air. "I'm having a hard time believing it. You know what pisses me off more than anything? I really liked you. You ticked all the boxes for the sort of guy I'd like in my life. I should have realized it was an act. No one's that good. How did I miss that you have the two most hated traits in a man? I didn't see it. But thanks for the lesson in never trusting, about proving me right to stay away from men for that reason alone. I hate liars and bullies. You're both wrapped in a..." She was about to say a well-muscled body, but the memory of his hands on her body caused nausea to well. "A... an overblown ego."

"Asher, please."

"Please? Please what? Listen to you? I have let you explain. I'm not listening anymore." She shook herself, trying to find the energy that had seeped out of her to be gobbled up by the shaggy rug she stood on. The same rug he'd stripped her naked on just a few hours ago. "I'm going home."

"I'll drive you."

She shook her head. "Stay away from me. I don't want you anywhere near me. I don't want you pretending I mean something to you."

He tried to stand up again but seemed to change his mind when she glared at him. "Asher, let me..."

She continued in a voice that didn't even sound like her. "I'll see you at the next shift. After that, you're gone. Good luck finding my brother."

She turned, stalked to the front door, scooping her bag and phone as she passed. She didn't care that his shirt was all she wore, didn't care, she was vulnerable without him by her side.

Didn't care she was walking in the freezing cold. He would not see her cry, would not see the pain ripping through her heart.

As she stumbled up the driveway, she punched in the auto dial she used for emergency patient transport which put her at the head of the queue and didn't ask question. A cab must have been in the next street because it was pulling up as she reached the footpath.

Asher climbed in, gave the driver her address, and caught his glance in the rear-view mirror as she settled into the seat.

"Are you okay? Do you want me to call the cops, or that hot line for you?"

She realized what a mess she looked and quickly ran her fingers through her hair.

"No, no." Hell no, she'd just left a damn cop. "I'm fine. Just...just some bad news. I'll be fine when I get home." Liar! He didn't seem convinced but let it drop and she turned to stare sightlessly out the window. The ache spread inside her, filling every tiny space. A sob choked her as she struggled to keep it in.

He dropped her home within a few minutes. She paid the fare, grabbed her stuff, and stumbled to open her front door. Inside she tapped the buttons to switch off the new alarm she'd had installed at Mitch's insistence. Shutting the door, she slid down the timber until her bum hit the polished floor. Then all the pain she'd been holding back, since she'd found that damn folder, burst through and she sobbed uncontrollably.

CHAPTER 20

M itch watched her storm out the bedroom door. He dropped the sheet, grabbed jeans and a shirt, and struggled into them. He didn't worry about shoes as he flew out of the apartment and into the parking lot in time to see her climb into a cab. *You should have told her*. He couldn't believe how this played out. He was lower than a snake's belly. Rushing back inside, Mitch grabbed his shoes and the keys to his truck. He shouldn't have let her go. Somehow, he should have kept her in his apartment, made her listen. *You're a coward*. His mobile rang.

"Buchanan." He shoved his feet into his shoes.

"Mitch, it's Ryan. We've got a sighting on Jones."

Mitch shut his eyes. What to do. His job? Or chase the woman he loved? He ground his teeth and pinched the bridge of his nose. "Where?"

"Loitering around Asher's. I got the car registration."

Mitch snatched a pen from the hall table and wrote the number on the back of his hand. "I'll get the boss to check for an address and to pull up the street cameras, see what we find. When did he leave Asher's?"

"Thirty minutes ago, he took off like a shot."

"Okay, I'm on it."

"How did your night go?"

Recollections of Asher wrapped in his arms, laughing into his face, kissing him, touching him. He shook his head. "Better than I hoped for." Images flashed. Asher slapping the folder against his chest. Asher barely holding in tears. Asher getting into a taxi, wearing only his shirt. "And worse than I could imagine."

"I'm confused, man. See you tomorrow."

Mitch cut the connection and headed out the door. This is what he should have been doing, chasing Jones until he found him. And keeping Jones's sister safe that way, not falling in love with her and leaving her vulnerable.

An hour later, Mitch pulled into the truck stop halfway to the Gold Coast. On arriving, he checked the parking lot, pleased to see the Commodore sedan with the matching registration number hadn't left. Mitch climbed out of his truck and headed toward the eatery. He sighted Jones through the window. Not bothering with stealth, Mitch stalked to the booth and stood beside him.

Jones stopped chewing and glared at him. "Well, well, if it isn't my sister's bodyguard. Mitchell Buchanan. Hot shot defense force investigator."

"Corporal Jones. Oxygen thief." Mitch threw back.

"Took you long enough to find me." His gaze darted to the exits before settling on Mitch.

Mitch recognized the look—Jones knew there was no escape. "Finish your meal. Then we talk." Mitch slipped into the booth beside him, blocking his escape and so he too could keep an eye on the entrance and the rest of the room.

A server took Mitch's order, but he didn't respond to her friendly banter as she slipped the mug of coffee onto the table. He wasn't in the mood for chatter and needed to keep his attention on Jones.

"What are you going to do with me?"

Personally, I'd take you out the back and pound the living shit out of you for the pain you or your buddies caused Asher. But orders were orders. "Take you to the hospital. The doctors will check you out to make sure you're in reasonable health. From there, they'll transfer you to a secured facility for interrogation." Mitch picked up his mug and sipped the hot brew.

Jones continued forking bites into his mouth, talking around the half-chewed food. "What about Asher?"

"I'll inform her you're safe. The rest is up to her."

"She won't care. She never cared. The only person in that bitch's life, is her." His gaze shifted around the room, then he whispered. You know they're using her to get me, don't you?"

No shit, Sherlock! "Why do you think I've been hanging around?"

Jones swallowed his mouthful and looked Mitch directly in the eye for a full second. "If I tell you everything what's in it for me?" And then belatedly asked, "And her." Jones's eyes searched the room as if he expected to see someone.

Mitch shook his head. Always looking out for number one. How could Asher even be related to this creep? "Once you're locked away, they won't be watching her waiting for you, will they?"

Jones shrugged. "They know I sent her the information they want. She won't be safe 'til they find it."

"Finish your food. It's time to turn you over to the army."

CHAPTER 21

ater that morning, Asher hung up the phone and wiped her eyes. *Stop crying!* She grabbed a tissue and blew her nose. Bridget had been blunt, as expected. According to her, he hadn't lied. He'd omitted, and not by choice. He'd been under orders.

It didn't make any difference. Mitch had tried calling her, numerous times, but she refused to answer. She would not speak to him. Not today, anyway. Today she was choosing misery and reflection for company.

Rolling onto her side, Asher grabbed another tissue off the bedside table and settled on her back, staring at the ceiling. His big, warm body had covered hers and filled her with gentle heat. His touch had been light, caressing. He'd been a generous lover. He'd bathed her pain away. *It was sex. Nothing more.* She let the emotions escape—didn't have a choice really—and cried herself to sleep.

The ringing of a phone dragged her awake, and she picked it up. "What?"

"Asher, It's Lily, Nikki's gone into labor."

"I'll meet you at the hospital." Asher stood and grabbed some clothes.

"Are you okay?"

"Yup," Asher lied. "On my way."

Ten hours later, Asher dragged herself back into her bedroom, flopped on the bed, and sucked in a breath. She picked up the phone and tapped in Lily's number. Asher insisted Lily go home to the other girls by promising to call her about Nikki and the baby as soon as she could. Lily answered on the first ring.

"It's a girl."

The older woman burst into tears, and Asher joined her. Seemed like all she'd done for the past day was cry. At least these were happy tears.

"And she's, okay?" Lily's voice wavered.

"They're both fine." Asher pulled the elastic from her ponytail and finger combed her hair. "She's being kept in for a few days. I told her you'd visit with the girls in the morning."

"I've never been so worried. She was a few weeks early, and you'd said the baby was little. Did she say anything about adoption?"

Asher hesitated. "No, we didn't discuss that. I'm sure she'll tell you when she's decided. I need some sleep. See you soon." Asher disconnected, dragged off her clothes and lay back on the bed. She shoved Mitch's face out of her mind and curled into a ball.

The ringing of the phone dragged her out of sleep again. She stretched out and picked it up. "Hello."

"Doc Asher, you have to get me out of here. He's going to take my baby. He won't let anyone help me."

"Charli?" Asher pushed her hair out of her eyes. The clock glowed two a.m. "Why are you whispering? Where are you?"

"At central."

Asher heard her tortured breathing. "Why?"

"The baby's coming. He won't let me leave."

Sickness clawed at Asher's belly. "Are you with Travis?"

Charli started sobbing. "He told me he loved me, and he was lying about giving our baby to someone else. So, I snuck out to meet him. He tricked me."

Asher struggled to breathe.

"He's coming back. You've got to come. The pain is coming again. Please help me." Her scream filled Asher's head as the phone went dead.

Asher immediately dialed the police emergency number, put her phone on speaker, and laid it on the bedside table as she stepped into jeans and the sweatshirt she had on earlier. She gave the operator the address and asked for an ambulance to be dispatched. Then she dialed Mitch. No answer. Was he ignoring her call? She hadn't seen him since she stormed out on him after their night of sex and the crap that followed.

She tried his number again. "C'mon, Mitch, answer." Still voice mail. Next, she tried Bridge, then Ethan, then Bridge again. She massaged her temples.

The agony in Charli's voice chilled her. What if something happened to her or the baby because I didn't get there fast enough? The dread that pooled in her stomach lurched to her throat. She pushed it away. Even though she'd been told never to go to Homeless Central because it was deemed way too dangerous. She had to go. An innocent baby could die if she didn't.

Asher hated that squat. It was a huge, old, abandoned factory, surrounded by a spiked metal fence topped with barbed wire. Every time she drove by shivers raced along her spine. She knew the homeless had a hierarchy. She hoped some of them knew of her business and would help find Charli.

She grabbed her doctor's bag, phone, and keys and bolted out the door. In the car, she called Mitch, this time leaving a message, repeating the message on Bridget's phone. "I won't go in by myself. I'll wait for the ambulance and go in with the paramedics. Please, please hurry." She disconnected then dialed Lily's number.

Lily answered on the second ring. "Charli's gone." Asher heard the tears in her voice.

"I know. She's at central. I'm going to get her."

"Oh Lord, Asher. Stay safe. Have you called for help?"

"Yeah. I have to go." Asher cut the connection as Lily said goodbye.

Asher stomped on the accelerator too hard, and almost lost control of her car as she pulled out, fishtailing onto the road as she did. With her breath wedged in her throat, she eased her speed and headed toward the pit of misery she called Homeless Central.

She arrived at the old distillery and sagged with relief when she saw the strobing ambulance lights. Grabbing her bag, Asher scrambled out of the car and bolted for the ambulance. "Did you find her?" She rounded the open door and froze. The paramedics were inside, blood oozing from their heads.

She sucked in a breath, stepped into the cabin, and leaned over, checking the pulse of the driver. Thready. The second was the same. She had to get help. With trembling fingers, she grabbed the two-way. "This is Doctor Asher Jardine—"

Her head yanked back as someone hauled her out by the ponytail and threw her to the ground. Trembling, she rolled over, pushed herself to her knees, and tried to stand. Pain sliced across the back of her head. She groaned and collapsed. Vomit rose to her throat. As her vision spotted and darkness spread its cold cloak around her, she prayed Charli would be okay.

CHAPTER 22

M itch and Ethan strode out of the office where they'd met with the police service and the Sentinel Bureau. Mitch was still pissed off about Jones. He had him in his grasp. Had escorted him personally to the military hospital where he went AWOL less than six hours later.

"I can't believe Jones just strolled out." Mitch said as he stabbed the button for the lift.

"Now he's officially AWOL. We can look for him. There's an all-points bulletin out. We'll get him."

"I wish I could be as confident as you are, Ethan. He's avoided capture for two weeks. Then we find him, and he escapes from a military hospital. Jones has a real agenda."

Mitch checked his watch. Two a.m. Too late to call Asher now. He sighed. He'd called earlier, she didn't answer. He should have left a message. She'd want to know they had found her brother. Then let him escape.

"Let's get home." Ethan slapped Mitch's back. "As I've said, we have guys looking for him. We'll find him."

Mitch hadn't spoken to Asher since she'd stormed out. She hadn't answered or returned any of his calls. Even though it was less than twenty-four hours, it seemed like forever. He'd see her tomorrow at Mates and Eats. Maybe she'd talk to him and let him explain. And apologize. He should have told her the truth, screw his orders. He shook his head. He should never have let her leave.

They were heading down the freeway when Mitch's phone beeped. He ignored it. Then Ethan's. Coincidence? He watched Ethan in his peripheral, saw the tightening of his mouth. "What's up?"

"It's a message from Asher. Charli called Asher begging for help. She's in labor, trapped in that pit of homelessness. Asher's called an ambulance and is going to meet them there."

Mitch stomped on the gas, pushing to a hundred in seconds. As Mitch drove, Ethan spoke into the phone arranging for police protection for Asher and the paramedics.

"The guys from Ridgeleigh are organizing a car to get out there. They'll be on the scene in less than five. Mitch, she'll be okay."

He nodded and switched lanes. Asher knew not to go there... she was aware of the danger.

"I'm going to call Asher." After a few moments, Ethan swore and dropped the phone onto his lap. "No answer. It means nothing. You've seen the size of that place, probably no network coverage."

They were less than ten minutes out when Ethan's phone rang. He answered immediately and went quiet.

Mitch gave him a quick glance. "What?"

"They found Asher's car parked by the ambulance. The paramedics are injured and unconscious."

"Asher?"

Ethan shook his head.

Mitch punched the steering wheel before tightening his grip and pressing harder on the accelerator... He gnashed his teeth as frustration gnawed at his gut. *I should have kept her safe.*

They pulled into the now overflowing parking lot. Cops were everywhere. Mitch leapt from the car before his next heartbeat. When one of the uniform boys grabbed him at the corded off area, Mitch realized he was an agent with a military organization and had no jurisdiction here. He turned to Ethan.

"He's with me."

The young officer released Mitch and stood back.

Blue and red lights strobed the roped off area around the ambulance. Mitch stood to the side and watched the paramedics work on their downed mates. Memories of moments with Asher flashed through his mind in tandem with strobing. She had to be okay!

"He's breathing. Unconscious. He's good to go."

As useless as he felt, Mitch stayed to the side and let them work.

It didn't look good. A group of homeless people lurked in the shadows. Mitch recognized a few of them from the charity van, others whom Asher had treated. They wouldn't meet his eyes. All she's done for them and not one of them would offer information that might help find her. He shook his head.

Ethan stepped up beside Mitch.

Mitch gripped his arm. "We need to find her, man,".

"I know." Ethan clapped Mitch's shoulder. "We're all over it." With that, he turned and stalked toward the patrol car. "McEwan, you got the schematics?"

"Pulling them up now, sir." The young officer opened the laptop and started pressing buttons.

The injured paramedics were transferred into another ambulance. Mitch watched until distance ate its lights and silenced its sirens before striding across to Ethan and the other police officers hunched over the front of the car. Mitch edged closer. He may not have any jurisdiction here, but they would not leave him out.

Ethan's voice rang clear. "Whoever snatched Doc Asher knows this area. We need to be careful. We've contacted the electric company to get lights on."

All eyes turned toward the dilapidated building. Gaping holes for doors. Buckled metal walls. "How is that roof still up?" someone muttered, the others grunted a response. The graffiti on the walls spelled messages Mitch didn't want to understand.

"Sarge."

"What, Donaldson?" Ethan growled.

The young officer's Adam's apple bobbed at a frantic pace. "It's going to take hours to get electricity connected. They need to do a safety check first."

Mitch shook his head. They couldn't afford to wait any longer. He was going in. He had to find Asher. And Charli. He pulled out his phone and reread the text.

Charli called me, screaming in pain. Told me she was at central. I've called the ambulance. I'm meeting them there. Please come. I'll wait for you.

Mitch's heart kicked hard. Even in all her hurt and anger, she still trusted him to help Charli, and he wouldn't let her down. Mitch continued scanning the area and noticed a specter step from the shadows into the circle of light. He recognized the bearded bloke from the mobile clinic. The guy headed towards him.

"I'm Rick Mason. You're the doc's bodyguard?"

Mitch nodded.

"Didn't do a very good job of protecting her, did you? I warned you both somebody was out to get her."

"I know." Mitch kept his tone even. That he let Asher down made him sick. As much as the homeless guy's comments stung, Mitch wouldn't defend himself. He deserved them.

"It was a set up, so he could get her." He fidgeted on the spot. "He smashed those ambulance guys good and proper."

"Do you know who he is?"

Rick shook his head. "No, but he's off his nut."

"Do you know where Doc is?"

The other fellow just stared. Mitch controlled his temper. He wanted to grab him and shake an answer out of him.

"He carried her away. She's somewhere in there."

"Come with me." Mitch motioned toward Ethan.

Rick nodded and followed slowly.

"This man has information." Mitch didn't want to run everything by these cops, but he knew they stood a better chance of finding Asher and Charli, if she was even here, by working together.

Ethan nodded, and both men stepped closer and peered at the open laptop. "We're going to break up into pairs," Ethan stated loudly. "You two." He motioned toward the junior constables and shook his head. "McEwan, go with Donaldson, Anderson with Peters." They stood in a semi-circle around the car, peering at the computer screen, studying the plans.

"It's different here." Rick pushed in and ran dirty fingers along the screen. "There are walls there now. They've boarded up different areas."

Ethan strummed his fingers on the laptop. "Anderson, Peters, you two, start here. Make sure you stick together. McEwan, Donaldson, enter through here." He tapped the screen showing a side door. "Mitch, you go with Rick. Grab your stuff. Pick up lights. Keep your weapon holstered. Let's go."

"We're coming for you, Doc," Mitch muttered. "Stay strong." He prayed they'd get to her in time.

CHAPTER 23

Asher lifted her head, and grunted as pain stabbed her temples. Her head throbbed like crazy. Someone had bound her hands behind the chair. She tugged to get free, but the bindings didn't budge. What on earth were they using? She tentatively moved again, and a burn travelled up her arms. Cable ties probably. Must be careful she didn't open a vein or artery trying to get out of them.

She took a breath, then gagged as the smell of decay filled her nostrils. The stench so putrid, it soured her tongue. Dim candlelight lit the room. Bags of garbage everywhere, food spilling from the torn plastic on the floor. *What was that wriggling in there? Rats? Mice? Did it matter?*

Something white squirmed over the filth. Rice? *Oh my God.* Maggots crawled across the grimy concrete floor. Bile rose in her throat. She bowed her head again, hoping to bury her nose against her own skin, to take away the stench pervading the air, seeping into her pores.

She put her legs up onto the chair, away from the maggots and vermin.

Tremors shook her body. She bit hard on her tongue. No way was whoever had her trussed up here going to see they terrified her. No way. Someone would be here soon. She'd left voice mails.

Mitch. Please, hurry.

A long, agonized moan reverberated somewhere in the building, followed by cursing. *Charli!* She sounded close. If Asher could get rid of the ties around her wrists, she could get to her and help. She tried again to free her hand, but the bindings bit in even further.

Footsteps. Asher lifted her head and tried not to breathe in too heavily.

"Not so tough now, are you, bitch?"

She recognized the voice. Travis, Charli's boyfriend.

He crouched before her and touched her face.

She didn't flinch, just glared at him. Wishing she'd let Mitch pulverize him. She sucked in another small grab of air. The stench was moving her stomach slowly upward. Asher swallowed it back down. She wouldn't let this excuse for a man see her discomfort.

Asher tried to see past the dirty rag that served as a door into the gloom for Charli. "Where's Charli? Please let me check her."

"No way. Bitch is going to have that baby, then I'm taking it. I don't care about her. She left me after I'd already spent the money. The baby belongs to those people, not her."

Asher struggled to free her wrists from the ties holding her. She wanted to be on her feet. She'd even ignore her urge to pummel him just to get to Charli. "That baby could be in distress." The mother certainly was, if the last cry was a guide. "It could die, then you'd have nothing."

A heart wrenching wail echoed from another room.

"Charli," Asher screamed. "I'm here. Remember, breathe it through."

Another deep, agonizing wail raised goose bumps on Asher's skin. Travis just laughed, pushed his way through the dirty curtain, and disappeared.

Eventually, the wailing settled. Asher heard deep breathing, then gagging. She wasn't surprised. It was filthy here. No baby deserved to be born in this place. Asher shuddered. She had to get free.

She wriggled her wrists. The binding charred her skin. The blood seeped from the wounds she was creating with her need to be free. It didn't matter. She had to save the baby and Charli.

"Keep breathing, Charli." Asher counted. She was up into the two hundreds when the low pitch wail started again.

Three to four minutes between contractions. Surely somebody had found the ambulance by now. Ambulance drivers were never out of contact that long. Her time working alongside paramedics taught her that. Someone would be here. Soon.

Mitch's face flashed in her mind, all serious, those chocolate brown eyes melting every time he looked at her. Even after she told him about her miserable life, all she saw was compassion, no judgement. He'd held her as she cried. For the first time in years, she'd felt cleansed, and maybe she could forgive herself. And Mitch, for his deception.

Travis pushed his way back in, spewing vile remarks about Charli, Asher, and women as he paced the claustrophobic space. She stopped listening, instead concentrating on Charli's next wail, and straining for the sound of rescue.

Footsteps. At last. Someone was here.

There in the doorway, a silhouette. Asher's stomach clenched as she squinted, trying to make it out. Not overly tall or powerfully built. Not Mitch. She peered harder, but darkness cloaked him.

Motor mouth kept up his vile taunts. Shadow crept forward. Asher didn't dare breathe hard. Is he here to help? She gnawed at her lip as he raised an arm, banging it down hard on the younger man's head. Asher winced at the sound. She didn't know what he'd hit him with, but it had cracked his skull, at least.

This much violence, the smell of blood tainting the already foul air, and Asher lost control of her stomach. She tried to turn her head to the side, but some of the vomit splashed her jeans. When the spasms eased, she coughed, and spat, and lifted her head. Travis lay unconscious at her feet. Charli moaned somewhere in the distance.

Shadow grabbed Travis's ankles and dragged him through the curtain. When he returned and stepped into her sight, she forgot to be afraid. "Thank you. I'm so glad you're here. Please, please cut me loose."

He leaned forward and glared into her eyes. And the sick sweet smell of cheap cologne caused her to gag. "Just a little too much cologne." The words from Paul Kelly's ballad, *How to make Gravy*, danced wildly through her head. *Oh Lord, now I'm getting hysterical.*

For a heartbeat she thought it was Greg, it wasn't. She'd never seen him before. But she'd smelled him. *Be brave.*

He lifted a torch, turned it on, and shone the light into her face.

She squinted. "Turn it off, please. Untie me, I have to help Charli."

"Your brother said you always put others before yourself. Thought it made you a hero. I recon you're both too damn stupid." His voice was deep, gritty.

She recognized it. He was the guy who'd threatened her the other day. That meant he wasn't a rescuer. Asher shook her head. *Not now.* Please not now. "Please untie me. That young girl's terrified."

"Don't care."

She dragged in a breath. He leaned close to her. His sickly sweet after shave almost as nauseating as the noxious smell surrounding her.

"Please, let me help her," she begged.

"Always so busy looking after everyone else, you don't have time to care about your brother. He's very disappointed in you, Asher. Very disappointed. He thought you loved him."

She froze in her chair and stopped pulling her wrists. Instinctively she knew shadow man wouldn't let her go, even if she got free.

"You won't even tell him where the letter he sent you is." The calm reasonableness of his voice was laced with venom. "You're making his life very uncomfortable."

"I received nothing from him."

He slapped her. The strike made her ears ring. She shrank into the chair and screwed her eyes shut. The sound of wind blotted out his voice for a second. Had he damaged her ear drum? She refused to acknowledge the pain in her head and arms.

"I need that letter." He pushed his face against hers.

"I don't have it." Her voice sounded weak. Although she braced for the next blow, the ferocity spotted her vision, anyway. She heard voices. *Were they in her head?* They grew louder. She recognized Mitch's deep pitch.

"I'm in here. I'm here. Help—"

Her abductor grabbed something from his pocket, then shoved fabric into her mouth.

"Shut up." His voice dipped to a harsh whisper but maintained its chilling authority. "Come with me quietly, and I'll let the kid's baby live. Your choice."

Realization came fast. He'd done this before. Asher spat the material from her mouth, and feigning compliance, nodded.

"Smart choice. Your brother knows you so well."

"Just let me check her."

The instant he cut the ties Asher leapt to her feet.

"Stupid bitch." He growled before bringing the torch down on the side of her head.

The world faded away.

CHAPTER 24

Mitch shone his torch around the vastness of the condemned factory. Haphazard partitions divided the space. Rusty iron, old timber, and bits of plastic turned the place into a rabbit warren. Black plastic that shivered in the wind covered glassless windows. Vermin feces patterned the cement floor. Something crunched beneath his boot. He didn't look.

"It's not what I expected for Homeless Central. Where is everybody?"

Rick shrugged. "They don't want to be seen."

Mitch was glad Ethan had insisted they take a torch from one of the squad cars. It was like midnight in here. Some rooms had candles or an odd kerosene lamp. The fire risk didn't bear thinking about.

Mitch followed Rick deeper and deeper into the labyrinth. The further they went, the stronger the stench. Things rustled in the shadows. People? Vermin? He couldn't tell.

A scream bounced off the floors and ripped into his chest. The two men looked at each other.

Mitch shuddered as he remembered the last time, he'd heard someone scream like that. He pushed the ugly memories behind him. He had to find Asher and Charli. Another scream. "This way." He shoved past Rick and moved toward a corridor with Rick at his heels.

Mitch tore down a tattered cloth that passed as a divider and moved deeper into the maze. Another scream. Longer, deeper. He caught his breath. *Hold on Charli.* He pressed the two-way. "There's someone screaming. Trying to find her."

"We heard it too. We're coming to you. Keep communications open."

The maze was never ending. The screaming now was almost constant. Mitch battled the temptation to lean on the rickety structures to see if they'd fall like dominos, but then they'd never get through.

"Doesn't sound good." Rick stepped up beside Mitch.

Mitch nodded and moved on. The screaming shredded his gut. Guilt sat squarely on his shoulders. He should've found Greg earlier instead of using Asher. He did what he thought was right. *How did that work for you?*

He drove himself harder, could hear stumbling behind him. The shrieking crimped his spine. "This way." Their torch light illuminated the narrowest of paths, but Mitch strode on. In his peripheral vision, he glimpsed a difference in the darkness. He veered to the left and burst through the Hessian cover into a room not much bigger than a cupboard. What he saw soured his gut.

"Charli." He stepped to her side and knelt.

Sweat lathered her face. Her eyes wide with fear and pain. They'd tied her feet and hands to the posts of a filthy bed. Her boyfriend lay on the floor next to a doorway, blood oozing from the back of his head.

Mitch felt for a pulse. "He's alive." He hit the two-way. "I've found the kid. We need a paramedic. The young woman's in labor, and there's a male, unconscious and bleeding. Rick will wait in the hallway, so you have a marker. Be quick."

Mitch placed the two-way on the floor and reached toward her, slowly, so as not to spook her any further. "It's okay, Charli. I've got you. You're safe." He worked to free her arms from the filthy rags holding her to the bed.

Charli whimpered as he helped her to sit. As he swept her hair back off her sweaty face, Charli screamed, and her body bowed as a contraction ripped through her. "Don't leave me here, don't leave me." She gripped Mitch's hand as she did the first night he met her, and almost crushed his bones.

"Paramedics are coming." Rick knelt by Travis.

Mitch shone the torch over Charli. Blood drenched her legs and the bed. He sucked in a deep breath.

Charli's moan came deep from her soul as another pain started. A pitiful mewling morphed into a high pitch wail.

At the sound of wheels on cement, Rick stood and strode to the fluttering cloth to signal the paramedics. A medic entered the room and bent to check Charli. Mitch stood.

Charli didn't release his hand. "Don't leave me." She begged

He sank down onto the edge of the bed and squeezed her hand. The paramedics' words droned on as they examined her. Mitch was torn. He wanted to be here, holding the kid's hand, because he knew Asher would want the kid comforted, but he was desperate to find Asher.

Mitch looked at the terrified kid. "Charli, where's Doc?"

Tears tracked down her sweaty face. "I'm sorry. I didn't want to call Doc." Her voice cracked. "But, they said they'd take my baby if I didn't. I'm sorry." As the paramedics loaded her onto the trolley, she continued. "I didn't see her." She sucked in a big breath. "She called out to me, but I didn't see her. I've been alone since they brought me here."

"Who tied you up?"

She scowled at her boyfriend. "Him and some other guy."

Both patients were ready to transport, one screaming as a contraction ripped through her, the other deathly quiet. "Let's move." They rolled the trolleys toward the exit.

Mitch's anger deepened to uselessness. Where had he taken her? And who was he? Or they? *If Charli had heard Asher, she had to be close.*

"I need to find Asher." He shone his torch. Light bounced off a wall constructed of white manure bags. Back in the hallway, he masked the light from his torch and searched for a lighter shade of dark. He followed his hunch and shoved through another Hessian doorway.

A chair. Broken zip ties. Blood stain on the floor. He directed the torch light and saw more drips of blood every few meters. *Asher's blood?*

"This way," he said. His blood grated like ice in his veins. He had to find her. She'd only been in his life for a few weeks, and he couldn't imagine his life without her in it.

CHAPTER 25

Asher squinted and slowly raised her head. She shook it to clear her vision. Didn't work. Her mouth tasted like rust. Her whole body throbbed in pain. *Just close your eyes, Asher.* Fear kept them open. The room was brighter. She turned her head and noticed lit candles. Everywhere. The cloth draped over the doorway looked different.

He'd moved her. The chair he'd tied her to was more upright than the last. And the bindings weren't so tight. Maybe he realized she wouldn't have the strength to escape even if she could get them loose. But she tried the binding, anyway. Not cable ties this time. At least she wouldn't risk cutting open an artery trying.

She'd try to escape again in a minute. Once her vision had cleared and she worked out where she was. A sickly-sweet smell? Practically worse than the stench. Mister stinky cologne—she almost giggled—was pacing. Obviously waiting for someone. Who? She couldn't think, her head hurt too much. She needed to gather her thoughts. She had to escape and find Charli. *She'd heard Mitch, hadn't she? It hadn't been wishful thinking or the blow to her head? Maybe he'd helped Charli. Charli? Where was Charli? Had Mitch helped her? The only other reason she couldn't hear either Charli or a baby was unthinkable.*

Her stomach roiled and spasmed again, but there was little left now. *You'll be okay, you'll be okay*. Hot stinging tears seeped past her lashes and dribbled down her face. She wanted to howl but didn't have the energy. She closed her eyes. Maybe after some sleep, she'd be able to get away.

Footsteps. She pried her eyes open, but her vision was blurry. Stinky Cologne must have heard it too because he stopped pacing. She slowly turned toward the sound.

Greg.

Her heart thudded quicker. He'd come to help. She raised her head a fraction. The men faced each other, anger radiating from them. Their garbled voices filled her skull. She wished she could make out what they were talking about. Her eyes threatened to close, but she forced them to stay open. Words floated over her.

Liar.

Traitor.

Con man.

Focus, Asher.

The voices grew clearer.

"Here, have it." Greg handed over a metal box.

Was that the information he wanted? Could she go now?

Mr. Stinky Cologne sifted through the contents, then looked at Greg. "There's stuff missing."

Greg pulled a gun from the back of his waistband and pointed it at Mr. Stinky Cologne. "Not my problem." Then pulled the trigger.

Asher gasped.

Greg moved toward her. "Shame you had to see that. You should have stayed unconscious." He pointed the gun at her. "It's all your fault." He waved his other hand across the room in the body's direction. "If you'd have just given me that stupid letter, it wouldn't have come to this."

She swiped her tongue over her sandpaper lips and shook her head. "Can I have some water?"

He waved the gun in her face. Her little brother was holding a gun on her. Is he going to shoot me? Bile rose in her throat. She didn't want to die.

She looked at the cold instrument of death, then into the eyes of the man wielding it. None of this made sense. "Please. Greg, I don't have any letters from you. Just let me go."

He stared at her. "Are you deranged? You should be sobbing, begging me to let you go."

She leaned back in the rickety timber chair. "Please, can I have some water?" Asher squinted at her brother. He looked the same, but he was so different. Pain stabbed her temple. She bowed her head and threw up what was left in her stomach all over Greg's jeans.

For what seemed like an eon, he stared at her before cursing and moving away.

Fear sat like a lead weight in her chest, and every breath became a struggle. Her head fell forward. Sleep, or something darker, eased her into its warm embrace.

"Asher. Asher."

Sounded like Mitch. Funny how he kept coming into her mind. She missed him.

"Doc." A slight shake on her shoulder.

She forced her eyes open.

Mitch stood by her side and touched her face. "I'm getting you out of here." He crouched by her feet and loosened the ties binding her to the chair.

"Ouch, that really hurts."

"I'm sorry." He gently massaged her marked wrists.

The loosening of the binding allowed the blood to flow freely into her hands and fingers. She whispered past the pain of pins and needles electrocuting her wrists. "Thank you." She reached out, touched his face. He captured her hand, pressed his lips to her fingers.

"You smell so clean." She whispered, then darkness once again, claimed her.

• • • • ● • ● • • •

"Asher." Mitch shook her shoulder. No response. Another gentle shake. A soft moan. He shone the torch briefly on her face. Eyes closed, bruised, blood dried in her hair. He shut his eyes briefly, drew fetid air into his lungs, and continued his examination.

Two massive lumps just above her temple. Anger surged through him, fired his blood, and he clenched his fists. *Keep calm. Get her out.* He dragged another breath and whispered, "Let's go, Doc."

"I'm so tired." She flopped back into the chair.

Mitch reached to scoop her into his arms.

Behind him, an icy voice demanded, "What are you doing with my sister?"

Mitch froze, then turned to face Jones, making sure he put himself between Asher and her brother. "Getting her away from you."

"Not happening. She knows too much."

Mitch eased closer to the chair and Asher's warmth filled him. "I'm taking her out. There are people out there who can help her."

"Take one step, I'll shoot."

Mitch stiffened. His brain went into warp mode as he assessed his options. From the files, he knew Jones was a lousy shot. But this was close range and there was a dead guy in the corner still seeping blood from where his brain should have been. This close, if Greg shot and managed to hit him, the bullet could travel through and hit Asher.

As his mind raced, he examined the man in the doorway. Greg's pupils dilated, and his eyes darted everywhere. Was he having a flashback? At this moment, did he even know what a sister was?

Cops would have heard the earlier shot and would have their guns drawn. But no doubt they were struggling to navigate this maze, as he had. Although technically still a soldier, Mitch didn't have a weapon. He hadn't since he started working with the Sentinel Bureau. It wasn't necessary in his role working amongst the general population. He wished now he had a gun. Because if he had, this fight would be over.

"There are cops combing this building looking for you." Mitch said as he turned slowly around again and whispered into Asher's non swollen ear. "You'll have to stay there for a second, Doc. Trust me, it'll be okay." He was taking an enormous risk that he'd be able to fulfill that promise. And she'd told him in no uncertain terms that she didn't trust him, anyway. Still, he hoped it was a feeble nod that he felt against his arm.

Mitch kept his tone even as he said out loud, "Jones. We know you're suffering from PTSD. Let me take you back to the hospital and get professionals to help you." The torch weighed heavily in his hand. Was it enough to save their lives?

Greg's voice matched the gun waving in Mitch's direction, cold and lethal. "If I go back to the hospital, I'm a dead man."

Mitch continued shielding Asher's body as he felt her moving on the chair. "You share the information you have, and they'll keep you safe." He took a tiny step to the side and held Asher's hand. He'd seen another cloth covered door. A way out. He'd only need a second. He released Asher's hand.

"I said, don't move." The pitch of Greg's voice grew shriller. He was losing it.

Ignoring him, Mitch moved slowly and stood before Asher. He glimpsed down at her. So, pale. Dried blood on her temple. Eyes dazed. She needed medical help. He had to time this crazy plan to perfection, or neither of them would get out of here. He tipped Asher's chin and looked into her eyes. And spoke barely above a whisper. "I've got you. We're getting out of here. Trust me."

"I warned you, don't move." Greg snarled and stepped into Mitch's space, waving the gun in his face.

It was the opportunity Mitch had wanted. In his next breath, he swung the torch flush against Greg's temple so hard, he swayed on his feet. Mitch ruthlessly followed the blow, with a kick to his nuts that sent Jones sprawling to the ground. Mitch turned back, scooped Asher from the chair, tucked her against his chest, and bolted toward another Hessian filled exit, ignoring the pain stabbing his leg.

"Give me my sister," Greg roared from his position on the floor.

Not in this lifetime.

Mitch ran, weaving his way through the maze of rooms, back the way he came. But instead of heading out, he realized he'd moved deeper into the bowels of this prison.

With minimal lighting.

He stood motionless in the middle of a room and squinted into the darkness. Slivers of light flickered through the fragile Hessian walls. He'd have to make his way back. He knew there were people looking for them. If he hadn't left that damn radio behind when he found Charli, his problems would be sorted. Now, all he had to do was find them. But first, he needed to get his bearings. His adrenaline was ebbing. Asher was becoming a dead weight.

"Mitch." Her voice was faint.

"Hi."

"Greg killed that guy. Just shot him." A shudder ripped through her body.

"I know. There wasn't anything I could have done to stop it, without giving my presence away."

"Mitch." Another tug on his shirt.

"Doc."

"I'm going to throw up."

He eased her out of his arms and sat her beside him on the filthy floor. She rolled onto her side and heaved. Mitch stroked her back. The sour smell filled the already tainted air. She heaved again and again.

"You'll be okay." He whispered as he continued to stroke her spine.

The spasms eased. She rolled back toward him and rested her head against his thigh. "I need a drink."

"I don't have any water."

"I'm talking bourbon."

He laughed. "That's my girl. Let's get out of here."

He stood and held out his hand. "Are you okay to stand?"

She nodded. "Yup." And grabbed his hand. He helped her up and pulled her close as she weaved unsteadily on her feet. "I've got you." He scooped her against his chest and began walking, then stumbled. as his injured leg threatened to give out. She put her arms around his neck and snuggled her head against his shoulder. Even with a gammy leg, he could carry her like this forever. "Let's get you to a doctor."

Mitch strode toward the first glimmer of light. A candlelit path. He didn't notice it on the way in. A set up? Paranoia? He shook his head. All he needed to do was find help for Asher. He wished again he'd remembered the radio before leaving Charli.

"You didn't really think I'd let you escape, did you Buchanan?"

The treasure Mitch held in his arms shuddered. There was no way he was going to let him get Asher. He'd die first.

The candles flickered from different positions around the room. Mitch looked at Greg, who held a kerosene lamp in one hand and a gun in the other. Demented was too mild a word. Weapons grade crazy, was a more apt description.

"Put my sister down. You walk away. Simple."

"Never going to happen." He placed Asher on the ground beside him. She wobbled, so he gathered her closer to his side and she wrapped her arms around his waist. He met Greg's gaze. "How about, I turn around, and you walk away? That's just as simple."

"No, Mitch," Asher protested weakly.

"Shh. It's okay, Doc."

Greg waved the gun in their general direction while Mitch held his breath and prayed Greg had enough control to not fire accidentally. "That bitch has something I need."

"You killed one of your accomplices. You won't get away with that. It doesn't matter what you give them, they're never going to trust you. So, you might as well just disappear. I have friends outside who can make that happen."

Mitch didn't take his gaze from Jones and noticed the tremor in the other man's hands. He gauged the distance between them. One solid kick to Greg's wrist should dislodge the gun.

Greg waved the gun again. "Give me the letter, bitch."

She lifted her head to face her brother, stepped away from Mitch's side and spat. "Go fuck yourself."

Greg recoiled as if she'd hit him. It was the distraction Mitch needed. He spun on one leg to smash his boot against Greg's wrist. He heard it snap, then a bellow of pain. The gun hit the floor, spun, and slid under a partition.

"You're going to die. I'm going to fry you both."

Mitch half supported, half dragged Asher through the nearest doorway, but glanced back in time to see Greg throw the kerosene lantern after them. Glass shattered, followed by a whoosh.

Mitch scrabbled, trying to recall the plan of the building. Finding the nearest exit was the best he could hope for.

"Sorry, Doc," he muttered. "This isn't romantic, but it's efficient." He lifted her right arm over his shoulder, squatted, and pulled her across his shoulders in a fireman's carry.

Pain lanced his knee and thigh as he pushed himself upright and moved forward. A breath hissed from between clenched teeth. The blinding pain intensified with every step. He moved as fast as he could, stepping over rubbish and around fallen beams. He didn't need a torch anymore; the flames had taken hold instantly and were already lighting the roof, so he could follow the gable toward an outside wall.

He plowed on, aware of the precious weight across his shoulders but much more aware of the increasing heat behind him and the acrid smoke of burning plastic interfering with his breathing. *Faster, faster*.

Above the sound of the flames, he heard voices, scared voices, screaming, the invisible people of Homeless Central. They surrounded him, but he didn't have time for them. He couldn't save them all. *Keep her safe*. He ran through the maze and kicked rubbish out of his path. *Keep moving*.

He reached an outside wall and stumbled down the length looking for a way out. Sirens wailed over the roar of the fire, but even fire fighters would do no good without a door. He turned and eased his way along the wall, heading toward a corner, staggering around abandoned shelves and benches.

There, a clearer space. He headed for it as fire sucked the oxygen out of the air and replaced it with poisonous fumes and smoke, while the radiant heat singed the skin on his face.

A door. He glimpsed a lever to the side and pushed on it. It didn't budge. He bellowed out his rage then forced the lever with all his might and almost fell through the opening.

He tumbled out into the fresh air and sucked a lungful of it as he lurched down a cracked concrete path away from the heat and toward the overgrown parking lot with flashing lights in the distance.

The crackling and hissing of the fire grew louder behind him as he struggled to move, but he didn't turn to look. He staggered as an intense pain knifed his injured leg. "Adrenaline could have lasted longer," he muttered as he slowed to a limp.

"Thank God, Mitch. You got her out. You're safe. Put her down." He recognized Bridget's voice.

He lifted his head to face Bridget as a paramedic reached for Asher.

"Don't touch her." Mitch snarled.

"It's okay, Mitch, they're here to help." Bridget spoke to one of the paramedics. "Get another trolley, I'll stay here."

"Mitch, let me help you," Bridget's gentle voice insisted. "We need to check her and make sure she's okay."

He nodded. "She's hurt. She hasn't argued." Mitch released his hold on Asher to allow Bridget, who moved behind him with the other paramedic, to lower Asher to the trolley.

"Not me." The hoarse croak came from Asher as she lay on the trolley. "Check him. He's got smoke..."

"Stop diagnosing and start breathing. Both of you." Bridget slid a sheet over Asher. "She needs oxygen." The paramedic placed the mask over Asher's face.

Asher lifted the mask. "Charli?"

Bridget replaced the mask. "Transported to hospital. I don't have any more information."

A rattle drew Mitch's attention as they pushed another trolley across the broken ground.

"You get on that one." Bridget pointed to the empty trolley.

He shook his head and coughed uncontrollably. "Not leaving her," he croaked when he could get his breath.

Bridget fisted her hands on her hips. "Mitch, sit down before you fall."

The paramedic grinned at him conspiratorially. "Better do as she says. She's mean and scary." He pushed on Mitch's shoulder and, before he could argue, he found himself flat on his back with an oxygen mask over his face.

The last thing he remembered was Bridget demanding, "Transport them together."

CHAPTER 26

Mitch came to, lying on a trolley. The ceiling sped past as they rushed into the emergency room, surrounded by paramedics, nurses, and noise. He coughed and hacked. His lungs were on fire. He turned his head and saw Asher being wheeled in. Her eyes were closed, her face a kaleidoscope of swelling and discoloration. Blood matted her hair. What was worse, she was silent and still. Dread clutched his heart. "How's Dr. Jardine?"

No reply.

In the cubicle, doctors surrounded him, and one pushed a stethoscope onto his chest. Medical terms he didn't understand floated around him. A needle slid into his arm, and he fought the immediate sleepiness the medication induced.

It was pointless. As his eyes shut, he saw them pull the curtain across Asher's cubicle.

The throb in his thigh dragged him back to consciousness. Oxygen hissed into the mask covering his nose and mouth. He looked around. A pole holding the bag of fluid hung over him and ran down to his arm. He hated drips. From the brightly lit space, he realized he was still in the ER.

While he was out of it, they'd taken his clothes and replaced them with a standard hospital gown with tie up undies. At least he wouldn't have to worry about his butt hanging out every time he moved. He needed to find Asher.

He sat up, swung his legs over the bed, clenching his teeth against the pain that traveled like a steam train up the full length of his leg and back down. *Wonder how long it's going to take to heal now.* He didn't care. It didn't matter, he just had to find Asher.

He pulled off the mask and left it hissing on the mattress. Sweat beaded his brow when he pushed off the bed and for once, grateful for the IV pole, moved toward the curtain. Not that far, but every step felt like a marathon. He limped heavily across the emergency area toward the nurse's station.

The nurse was on the phone. He leaned on the counter to take the weight off his leg and looked around. Lots of cubicles with empty beds. Orderlies pushed patients in wheelchairs. Cleaners mopped floors. People stood around chatting. Then he saw a face he recognized.

"Bridget." His voice was barely above a croak, but it must have carried.

She hurried across the tiled expanse and pulled him into a hug. "Why are you up?"

"Looking for Doc." He could barely understand the words himself and ended up with a coughing fit that hurt his chest as much as the pain in his leg tortured him. He sucked in a raspy breath to ease the agony stabbing him. It didn't work. "Where is Asher? How is she?"

"She's holding her own. Mitch, you look dreadful. Sit." She pointed toward a plastic chair.

He rolled his shoulders. "I don't want to sit. I need to find Doc."

Bridget shook her head. "You need to sit before you fall. I'll get you a wheelchair."

"I don't..."

She didn't listen, just bustled away and was back in a minute with a wheelchair. "Sit."

He didn't argue and couldn't stop the sigh of relief escaping as he sank into the seat.

"I'll take you to her." With that she wheeled him down a corridor leading away from the ER.

"Is she seriously hurt?" He'd seen how dreadful she looked when they wheeled her in.

"Doctors say she'll be fine. We're here." She pushed him through the open door to face a washed-out, blue curtain. Bridget pulled the curtain back. He closed his eyes and calmed his breathing. *Bridget said she's okay. So, open your eyes and see her for yourself.*

"I'll wait back here. She's in and out of consciousness and drugged to the max. Just talk to her."

Mitch nodded, then opened his eyes and took in the still figure under the sheet. He wheeled over to look at her battered face and shook his head. The pain attacking his leg was nothing compared to the pain cracking his heart. He clenched his fist and punched his legs as sheer frustration ate at him. Never in his life had he felt so useless.

Unclenching his fist, he leaned forward and stroked her brow. No response. He took her hand, cradling it in his. "Please be okay." He pressed his mouth to her palm. "Forgive me for not keeping you safe."

Nothing.

"I hope you can forgive me for not being honest with you." He stroked her brow.

Her breath came in shallow puffs. Her dark lashes fluttered, and she turned her head toward him. She opened her eyes and stared at him but didn't say a word.

He held her gaze then leaned forward and kissed her fingers. He cleared his throat and whispered. "I'm glad you're okay. Doc?"

"Mitch." She swiped her tongue over her cut, swollen lips and winced. "Thanks for getting me out of there. I appreciate it." Her voice was huskier than usual.

And so cold.

"Please go."

He reeled back in the chair and met her gaze. Her eyes were dull, and she looked like a shadow of her usual self.

"Doc. Let me…"

She shook her head and winced again. "No. Just go. I don't want you here. Go away. Don't come back."

"Asher. Please." He reached his hand toward her.

She sighed and turned away.

Mitch wheeled out of the room. As he passed Bridget, he said, "I'll go back in later and try again."

The minute he entered the hallway an orderly grabbed the handles of his wheelchair. "There you are. You're supposed to be injured, not gallivanting around the place getting everyone agitated."

Mitch had never felt less like gallivanting in his life.

"There's a bunch of military boys here, I don't want to argue with," the orderly continued. "They're here to take you away."

Mitch slumped in the chair. Great.

But right now, he really didn't care where they were taking him.

CHAPTER 27

Two months later, Asher stood at the door of her shiny new ambulance and looked toward the waiting area. Only one patient left, and he had his back to her. The sight would normally have filled her with satisfaction for a job well done. But somehow it didn't anymore.

She glanced behind her at the pristine, completed, miniature surgery. It was perfect, of course, thanks to the insurance. But it didn't give her the sense of achievement that the "cobbled together with her bare hands" old one had.

She sighed. Maybe when it wasn't so new and shiny, the old feelings of pride would come back.

She stepped down. "Next please."

"That would be me."

The man stood and turned towards her, carrying a take-away cup. He handed it to her, but the cheeky grin that usually accompanied him was missing. His mouth a harsh, straight line.

"Ryan. How wonderful to see you." Asher smiled in delight.

He didn't return it. "We need to talk."

"Okay." She bit her tongue to stop asking after Mitch as she sat with Ryan in the empty waiting room. "How's Mitch?" She cringed as snippets of her sending him away that night struck her. No wonder he'd never answered her calls.

"Do you care? Or are you being polite?"

Asher leaned back in her chair. "I care. Of course, I care." She twisted her fingers together. "I more than care."

"Okay then. If you're not lying, he's a hot mess. Lost weight, looks like death. He's had his leg operated on again, and it's taking forever to fix. Got enough metal in there now to set off every metal detector in the state. He needs a doctor." Ryan leaned toward her, staring her in the eyes. "He needs you."

"I've tried." Her voice hitched as she swallowed back tears.

Ryan looked as if he didn't believe her and handed her a slip of paper. "Try harder." He stood, turned, and stalked into the night.

Asher sat by herself after he'd left. The paper he'd given her scrunched tightly in her fist. If Mitch had been in the military hospital having more surgery, that would explain why she hadn't been able to find any record of him after he left the emergency room and probably why he wasn't home when she called around.

But that didn't explain why he hadn't answered her calls or texts. Hope flared, and she quickly smoothed the piece of paper Ryan had given her. Mitch's number hadn't changed. She sighed. Unless Ryan was wrong, and he didn't want her to find him. For him, it was probably just a job that went wrong and hurt his pride.

Or maybe not.

Her driver dropped her at home. Inside, Peaches launched himself at her. She sat down on the lounge chair, with her tabby on her lap, and rifled through the mail she'd collected on her way in. She stopped on the one stamped Defense Dept.

Didn't look like an official letter, just their yellow stationery. Her heart soared. After what Ryan said, could it be from Mitch?

She turned it over, read the return address.

Greg Jones.

Her heartbeat slowed. And she hated her brother all over again for getting her hopes up, no matter how fleetingly.

She didn't want to open it. What he did to her, to Mitch, to them.

Mitch's image filled her mind. Big. Strong. Gentle. Those gorgeous chocolate brown eyes.

She missed him. Every minute of every day.

Every time she'd try to call, and he didn't answer, negativity overwhelmed her. Thoughts like, why would he want to see a woman whose brother tried to kill him? Really, why? Why would he want anything to do with a woman who threw him out after he'd saved her life? A woman who wouldn't listen.

She'd eventually visualized him moving on with his life, finding some appreciative woman to spend his time with. But if what Ryan told her was true, would it hurt to see him? What was the worst that could happen?

He could tell her she was an ungrateful bitch, and he never wanted to see her again. "So what?" Her heart said his rejection would kill her. Don't overthink it.

In the meantime, she dropped Peaches onto the floor and opened Greg's letter. It was brief and to the point. He was in the psych wing of the military prison—he called it Stalag 19—waiting for his Court Martial. He'd already pleaded guilty, so he was going to be there for a long time. The shrinks were working on him, not that it would do much good in there. After he'd spilled his guts, they'd found the rest of the team and they were being held somewhere else in the Stalag, also waiting for a court martial. He hoped their paths never crossed.

He finished by saying Mitch had contacted him and said he'd accepted that he wasn't in his right mind and hoped he'd get better one day. Greg said he hoped the same for Mitch's leg. Asher didn't believe a word of that part.

He'd signed it simply "Greg." There was a PS though. "The shrinks said I have to write letters. You're all I have left. I don't expect you to reply."

Asher felt a sliver of sympathy. It quickly passed. After what he'd done! And he was way too much like her father for her to forgive him. But maybe, just maybe, a long time from now, she might think about it.

Her eyes skimmed to the end again. Mitch had contacted him and said he'd understood Greg wasn't in his right mind. Did that mean he'd forgiven Greg? After what he'd done? And if he'd forgiven Greg, could he forgive Asher too?

She put aside Greg's letter and fished the neatly folded scrap of paper out of her pocket. She rested it on her knee and looked down at the cat rubbing his face against her legs. "What do you think, Peaches? Should I put my heart and my soul and my pride on the line and see him?"

The cat jumped up onto her knee and head butted her forehead.

She sighed. "You're probably right."

CHAPTER 28

Mitch lay on the massage therapist's table and swallowed back a groan. The woman's ancestors would have done well in the Spanish Inquisition...as torturers. Her thumbs were like corkscrews.

"That's us done for today, Mitch. Make sure you follow my instructions." She wiped her hands on a towel. "And don't miss any of the exercises, or you're going to be in that brace even longer."

Mitch grunted and sat up slowly, swinging his legs over the edge of the table. He watched as the therapist attached his brace and grimaced as she tightened a strap.

"You are healing." She pulled another strap tighter. "I know you're frustrated because it's slow, but you are progressing. I've written your appointments on here." She handed him the business card.

Mitch eased himself to the floor and almost smiled as the pain bit through him. It was about the only thing in his life he felt. Pain. In his body. And his heart.

As she packed up her equipment, he shoved the card into his trouser pocket, grabbed his crutches and moved to the double glass door to his veranda. No steps. He was grateful for that because they were a struggle. Leaning against the wall, he slid open the door and hobbled outside.

"See you in two days," his therapist called after she'd manoeuvred her table through the door.

"No worries." Mitch gave a mock salute.

"Remember, do those exercises every day," she threw over her shoulder as she moved to her car.

"Yes, ma'am." Mitch edged toward the balcony rail and sucked in a lungful of fresh air tinged with liniment. He'd been here on the grounds of the Sentinel Bureau, at a private rehab unit, since being released from the hospital six weeks ago. He scanned the area. Birds chased each other between tree branches, chirping and calling as they moved. Further up the drive stood a huge fully equipped gym specifically built to help injured soldiers rehabilitate. There were a dozen or more huts like his scattered around the property. Mitch hadn't ventured further than the BBQ area, but lately, he didn't feel like socialising. Sure, his mates, Nic, Pete, and Ryan, came to visit. They brought pizza and beers, talked garbage, listened to music, then left. After their last visit, Mitch had ordered a couple of bottles of Johnnie Walker via a delivery app. That was all the company Mitch really wanted. *He* wouldn't have cared if his mates stayed away.

His phone beeped. Mitch balanced himself against the rail, withdrew the phone from his pocket, unlocked it, and clicked the message.

Reminder. Your appointment with Dr. Atkinson is at 2 p.m. tomorrow. He almost threw the cell into the driveway. *We have arranged your transport. A driver will pick you up at 1:30. Reply Y or N.*

He hated these weekly shrink appointments. Hated having to be picked up and dropped off because his rehab had gone pear-shaped, and he could not drive. That he and the psych went over the same shit, with no resolution, frustrated the hell out of him. Hated that she asked the same questions in a roundabout manner, and he gave the same replies. Mitch despised it. But it was a requirement. So, he did it. He clicked the message off and shoved his phone back into his pocket.

After a few minutes of letting the sun warm his bones, he manoeuvred back inside, shut the door, and pulled the shades. He didn't want to be disturbed. People were telling him what to do and when. And all he wanted was to sit and have a drink or three.

Settling back into the leather recliner with his injured leg out straight, Mitch picked up his phone and unlocked it. No new messages. No new emails. With a shake of his head, he opened his social media pages. "Welcome to your new life," he muttered as he scrolled through pages on the screen. Cute dog and cat photos. *Put it down, Buchanan.* Recipes for food he didn't want in languages he couldn't read. He shut off the phone and dropped it onto the table beside him.

The bottle of Johnnie grabbed his attention. He looked at his watch. Way too early for the heavy stuff. *So, what are you going to do? Sit here and go bonkers. Get a life, Buchanan.*

Mitch hated that damn voice. With a passion. Refusing the draw of alcohol, he reached again for his phone, and because his life couldn't get any worse, went to missed calls. Asher had called him many times in the first few weeks. Then, as time passed, the calls grew less. *Why had she called him? But the bigger question: why didn't I call her back? Because you're gutless.* Mitch grabbed the bottle, unscrewed the lid, and sculled. *Because you're no damn use to Asher.* He took another swig.

• • • • • • • • • •

Someone wrapping sharply against the glass sliding door dragged Mitch from his drunken slumber. He straightened in the chair, eyed the now almost empty bottle, and scowled. Still, the rapping went on. He looked around, saw a silhouette on the blinds, and yelled. "What!?"

"Hey, man. It's me."

Mitch shook his head, hoping to clear the fuzziness. He stood slowly, grabbed his crutches, and eased his way to the door, unlocked it, and slid it open.

"Ryan. What's up?" he asked, with zero interest in the reply.

Ryan stepped into the room and waited as Mitch shut the door and manoeuvred his way to the kitchen.

"Drink?"

"No. I'm okay." Ryan met Mitch's gaze before offering a large yellow envelope. "From the Colonel. I thought it would help if I gave it to you personally. "

Mitch rested his crutches against the kitchen bench and took the envelope, lifted the flap, and began pulling out a sheaf of papers. Below the Sentinel Bureau logo was a big, bold heading. VOLUNTARY MEDICAL DISCHARGE. He lifted his gaze and stared at Ryan.

"Voluntary?"

Ryan shrugged. "A better payout."

Mitch repeated. "Voluntary?"

Ryan shrugged again. "You know what voluntary means around here. Take it or leave it... Or leave."

Mitch angrily hurled the envelope across the room. The forms half fell out, and the heading, Medical Discharge, branded his retina. "Then piss off and tell them they can shove their fucking package up their ass. I'm not spending the rest of my life sitting around being useless."

Ryan headed for the door but stopped halfway. He turned around, crossed his arms, then met Mitch's gaze with the steely stare of a man about to deliver some tough, unwanted advice. "Then I'll see you after your next medical review when you're demoted to being useful by sweeping the canteen floor for the rest of your life." He sighed heavily. "Think about it, man. It's a decent package. You could do something useful with it." He turned toward the door but looked back. "Or buy yourself thirty crates of Johnnie and a coffin. Cause that's the way you're headed. Your choice."

As Ryan closed the door, he looked over his shoulder. "We'll come for a visit on Friday. See you around two."

"Whatever." Mitch stumbled to his chair, sat, grabbed the bottle of Johnnie off the table, screwed off the top, but set the bottle on his good knee. He leant back and tried to concentrate on the pain in his leg, but even with his eyes closed, all he could see was the open bottle and the envelope spewing the papers for a medical discharge.

Medical discharge. And be a cripple for the rest of his life. He looked at the Johnnie. But isn't that what he'd just been thinking? That he was of no use to Asher? Especially no use to Asher! He checked his phone again, but no more messages from her. By now she'd probably heard what a useless man he was. By now, her medical practice was probably booming again. With no use for a security guard who couldn't even walk without crutches. He glanced at the damn yellow envelope. And now, no use to the Bureau either. If he left the Bureau, what would he do? All he'd done all his life was take orders. Each promotion had given him validation to keep going to the challenge of the next level. And every investigation completed had given him a sense of wellbeing at a job well done. But the jobs had always been orders. Someone else's decision. Not his own. He lifted the bottle of Johnnie to his lips but couldn't drink. It had been full this morning. He didn't even remember drinking it. Like the rest of his life since the fire–he lived without remembering. Lived without living. Just existed.

He put the bottle back on the table.

Is that what his life would be like from now on? Johnnie he wouldn't remember for breakfast and soaps on TV for dinner? He hadn't always been like that, had he? He'd had jobs to do. Important jobs. But the jobs had just been orders.

Not like Asher. She knew what her next job would be because she was the one who decided what it would be. She had her life mapped out. Whereas he didn't even know if he'd even have dinner, let alone what he'd eat.

Well, at least that was something he could do something about. Make one decision, at least. Maybe then he could make another one. Damn, that's what the bloody shrink had said. Couldn't be right, could she? Only one way to find out.

Mitch manoeuvred himself out of the chair, grabbed his crutches and hobbled toward the kitchen. He cobbled together the makings of a BLT and got busy cooking dinner. After eating, he looked around for another decision to make. He noticed his wilting plants, grabbed the spray bottle, and made his way through the tiny unit and watered his girls. He might not be much use to anyone else, but they depended on him. And it was another decision. Things were looking up.

Right now, the plants were the only things that gave him any semblance of joy. And he was doing a great job of ignoring them to death as well. He wondered if Asher had bought any plants. If things hadn't gone down the way they had, he would have bought some for her on the way back to her house. But it went wrong.

He put the spray bottle back on the bench, trudged through to the lounge and settled again onto the recliner. Then picked up his phone. Again.

He knew his melancholy was eating at him and slowly driving him nuts. That he was using alcohol as a crutch to get through a day sickened him. He had always believed he had his life under control. But not anymore. He was losing the plot. And he'd seen other returned soldiers' lives ruined because they didn't have a plan for life outside the military.

And here you are, Buchanan, sitting on your ass, not knowing what you're going to do tomorrow, let alone the rest of your life.

He looked around the minimalist, planned-for-efficiency room as if it would give him the solution to planning the rest of his life. Boring.

This accommodation was courtesy of the Sentinel Bureau and was only temporary. Whether he left the Bureau or not, he'd soon need somewhere else to live. When it became obvious it would be months before he could live on his own again, and probably never manage the stairs at his old apartment, Ryan and the others had arranged for the bureau's legal eagles to break his lease and moved the stuff he wouldn't be needing into storage.

Time to start house hunting. At least money wouldn't be an issue. His Afghanistan bonus, compensation, and pay for the last ten years was still in the bank. He could rent a place by the sea, or way out in the sticks where nobody would bother him. Or he could even buy a house. He'd always known his job meant he would never be staying in one place for long so never actually owned a house before. He could even buy a mansion if he wanted. On the other hand, staying in one place vacuuming and mowing the lawns. Not for him.

Or he could buy a Porche like other blokes. Or buy another old bomb and do it up like he used to with his dad. Only that wouldn't be any fun without his dad. Or he could give it all away. To a dog's home or something. Without kids or family, that's probably where it would end up anyway. Do it now and cut out the middleman.

So, what was he going to do this his time and his money?

He sighed heavily and thought about opening another Johnnie. Whatever he did, he'd need somewhere to live. Ground level. Practical. Boring.

He changed his phone onto a realtor's ad and flicked through the pictures of units. Nothing caught his eye until he glanced at the picture of a dilapidated unit block. Why would that grab his interest? Neither practical nor boring. Then he remembered Asher's vision board, and the decrepit block of flats she had down as goal two.

A thought struck like a thunderbolt. Mitch straightened in his chair. Expanded the ad. There were eight units. They looked cruddy and would need work, but they were cheap. Buy them for Asher, bulldozed into his brain. It's what she wanted. They'd been on that vision board of hers. He could buy them, give them to her, and Asher's first vision board would be completed. And he would have done something useful with his life. And for the first time in ages, a smile tugged at his mouth.

"We have a plan." He did a little jig in his chair, then stood.

Friday morning, he placed all the pictures and newspaper clippings onto the cork board as best as he could remember to make his replica as close to Asher's vision board as possible. It looked good. The only piece he'd changed was the block of units. He couldn't find the one she had, so had substituted the ones he'd bought.

The realtor had picked him up and taken him to the unit block, not too far from Mates & Eats. And they were as pathetic as they looked in the photo. But the vision that filled Mitch's mind was the renovated result. And how it would help Asher complete her first vision board. Make her happy. He bartered with the agent and got the price down to where he could cover the cost. So, he bought them.

Now, all he had to do was give them to Asher. He thought of giving them directly to her foundation anonymously, but that sounded complicated. Besides, doing it in person would give him a chance to see her again. To see for himself how she was doing. And if he was honest about the niggle at the back of his brain—see if there was a glimmer of a chance that she might have forgiven him enough to let him hang around on the edges of her life.

"So, what do you guys reckon?" Mitch held up the recently completed vision board, looked around the table, and met the eyes of his closest friends.

Ryan met his gaze first. "It's a great idea, but I think you've left your run a bit late."

"What are you talking about?" Mitch lifted the heavy cut tumbler and took a sip of the double Johnnie.

"She's throwing it in."

"What? Are you kidding?" Mitch's heart rate kicked up a few notches at what he was hearing.

Ryan held his mate's gaze. "I spoke to her a couple of nights ago. She's had enough. Moving on."

"You spoke to her? Why didn't you tell me."

Ryan shrugged. "I'm telling you now."

"I don't believe Asher's giving it away. She loves what she does."

"Not anymore." Ryan kept his gaze fixed on Mitch and repeated. "As I said, looks like you've left your run a bit late."

Mitch shook his head. "After all she's gone through to build that service, she's going to walk away? I don't believe it."

Pete picked up where Ryan left off. "Got that upgraded ambulance through insurance. But reckons it's not the same. No sense of self in it."

Nic took a swig from his beer. "Yeah. She reckons she's going to start again elsewhere. Another state. Muttered something about Doctors without Borders."

"I don't want her to go." Mitch stated before he could stop himself as he massaged the growing pain in his leg.

"It's her life, her choice. Asher will do what she wants. We all know she is one strong, stubborn woman," Pete said.

The three mates laughed, and Mitch glared at them.

"You know what's funny, Mitch? We saw the spark between you two. She could have been yours, and you were too damn gutless to chase her." Ryan crossed his arms over his chest.

Mitch froze. He wanted to argue. Deny the statement. But couldn't. He knew he'd screwed up. And it ate at him every single minute of every damn day. Mitch stood up and dragged himself to the window to stare into the late afternoon sunshine. Pain lanced through his thigh. Not enough to chase the pain from his heart, though.

If only he'd answered her calls. Or called her instead of wallowing in what ifs. An additional set of 'what ifs' pounded inside his head. What if she didn't hate him? What if he could explain his feelings to her? He leaned his forehead against the glass. What if he told her how he felt? What did he have to lose?

Asher.

And that thought spurred him into action.

"I need to go see her."

"I'll drive you."

"Not tonight. I need to sober up first."

His three closest mates looked at him, then at each other. Ryan shrugged, then spoke. "Glad to hear it. We've been concerned. Whenever we visit, all you do is drink straight scotch. You hardly eat. And man, you reek."

Mitch knew Ryan was right and hated him for bringing it out into the open. Mitch dragged himself back to the dining table and eased into a chair.

"So," Ryan continued. "I agree. Leaving it until tomorrow is the right choice. Hell, you've left it nearly two months already, so what difference will one more night make? I'll pick you up at eight in the morning, take you over to Asher's."

Mitch nodded, then stood. He looked at the bottle of Johnnie, grabbed it, eased his way to the sink, and poured the contents down the drain, then threw the empty bottle into the trash. Leaning against the sink, he looked at his three mates. "There's steak in the fridge if someone wants to light the BBQ. I'm going to hit the shower. I won't be long."

Mitch looked at his group of friends. Then zeroed his gaze in on Ryan. "I appreciate you coming to see me the other day with the news. You're a good friend."

"Actually, we drew straws who would bring them to you." Ryan smirked. "I lost."

Mitch shook his head, and all four of them roared, laughing.

The next morning, Mitch and Ryan sat in the parked truck outside Asher's home.

"If you're not ready, I can take you back to your place. You don't know if she's here. She could be out at breakfast. Or not home from a date last night."

"I swear, if you poke me once more with Asher's love life, I'll throttle you." Seeing the glint of humor in Ryan's eyes, Mitch grimaced. Thinking of Asher with someone else almost made him puke.

"Are you getting out?"

"In a minute. I'm still thinking this through."

Ryan sighed and leant back in his seat. "And that's your freaking problem. All you do is think. You've been stuck in that damn hut for eight weeks thinking."

"Recovering. "

"You're chicken shit."

Mitch glared at him.

Ryan raised his hands in mock surrender. "That's the first visible sign of life I've seen in your eyes in months. I'm sorry your injury hasn't healed. Even sorrier you're in constant pain. What I'm not sorry for is you hurting that bloody woman and not having the guts to put it right."

"That's why I'm here. To put it right." Mitch shoved his fingers through his short hair. "You think I don't know I screwed up?"

"We all know. Just didn't know how to tell you."

"Her car's here." Mitch pointed to the Ford Focus parked at the side of the house.

"Off you go then." Ryan elbowed Mitch in the ribs.

Mitch pushed the door open, turned, and slid gingerly to the ground. He turned back and grabbed his crutches from the car floor.

"Here." Ryan climbed out, grabbed the wrapped vision board. "I'll carry this for you, so you don't fall on your face."

Pain lanced through Mitch's leg with each contact with the ground. At the front door, Ryan placed the package on the ground and turned toward Mitch. "You look like shit. That's great. Asher, being a doctor, seeing you looking dreadful, means she won't throw you out."

Mitch shook his head. "That's good?"

"Do you want me to hang around?"

"No. I'll be okay." Before Ryan could say anything, Mitch added. "If she throws me out, I'll call an Uber."

Mitch leaned against the building and watched Ryan drive away.

What are you waiting for, Buchanan? An invitation? Mitch sucked in a breath and pushed the buzzer.

CHAPTER 29

A sher moved the photo of her new ambulance from the corner of the wooden board to the center. And back again. "If I can't even get a vision board right," she muttered to herself, "I might as well just give up and join Medicines Sans Frontières." Relaxing back in the chair, she looked at the board again. There was something not right, but for the life of her, she couldn't figure out what. The vision of her new life in Sydney should be exciting, not another frustration! She'd researched a dozen charities similar to Mates and Eats that would fall over themselves to get the services of a doctor with a mobile clinic, but she couldn't settle on any one in particular.

She was about to move the ambulance again when the doorbell started ringing. "So, help me if they don't take their finger off that bell, I'm going to go out there and rip it off." Unable to ignore the noise any longer, Asher shoved back her chair, stood, and stalked up the hall, Peaches at her heels. Why can't people just leave me alone? She'd told Bridge she didn't want to go out, didn't want to go shopping. She wanted to be left alone. There were choices waiting for her to make, plus plans to sort out. And a new vision board to create.

Looking out the window as she approached her front door, she saw no car in the driveway. Someone selling solar? She already had it. She already had everything she needed–except peace and quiet.

"Be nice," she told herself as she slipped off the latch, grabbed the doorknob, and wrenched the door open.

And froze.

Mitch.

She ran a professional eye over the man leaning on her door-jamb and shook her head. He looked dreadful. Tears stung her eyes. Ryan told her he looked terrible, but she thought it was just a ploy to get her to see Mitch. But no, Ryan hadn't been lying. Mitch had faded away to nothing. Lean to the bone. And a brace on his leg from ankle to thigh. Was that because of her demented brother trying to kill them? Because he'd carted her from a burning building?

She grabbed her breath and stared at his face. His beautiful brown eyes looked like mud.

"Mitch." She was thankful her voice came out strong.

"Can I come in?" A pause, as if he wasn't sure if he wouldn't get the door slammed in his face. He almost did. "Please?"

Asher continued to stare at him as she warred within herself. Yes? No? But when she looked deeply into his eyes and glimpsed the pain in them, she stepped aside and opened the door fully.

"Come through." She wasn't sure how the words would come out, but practice won, and it sounded like a professional invitation to a clinic.

Mitch reached down beside him and awkwardly picked up a wrapped parcel. Fortunately, it was in a bag with handles, and leaning on his crutches, he made his way into the living area, the parcel bumping awkwardly against the crutches. Why on earth was he trying to carry a parcel while he was on crutches?

Noticing him sway, Asher said, "Sit down before you fall down." Hearing the harshness in her tone, she added softly. "Sorry. I didn't mean to snap." She took his parcel and propped it against the recliner. She'd expected him to object, but he didn't. He must really be ill! As he eased gingerly into the chair, Asher pulled the lever and the leg support folded out.

"That feels better. Thanks." Mitch had no sooner finished talking when Peaches launched into his lap.

Asher stared at her traitorous cat as Mitch gently stroked his fur. Silence wrapped them in an uncomfortable blanket as they stared at each other.

He was exhausted and unnaturally grey. His lips looked dehydrated. Unlike the night they shared soul searching kisses. That night they'd been plump, healthy. Her belly knotted, and she blew out a breath. That time had passed.

The unresolved issues between them would remain unresolved.

Not knowing how to break the silence, Asher made her way over to the window and pulled open the curtains. She stared out, trying to pull her thoughts together. What if he was here to restart their relationship? Or end it? She shook her head and pushed both thoughts back into the compartment of 'too hard to think about.' The silence was becoming oppressive, so she squared her shoulders and turned back to face him. "Why are you here, Mitch?"

He closed his eyes, shook his head, then opened them, and stared into hers with such longing. Asher's breath hitched. Warmth stirred deep in her belly as memories of them locked together in passion taunted her. Concentrate!

"I, um, I came to apologize."

That caught her attention! "What for? Lying to me for our entire relationship? Carting me out of a burning building after I told you I could walk? Or not replying to my calls for months?" The harsh words were out of her mouth before she could call them back.

His jaw tightened. "All of them, I guess."

When he hesitated, she sat on the couch opposite. This had better be good. He'd turned her life upside down and inside out. Throughout the last few months, her emotions had been all over the place. Anger, gratitude for his saving her, anger again, regret for his injury, and frustration because of his lies. She was over it. "So, get on with it!"

He took a deep breath and launched into a pile of words as if he'd been rehearsing them. "I'm sorry I lied to you." He dropped his head. "Although mostly, I didn't really lie, I just didn't tell you the whole truth." He looked up again. "I wanted to. I even asked permission to fill you in, but management thought it would put you in danger. And in the end, I agreed."

Put like that, his argument actually made sense. Damn. She didn't want to stop being angry. It was easier than knowing he was suffering and feeling sorry for him.

He spread out his hands. "As for not letting you walk, they had beaten you half to death and you were in and out of consciousness. It was carry you out or leave you there to fry."

"What about your leg? How did you know it wouldn't give out, and you'd drop me?"

He shrugged again. "Either I got us both out, or we went down together. I wasn't about to risk living the rest of my life without you."

Asher snapped her head up at that. Was he trying to say something?

Instead of answering, though, he reached down and pulled the lever to let the leg rest down. As Peaches leapt from his lap, he started undoing the Velcro holding the brace on.

"Are you allowed to take that off?"

"Don't know, didn't ask. Hate the damn thing. It makes me feel like an invalid." He tossed the brace beside the crutches and levered himself out of the chair. As he edged to his feet, he wobbled, then fell back into the chair. "Damn this injury." His pallor had turned a decidedly bilious shade of green.

Asher reached across and laid her hand against his knee. His heat crept into her being. To cover the uncomfortably warm feeling the memory of having his body next to hers at other times had invoked, she went into doctor mode. "Have you eaten today? Had your meds?"

He rolled his head from side to side. "No appetite for anything much except Johnnie recently, but I'm off that too now."

"Memory killer and empty carbs. What about meds?"

"Mostly just pain stuff now, but it makes me fuzzy. I didn't want to be fuzzy today."

Asher crossed her arms. "Patients who don't take orders are the pits. I'll get you something."

She grabbed some mild pain killers from the cupboard and a glass of water and went back. "Take these. They'll only take the edge off, but at least they won't make you fuzzy."

The corners of his mouth tipped up a little. "Yes, Doc."

Why did hearing him say his nickname for her make her stomach get the jitters? She waited till she was sure he'd taken the pills and drunk the water. Taking the glass from him, she placed it on the table and said, "Not supposed to take meds without food. I'll find you something."

"Doc, I don't have much of an appetite."

"Okay, then. How about a hot chocolate?"

He nodded. "Then can we talk?"

Asher met his eyes. "Maybe."

"Doc, I appreciate you letting me in." He tipped his head and met her gaze. "I didn't think you would."

"I didn't either."

She turned and almost bolted from the room. While the kettle was boiling and the toast toasting, she leant her elbows on the sink, rested her head against her clasped fingers and closed her eyes. What was going on here? She'd convinced herself she was angry with him, and if he didn't even want to answer her calls to find out how he was, she didn't want to have anything to do with him. He could go back to his wretched job and lie to someone else. And she'd move to Sydney so she wouldn't see any reminders of the places they had been or the things they'd shared. She could almost drive down the street where he lived and look at his apartment where they'd shared such an incredible night together and not want to cry with a mixture of longing, betrayal, anger, and hopelessness.

A short while later, Asher carried the tray holding the hot drinks and buttered toast to the living room and placed them on the coffee table. Mitch had dozed off, obviously he needed the rest. A tinge of color shadowed his cheek bones. She reached out to push his hair back off his face but stopped herself. Her teeth latched onto her lip as her hand dropped to her side. She picked up her drink and walked back to stare out the window. He'd come here for a reason. So, when he woke, they'd have the conversation they should have had months ago.

Asher prayed for the strength to get through it.

Mitch woke with a start. He looked down and saw Peaches, but this time the cat was standing on his chest, eyeballing him. He smiled, couldn't help it. It reminded him of the first night he'd stayed with Asher, and that cat eyeballed him. Well, the same message was in his eyes again, and Mitch read it, loud and clear. 'You hurt her, and I'll scratch your eyes out.' Mitch stroked the cat's fur, and the vibration of his purr travelled over his torso. "I swear I'll never hurt her again." With that, Peaches stalked down to his lap, kneaded his thigh, curled up and went to sleep.

Mitch scanned the room and settled on Asher. His breath caught in his throat as he observed her unnoticed. He drank her in, every single bit of her. She was staring off into space, a soft smile on her face. *Is she thinking of me?* He scoffed at his own baffling thoughts, but he couldn't help hoping that maybe, just maybe, he had a chance to resurrect the feeling they once shared. After all, she'd allowed him into her home.

It must have been the intensity with which he was looking at her that made her turn to meet his eyes. She said nothing, just stared at him with those beautiful cobalt blue eyes. The ember of heat in his gut sparked into life with that look. It had been forever since he'd held her in his arms, but from the way his body still burned for her, it may as well have been yesterday.

"You're looking better." Asher said, her voice gentle.

He shrugged. "Feeling a bit brighter." He reached towards the mug on the tray, careful not to disturb Peaches. And noticed the slight tremor in his fingers. He made his hand into a fist before grabbing the mug from the tray and sipping. "Hot chocolate. Thanks. I haven't had that since," he gave her a smile, "since ages."

Their gazes locked.

Mitch sucked in a breath. "Time for talking."

Asher twisted her pinky ring, then nodded.

Mitch put his drink down. "I should have called you months ago. I've just been too gutless to know how to go about it."

He looked into her face. Noticing the flush on her cheeks, the lushness of her lips. He swallowed a groan and continued as Asher moved back to the couch.

"Doc, I picked up that phone to call you so many times."

"So why didn't you?"

"I'd remember the last conversation we had." He shrugged as if it wasn't the humungous thing it had become in his mind.

"Mitch, I was off my face on those stupid drugs."

He shook his head. "I realize that, Doc. I'm talking about the conversation we had when we found that damn dossier I had on your brother."

Asher gaped. "What? I thought you meant at the hospital."

"We'll get to that. But first." He struggled to his feet and clutched the back of the recliner for support. Once steady on his feet again, he hobbled the short distance to the couch and sank down beside her. and turned to face her. "Asher." He reached out and grasped her hand. When she didn't withdraw it, he reveled in the warmth of her touch.

He drew a heavy breath. "First up, I need you to know that my feelings for you had nothing to do with orders. My job was to find and bring your brother in. That had nothing to do with you. Me. Us." Another deep breath, then he continued. "What happened between us was personal. Something I never expected to happen." He shook his head. "Never happened before. It blew me away."

Asher stared deeply into his eyes. "Go on. I'm listening."

"When I first saw you, I thought I could handle it. You were fierce, a force to reckon with. I thought I could keep my personal feelings apart from work, which I always had in the past. But I was wrong, so wrong."

He rubbed his forehead, praying for divine intervention to make the words come out right.

"That night we spent together after the ball...making love." He shrugged, feeling lost and hot. She moved her hand, so her fingers were around his and squeezed. It gave him the courage to continue. "It was magical for me. I'd never been so at peace." He drew her hand to his mouth and kissed her knuckles.

"You should have told me everything that night. I shared my soul with you, but you said nothing." She pulled her hand from his, stood and stalked to the window again. What was so fascinating outside? Apart from not having to look at him.

"I wanted to tell you that I had fallen for you. Hard." He stood and limped heavily to stand by her side. "But I couldn't tell you that without telling you about looking for your brother. As I said, I'd even asked for permission, but they'd shut me down. I know you think I lied to you, and just used you to get to your brother." Mitch held her gaze. "Please, Doc, believe me, I never lied about my feelings for you. I wish you could understand it was just my damn job."

She said nothing, and the quiet stretched between them. Mitch couldn't stand it and stepped forward to embrace her. Just then, Peaches crossed his path. Not wanting to hurt the cat, Mitch lifted his injured leg and tried to step over him, but his leg gave out.

"Mitch," He heard Asher scream. In a moment she was beside him, propping her shoulder under his arm and guiding him so his fall was a slow circle that had him landing heavily on the couch instead of cracking his head on her coffee table.

And she landed right smack on top of him.

Silence.

Mitch couldn't stop the groan pushing past his throat. Asher, the woman he loved, was flush against him. He wrapped his arm tightly around her, holding her. His breathing was ragged. As was hers.

"Oh my God, Mitch, are you okay?"

He tightened his grip, then gently brushed his lips against her temple. "I've not felt this good in two months." He laughed out loud. Then words poured from him. "These last few months without you have been miserable." He repositioned them so Asher's body rested against the back of the couch, and he was on the edge.

"Mitch, please..." She looked everywhere but at him.

"Doc." He tipped her chin so she would meet his eyes. "Let me get this out. Please."

She held his gaze and gave a brief nod.

"I've been stuck in that rehab hut for months, kicking myself to hell and back for not finding your brother before he hurt you..."

"He hurt us," she interjected.

"And hating myself for not keeping you safe." He closed his eyes and then there was a slight weight on his lap. Asher's palm. He sighed as calmness stole into his being at her gentle touch.

He inched closer to her. "I want you to know that my feeling for you, the way I feel for you, had nothing to do with your brother. He was my assignment. But you, hell, woman, from the minute I saw you, I was a goner."

"Mitch."

"Please, Doc, let me finish."

At her nod, he continued. "You are amazing. Your strength, your compassion. You, you're just," he traced the outline of her brow, "perfect. To me, you're perfect."

He heard her scoff but continued. "Doc, I meant what I said. These past two months without you have been miserable. I tried hiding my emotions behind liquor. Didn't work."

She grasped his fingers. "You should have answered my calls."

The softness in her voice almost undid him, but he pushed through.

"Could have, should have, would have, if I wasn't so damn angry with myself for not keeping you safe. Because I felt I was of no use to you. Because I didn't feel worthy."

"Mitch. Stop. Please."

He lifted his head and met her eyes. "Doc, that morning you slapped that dossier on my chest, I wanted desperately to tell you the whole truth." He shook his head. "But orders are orders. So, I just let you go." Keeping his gaze on her, he added, "After you stormed out, by the time I got into my jeans, you were getting into a taxi. I picked up my keys to come after you when Ryan called to tell me that Greg had been sighted." He dipped his head, then met her gaze again. "I chose to go after your brother. I followed my orders, rather than follow my heart. And that almost got you killed."

"Mitch, you did your job. And then rescued me. You flung me over your shoulder, with no concern for yourself, and carted me out of hell, and I'll be forever grateful."

He held her gaze. "I don't want your gratitude, Asher."

She blinked repeatedly, then reached across to touch his face. "Well, what do you want?"

"You." The word spilled from him before he could censor himself. "Beside me, every day, every night. I love you, Asher Jardine."

Silence followed his words.

Her quietness ate into him, then she spoke, her tone gentle. "I wasn't expecting that." She moved closer to him on the couch, her hand still against his neck.

"What were you expecting?"

He felt her shrug. "That you wouldn't be interested in a woman whose brother tried to kill you."

He jerked back and almost tumbled from the couch.

Asher grabbed the front of his shirt with both hands and hauled him back.

They were face to face, a mere whisper apart.

"How could you have thought that?" He eased her hair back behind her ear.

"How could you have thought you would be no good to me?"

He smiled. "Point taken."

"Two months apart, two months we'll never get back." She let go of his shirt and trailed her fingers into his hair.

"Eight weeks of misery and pain." He took her other hand between his, brought it to his mouth and kissed her fingers, one by one.

"Sixty-two long, miserable nights, filled with trying to convince myself you meant nothing to me."

There was a pause, then Mitch said, "I can't do the math to figure out hours and minutes."

They laughed.

"Doc."

"Yes?"

"My leg's throbbing. I need to sit."

"Sure." Asher crawled over his body, and he sucked in a lungful of her apple scented shampoo.

When her feet touched the floor, she pushed to stand and reached out her hands. He grabbed them with care, and she gently eased him to a sit. Then she pulled the coffee table toward them, grabbed a cushion, placed it on the coffee table, then lifted his leg and released it on the support.

A breath hissed from between his teeth. "Thank you."

"I'll grab you some more pain pills."

He didn't argue. The intense throbbing through his leg wouldn't allow him to.

She was back in a few minutes, hand outstretched, pills in the palm. "They're only a low dose." She passed him the glass of water and settled beside him.

Mitch reached for her hand. She allowed him to hold it. "Asher, could you pass me the bag?" He pointed to the parcel beside the recliner.

She did.

He pulled out the parcel wrapped in brown paper and handed it to her. "For you."

Her eyes sparkled. "Thank you." A smile tilted her lips. "You didn't have to give me a gift."

He shrugged, "I know. Open it."

She started ripping the paper. Mitch noticed the sparkle in her eyes and continued talking. "I've never looked at my future. I had my career. Nothing else. I survived my life. I didn't plan it. It never bothered me. Until I realized I had nothing."

The ripping sound ceased. "That's crap. You have friends that jump off cliffs with you. Those kids at Mates and Eats looked up to you. And you help people. That's something."

"But I had no goals. No plans. And I realised I wanted a goal, or at least to share in one." He dragged in a huge breath as Asher pulled the remaining paper off her gift, gasped, then stared at him, open-mouthed. Eyes wide.

"Mitch, you made this?"

"Yup."

"How? Where did you find the pictures? The articles?" Tears filled her eyes.

"Phone calls to the local paper. They were happy to get me what I needed." He tapped his fingers on the arm of the chair. "Your vision board made more of an impression than I realised. I knew insurance would replace your ambulance, but I thought," he pointed to the board she hugged tightly to her chest, "that wouldn't be replaced. So, I made it for you."

"Thank you, it's beautiful." She swiped the tears from her eyes, then leaned down and kissed his cheek. "It's exactly the same."

"Except for the block of flats."

"That's not important." She said, as she hugged the board tighter against her chest.

"Well, to me it is." She raised a brow in silent question.

"I've retired from my position."

"What? Why?" Her eyes were wide.

"My leg would never heal."

He heard her gasp.

"Is it because of my demented brother trying to kill us?"

"Nah. It never healed from the injury I received in Afghanistan." He pulled her close. "The job at the sentinel Bureau was a stop gap. If my leg had healed as well as it was supposed to, it would never have given out that night. So, no, not because of your brother."

"Sitting in that hut, I realized my life had changed. I was miserable. Not because of this injury, but because you weren't with me."

He still held her against his side, so he leaned into her, kissing her temple. "I quit because I wanted a new life. With you, if you'll have me."

He turned to look at her. Tears were dripping down her face. He swiped them with his thumb. "Don't cry, Asher. I love you. I want to be with you."

"Okay. I'm sure I can handle being with you every day. For the rest of my life."

"That's where the block of flats come in."

"Go on, I'm so curious." She placed her hand on his chest.

"I am so proud of what you do, working for those less fortunate than us. Your compassion rubbed off on me. So, I thought..." He dragged in a breath. "If I bought those flats, I could do what you do."

"Mitch, spit it out. I'm going crazy here."

He dropped a quick kiss on her lips. "You offer a service to others. I want to do the same."

"So, you bought a block of flats?" Her eyes narrowed in concentration.

"I bought them for you."

She sat back, eyes wide. "Are you kidding? I don't need..."

"And I knew that would be your reaction." He smiled, "So, I bought them for me instead."

"Why?"

"So, I can be your partner in everything. I want to build my life with you, offering service to others, without ever having to leave you. What do you think? Good idea?"

She was quiet. That scared him. Asher was never quiet.

Then she hiccupped. "No, it's perfect. I can certainly work with you to make your vision come to life."

"And then there's this." He bent down and picked out another parcel from the bag, this one not wrapped and passed it to her.

It was a tiny leafy-green Madonna lily in a boot-shaped purple pot.

She raised her brow quizzically. "What?"

"That night, at my flat. The night we made love and laughed and talked, was the best night of my life. I offered to teach you how to grow indoor plants. Remember?"

Her eyes sparkled with unshed tears. "I do.

"Well, this treasure will be your first lesson."

Asher bit down on her lip.

"I'm hoping you'll forgive me for screwing things up between us before they really got started. Asher, I meant what I said, I love you and want to build a life with you.

"So, you give me baby plant and a declaration of love."

"I can throw in a block of flats, if you want them?"

She laughed out loud.

"Mitch." She scooted closer to him, resting her hand against his cheek. "Thank you for carting me out of that building." Her lips touched his brow. "Thank you for coming back into my life." Her lips trailed the length of his cheek. "Thank you for loving me." Finally, her lips settled against his in a brief, passionate kiss. "Buchanan, never leave me again."

"I won't, Doc." He kissed her long and hard, then broke away." So, about my plans for my future.

Asher eased closer so their bodies touched. "We can work on them later." Just before her lips covered his, she whispered. "Much later."

EPILOGUE

Two nights later.

"So, we're really doing this." Asher said, looking out over Mates and Eats.

"Yup." Mitch leaned his back against the bonnet of the ambulance, with Asher nestled between his parted thighs. In his hand, he held the signed contract for the dilapidated block of units they had such big plans for. They had spoken to members of the local council, and the plans were being submitted in the morning.

Asher turned in his arms. "Your idea of getting some of the young, homeless kids, working with the builders to get them a bit of work experience, and maybe even an apprenticeship, is brilliant."

He smirked. "I know."

She pulled his head toward her, and kissed him, deep and hard, then gave him a smile. "You're a genius to have come up with that idea." Then she kissed him again for good measure. As she came up for air, she saw Charli break away from the crowd, a sling across her chest. Asher stepped away.

The vibrant young woman tapped Mitch on the shoulder and smiled when he turned toward her. "Hey Mitch, meet

Mitch." She was grinning from ear to ear as she folded down the sling to show the dark-haired baby.

"Hey, Charli," Mitch said. "Is he named for me?" He reached over and gently traced the baby's hairline.

"Yup, Mitchell Ethan. Mitchell for you, Ethan for Bridget's husband. Because you both stopped those creeps stealing my baby. And I'm so grateful."

"Well, I'm honoured. Thank you." He touched the young mother's shoulder. "He looks strong and healthy. You're doing a wonderful job with him."

"Thanks, Mitch, I love being a mum." With that Charli gave him a wave and headed back to her friends.

Asher traced the smile on his lips. "Did she tell you of her plans?"

He shook his head. "No, just that she loved being a mum. She didn't mention anything about her boyfriend either."

"After he recovered in hospital, he discharged himself. Never heard from him again."

Mitch pressed a kiss to her lips. "So, what's her plans?"

"She's moving in with Lily on a permanent basis and going to finish school."

"That's terrific news."

Asher smiled. "I know. She's exceptionally clever. After having little Mitch, she decided to do her best by him, and that meant, finishing school. Lily enrolled her into a local high school, they have a childcare facility attached, so her precious baby can be cared for while Charli studies."

Mitch pulled her against his side. "I'd call that a win, win situation."

Asher smiled. "I know. Fancy a coffee?"

"I'd love one." Mitch draped his arm over her shoulder as they strolled slowly through the quadrangle toward the food van.

They stood with Bridge and Hamish as they sipped their hot drinks.

Mitch drew Asher close, pressed a kiss to her lips. "Life has a way of working out just the way it's supposed to."

She smiled and stroked her finger across his jaw. "That it does, my love." She looked around the area, saw the people who needed her service, her friends. Then back at Mitch, the man who loved her. "That it does."

CHECK OUT MORE GREAT READS FROM ROWAN PROSE:

Romantic suspense author Rosie Miles was born in Glasgow, Scotland, and was dragged screaming and kicking to Queensland, Australia, many years ago, where she still resides. She is a Romance Writers of Australia's Ruby Award-Winner for Romantic Book of the Year. She is active in the writing community, working within two critique groups, and has been a member of RWA Australia for over twenty years. In addition, she volunteers at her local library for Writing Fridays, overseeing different writers as they focus on building writing skills.